Excerpt

"She's mine!" a new voice bellowed, silencing those around her into stillness, as a behemoth shoved his way inside the menacing circle tightening around her. "Paws off! Lest you want them crushed for Christmas."

She's mine.

Susanna's eyes widened. Stomach jumped into her throat.

Shouldering his way past the others, the newcomer blasted straight to her. Her nerve-scrambled senses could only think: *Big.* That and *Welcome.*

At first glance, her rescuer looked as though he belonged with the soused tipplers, singing abused carols interspersed with lewd villainous remarks.

"She don't look claimed to me," Bearded Squirrel swooped in front of her and rasped, brandishing her bag from one finger, as though to mock how heavy she knew it to be. And to emphasize who had control of it now.

The one who'd just named her as *his* aimed his steely gaze toward the fellow and practically growled, knocking Squirrel Man aside and glaring at each of the reprobates who would do her harm.

As rough and wild as the weather outside, the blue tempest of his narrowed eyes burned hot, every bit as threatening as the men around her—only his ire was directed *toward* those who would steal what she did not choose to give.

Did she want to align herself with this sandy-haired, bristling stranger?

Do you have a choice?

Brute strength hauled her up against a wall of warm chest. A strong arm banded across her back as a gentle hand brushed over her head, past the fallen bonnet that no longer strangled (or if it did, she no longer noticed). His warm touch feathered over her head again and came to rest upon her shoulder. Comforting.

"Got delayed by the bridge, same as me." As he spoke, he tightened his hold around her.

Unbidden, a sigh slipped free. Tension eased from her aching limbs. Her forehead tilted forward, met the wool of his coat. Seemed her body decided to trust and relax into him before her mind could question further.

LADY RECKLESS

STEAMY SCANDALS
BOOK THREE

LARISSA LYONS

*To Belinda, the creative genius at Blurbs by Bel.
Working with you brought about extra excitement for working on—
and finishing!—stories. Thank you!*

Proofread by Judy Zweifel at Judy's Proofreading. Cover by Erin Dameron-Hill at EDHProfessionals. Blurb copy by Blurbs by Bel.

At Literary Madness, our goal is to create a book free of typos. If you notice anything amiss, please let us know. litmadness@ yahoo.com

NO Generative or other AI uses Permitted.

Author and Publisher reserve all rights to this content, both text and cover. No person or entity may reproduce and/or otherwise use this content in any manner, including for purposes of training artificial intelligence technologies. With the exception of brief quotes in reviews (one to two sentences in length) no other use may be made of this content without the Author and Publisher's specific, express, and written permission.

CONTENTS

AUTHOR NOTE ON CONTENT

While *Lady Reckless* has the fun and humor you have come to expect from one of my novels, there are also some darker themes that propel the plot and have affected the characters. In the interest of cautioning anyone who likes details before they read, items of note are listed below.

SPOILERS BELOW - SPOILERS BELOW - SPOILERS BELOW

OFF PAGE
-the heroine carried a baby nearly to term only to have it die a few months prior to the story beginning; this loss is still emotionally fresh
-references are made pertaining to past spousal abuse, both emotional and physical
-references are made to being bartered sexually by one's spouse

-a past accident/blast—in times of war—injured the hero, leaving him deaf

ON PAGE
-the heroine is threatened by a group
-heroine is threatened by an individual
-violence, in the form of a rollicking good fight between hero and villain

END OF SPOILERS - END OF SPOILERS - END OF SPOILERS

With that seriousness taken care of, enjoy!

Larissa

LADY RECKLESS

If adventures will not befall a young lady in her own village, she must seek them abroad...

— JANE AUSTEN, *NORTHANGER ABBEY*

1

BLUSTERY BEGINNINGS

December 1815

East Crossings, the Midlands

Leopold Michael Tucker, former captain of the HMS Restless, minded his back against the far wall opposite the entrance of Ye Olde Filthy Pig. Despite the effort it took to see himself stationed there, given the brimming crowd practically bursting through the walls, 'twas the only place a man could relax enough to enjoy a meal—or a pint—in a rackety place like this.

He should know. Before joining the navy, he'd grown up in taverns like this one—only never quite this overrun with seething, boisterous humanity, not for this many hours on end.

Wincing, he took another sip of the ale the

barmaid had delivered (along with a flash of bosom) and surveyed the probable purse-to-pound ratio of those lingering this eve, and this close to Christmas.

Ah, The Foul Swine, the officious name of the tavern known to all who frequented it, willingly or not, as The Filthy Pig.

He'd been here before, twice in the last six months, so he wasn't counted a complete outner by the locals. Still, it never paid to be overly complacent in a place of this caliber. Not when inebriation appeared the goal of many on a stormy night howling its way inside through the cracks around the plank windows. The gusts would have stirred the curtains had there been any. As it was, the candle nearest him gutted and left the scent of smoke wafting in front of his face and his corner dimmer than it was before.

His faithful companion snuffled and scooted closer.

Leo knew because he'd pried off one boot and placed the sole of his foot comfortingly against his canine's side. Ever since their last, fast jaunt into the cold, hours ago, Reaver had breathed regularly beneath the table, tucked away from the stray boot or flying beverage. The snuffle vibrated Leo's foot and brought a small smile despite the sour tang lingering on his tongue.

A frigid rush blew against his cheek. Today's icy, storm-drenched hours had turned the place into a dank, if not dreary, crush. Too many tippling, unwashed (unsavory, he feared) bodies of locals jammed in amidst the journey-worn and weary travelers stranded here, just like he was.

Not that he typically liked to be complaintive, but by now—and by design—everyone knew his horse had come up lame. He'd spent the day bemoaning his lack of fortune at the bar: Why couldn't the nag have stumbled tomorrow? Or yesterday? Or even seven miles back? But no, Nelson just had to go and slip on ice 200 yards from this piece of (and he kept this part to himself) broken humanity with its deplorable ale, stale bodies, loud braggarts and pendulous bosoms—the last he knew because of the immodest barmaid.

The one he had less than no interest in. Since the battle that felled both him and many others, his focus had first been healing, and then learning. Finding a way to contribute, to the safety and freedom of England, even if it was no longer as captain of his ship. Women? Pah.

Who had time to pursue such things? Especially when their body showed zero interest as well?

Stay clear of trouble, you sorry lout, and come see us for Christmas, his fellow, also "retired" captain had written. Nathaniel Oliver, his former first mate and long-time friend, knew him well.

Leo never *looked* for trouble. Didn't have to. It gravitated to him like gnats to a good apple crisp. Had since he was a lad. And reaching forty last month hadn't changed his allure, it seemed. Only the sort of trouble.

Swiping his tongue past his lips, he braved

another small swallow. No matter the size of the sip, the ale wasn't getting any better.

"Tastes like piss." The words whispered from him.

Switch to whiskey? once upon a time, one of his mates would have asked.

Something Leo would never hear again.

Sort of like the drunken, bellowed butchering of Christmas carols he'd witnessed the last half hour or more.

Watched. Not heard.

Now being deaf and all.

***

THE COACH limped into the sludge-mired yard of the tavern ahead of Susanna's methodical, slower pace. Her lack of speed hampered, no doubt, by her practically frozen hem (rather *sludged* itself), a few annoying, if minor, aches and pains, and the heavy valise weighing down one arm as much as the last hours threatened to weigh her spirits.

"None of that, now." She didn't even have to whisper the encouragement. No one was close enough to hear.

Her gaze followed the razed coach and skittish horses (except for the injured one that had been put down) being tugged toward the stable. The coach, and its battered and bruised occupants, shouldn't have been here at all, and wouldn't be, except for the teeming deluge the last day and a half that had flooded roads and rerouted her stage more than once. Along with the other passengers, she had been unceremoniously disboarded when the horses lost their footing (hooving?) on a treacherously slick, uneven portion, which ended up delivering the coach into a ditch—and most of its occupants into each other.

Take care to mind your safety at all times.

Susanna Oliver Mitchell would have snorted at that reminder—the refrain oft repeated by Sarah these last months, ever since Susanna became widowed at the ripe age of four and twenty.

The more worldly-wise Sarah had become Susanna's sister-in-law through marriage when Sarah's younger sister married Susanna's older brother. But after three daughters and thirteen years of marriage, Ellen had died nearly two years ago. Since then, and even before—when her health had declined and Susanna had given care and comfort where she could to her three nieces and the waning El—Sarah had taken Susanna under her wing.

To wit, with Sarah's own sister no longer hale and hearty, long letters and sisterly advice had come, welcomingly, Susanna's way. If it had been years too late to prevent Susanna's folly of a marriage and the calamities that came after? Well, 'twould not stop her appreciation for every piece of shared advice, no matter how she wasn't quite listening at the moment.

Mind your safety and never find yourself alone at night.

She would've laughed at the reminder—if she'd had the energy.

It seemed as the wind whipping her frame increased, the determined plod of her frozen feet did the opposite, their steady pace decreasing until it was all she could do to keep moving forward and not allow herself to be blown back the way she'd come. The other beleaguered travelers battling the wind buffeting them from all sides these last two miles had now overtaken her straggling form. *Mind your safety...*

Bother that. No one imperiled Susanna's safety. Not any longer, now that her husband wasn't around.

But the two-day adventure (*reckless* adventure, per Sarah) that should have seen Susanna safely delivered to her brother and his new wife's abode well ahead of Christmas Day had now become a two-and-a-half-day disaster, if one listened to the other passengers, and she still had yet a full day's travel remaining. For herself? She was simply tired and cold on this last of a long stretch, anticipating a warm meal and hopefully an available room to change out of these wretchedly sogging garments— assuming anything in her bag still remained dry.

With a loud whinny, the last of the horses and the dilapidated coach they dragged, disappeared inside the long stable/carriage house located a couple dozen yards from the inn's entrance.

Nightfall approached, or perhaps had already arrived—thick grey, roiling clouds had obscured the sun all day—but the low hum of visitors drifting out into the yard welcomed, as did the candles burning from the one- and two-story windows.

Her nose was numb. Eyes stung from the wind. Her bonnet sagged precariously, only kept from escaping by the ribbons tight across her neck. Her slippers were ruined and her belly hungered.

Yet she had not felt this free in years. This alive.

Adventure was hers this holiday and she was ripe to claim it. (Despite warnings and crushed coaches.)

The length of her steps increased. Christmas beckoned, mere days away, and after years of suffer—

Nay. She'd promised herself, when she'd seen Mr. Mitchell's casket lowered into the ground early this past fall, that she would suffer no more.

Rejoice, she would! In her freedom. In the season. In the—

As she reached the tavern inn, she squinted past the ice pellets blowing beneath her bonnet, attempting to make out the swinging overhead sign, the paint faded in places...

A black-and-white pig, and a grey duck? No... A goose? Chicken? The letters above and below more gone than not, but... Yes!

The Foul Swine
Inn & Tavern
Est. 1783

"Hmph. The *foul* swine?" She did hope that wasn't an omen; for nothing foul best spoil her holiday adventure.

Enough tragedy, some of it brought upon herself, most of it compliments of Mr. Mitchell, had already blighted enough of her not-quite-young-anymore life.

Take care and mind her safety?

Bah. Time for a little reckless enjoyment.

A few exciting hours before she climbed the lowered steps of another coach come morning that would deliver her to her destination. Time enough to mind her safety, her reputation and the guilt she still harbored well after that.

⸺◦⸺

THE SQUALLING nibbler fighting against its mama's efforts to soothe. The grumblers whining and wallowing over the inn's crowded conditions. The *clank* and *clump* of tankards, toasting each other when full or landing back upon the table once empty.

All things he "heard" with his eyes, not his ears as his lips and tongue battled down another swallow of pathetic ale. As his toes curled in their thick socks against the warm, furred body beneath the table.

But Leo had a suitable imagination (a wildly exuberant one, his mama would have claimed when he was a lad). So at times such as these, when surrounded by more people than any sane man might wish, he didn't miss having working wattles as much as one might think.

But later tonight? When he bedded down in the stable next to his horse for a handful of hours before dawn? Then, Leo knew from nightly, irksome experience, once he was by himself, the silence would fair scream at him, keeping him awake. Apart.

Alone.

2

ANOTHER PISS-POOR ALE OR A RELUCTANT RESCUE?

———⊃○⊂———

EASING past the open entrance into the courtyard, flanked on either side by low walls, Susanna's perceptions changed from hoped-for holiday merriment to teeth-grinding reality.

It wasn't holiday candles aglow and warmth that beckoned, but rather soot-grimed oil lamps in the upstairs windows, so depleted of fuel that the light given off through their smutted glass lamps was feeble indeed.

As she had pried loose wearied, benumb feet that stuck to the muddy earth as though it were paste, the last fifty yards had seemed five hundred, so that her chilled body's need of a warm respite had only magnified.

The carolers? The ones she'd thought so vibrant and revelrous? The ones singing to the heavens with such joy it had made her too-frozen-to-feel lips attempt to crack a smile through the light coating of frost?

Fuddle caps, one and all, she saw, approaching the heavy set of double doors leading into the foul, dingy-feathered tavern. Loud, rough men of varying ages and varying stages of inebriation, half in/half out of the building itself but all with hearty voices and lewd lyrics. Lyrics that made her icy eyebrows wing skyward now that she was close enough to hear *words* and not just a lively tune. The swillers also possessed hungry, hard eyes when they caught sight of her lone self dragging in behind the others.

Gulp.

Her feet wambled, as though to delay her arrival.

You ought not travel without a companion, Sarah had written, *not for any distance.*

Pah. Susanna was more likely to *be* the companion, now that she no longer existed in a state of wedded servitude.

"Wot's this now?" Blockading the entrance, one of the coarse revelers crowded closer. "A little chickadee come into our midst this night?"

She squirmed away from the outstretched hand and made it to the door, in time to grab the edge as someone exited, looking rather pea green and holding their stomach, racing toward the fence. Susanna didn't wait to hear the retching, scrambled past the doorway and inside, to the safety it promised. A room. A meal, and mayhap, if she were lucky, a bit of privacy.

"Oh ho, little bird," another voice rasped, more

refined than the last, but no less frightening—especially when accompanied by a bulky presence barring her way. "Eh, not so fast."

One of the men, not the largest, but the tallest, stained clothing and a black gap between his lips where a tooth or three belonged—lunged for her.

She jerked back and hauled her bag up between them. "Where is the proprietor?" she aimed her query toward the dim, swarming interior as a whole, raising her voice over the ragged group of seven or eight pressing in, crowding round and blocking the way forward—and back out.

Like flies at a summer picnic, the tavern buzzed with people. Standing, sitting, laughing, yelling. Aye, there were even some carolers—two parents with five wee ones were singing heartily, trying to appease the youngest whose face was screwed up, red and wet from crying.

"Who owns this establishment?" she called again, frustrated when her voice faltered toward the end. She firmed it and did a bit of yelling of her own. "Proprietor! Innkeeper! Please, I bid your assistance."

<hr>

REAVER THE IMPRESSIVE gave a light stretch against his human's foot. Impressive for his hearing, aye, but he also had a number of hidden talents as well. Ones he remained supremely confident of, whether they were visible at the moment or not.

He and the captain had been cooped up in this seething mass of humanity for hours. He felt the strain from the man he traveled with as the rain forced so many indoors.

His captain was impatient to be on the move.

Tedium didn't approach. It had already landed, and with a huge splat even worse than the stable horses made when they fizzled some foul-smelling wind or cacked a corkscrew.

Well, no...maybe the horse excrement *was* worse.

Which was neither here nor there. And Reaver didn't really want to be *here* any longer, either.

He was beyond ready for a good roll in the dirt. Given the weather of late, he would settle for a lovely squish in the mud.

But wait. His human's foot flexed against Reaver's flank. Well, ho ho. Something interesting was about to happen. Hopefully, something impressive...

Leo tensed.

Dread knotted his stomach, churned an urgency through him he wanted to ignore. Needed to ignore, for sake of his mission.

Stay out of trouble, Leo. No sense involving yourself, of doing anything worthy of note.

After all, though he'd griped and groused enough to explain his presence, beyond that, his goal was to blend. Go unnoticed, unremarked.

But trouble likes you. Have you forgotten?

Nay. Trouble *traveled*, it seemed. For what he watched, unfolding before him, was the sort of thing he'd expect to find in London or Portsmouth, not this far in, and in an outwardly sleepy village to boot.

Is that not why you are here? Following trouble...

Blast it all.

The fur beneath his socked foot vibrated. Growling? Or more snores? When the canine's body stiffened, he had his answer.

Trouble *was* afoot, by damn.

Leo, known the last dozen years as Captain Tucker, had remained in His Majesty's Royal Navy even after the cannonade and particular blast that knocked him on his arse, head bleeding, and stole his ability to hear and the rest of his seafaring career. Hoping the auditory loss was temporary— but now accepting that it wasn't—he had continued to work for the navy, though from a desk and land-locked, applying his experience toward strategics while learning new skills. One of significance.

Which brought him here—to this torpid-yet-sinister village off the main stage routes: his ability, up to a point, to make out what others were saying from across the room. As long as he had a clear path to their mouth—without a bottle or tumbler hiding their lips—and they talked long enough (or conversely, brief worked fine, if they spoke slow enough—which usually wasn't the case) he could scrape together what he needed, typically a place or date. A hint of their nefarious goings-on. Something to help his superiors direct their next actions. As to being here, specifically? At the weak-handed Filthy Pig?

He'd been following a crew known not for their polish or wits, but their greed. Their lack of law-abiding interest, the crimeful vulgarians. Hoping to glean useful information had given him a purpose in life again, one he relished. Even though, to the world he now inhabited, he was naught but one of many war-injured military men returned home to English shores with little to occupy his time, save whinging about the flooded roadways, the busted bridge and his lame horse.

His horse wasn't lame. Not one bit. And the stable master knew it, as Ol' Mikey also traced this crew's scambling acts, Mikey being a prime intelligencer himself, and only one of two other men anywhere within 100 miles Leo knew he could count on.

But, for the nonce, he was on his own.

In the four seconds since sensing trouble, he'd drawn on his boot. Now sat, muscles tight, attention affixed on the rabblers. One hand clenched round the tankard, the fingers of the other fisted below the table in Reaver's scrubby fur. The rangy group he'd observed all day (alert for the information he sought) had grown more soused and bolder with every song, every sip...

When he'd watched them daunt away the over-worked, ill-prepared proprietor once food ran out two hours ago (and seen the outworn word man take his harried wife and daughter upstairs, abandoning the brazen serving wench to whatever coin and calmness she could claim), he'd suspected something like this loomed.

The modest tavern wasn't on the primary stage route, but the flooded bridge that detoured travelers the last two days also ensured an influx of riff-raff, over and above the usual. While he hadn't spared a moment's surprise when the impinged family abandoned ship, neither had he planned for this:

A lass in need of a rescue.

"Well, hell," he whispered beneath his breath, wishing now he'd consumed more of the rottenish ale. Enough so that he would have slid into unconsciousness and out of responsibility.

But nay. Looked as though the bold-spirited, black-maned little miss didn't realize quite how deep she was sinking and might drown if he didn't rouse his reluctant self to jump in and swim out beyond his tidy, shadowed shore to save her...

⸻ ◉ ⸻

"Innkeep! I would bespeak a room." Confound it, no one was rushing to answer—or to come to her aid.

What did you expect? Not Sarah's words this time, but Susanna's own pragmatical mind arguing back with commonsensical certainty. *No one helped during the last seven years of miserable marriage either.*

Ah, but she'd not told a soul how sorrowful her

situation had turned. Easier to hide her woes beneath the beautiful trappings of the fanciful, uncomfortable home she had practically become trapped inside rather than admit her mistakes.

And with her brother off at sea and their parents deceased, Susanna had persevered, had accepted her lot, pretending it didn't suck at her soul, draining the very life from her, with every year that passed...

You did want adventure on this journey, did you not? Which is why you defied propriety and set out on your own.

Freedom, by God's grace. She finally had it now and would savor every experience she could. Would defend it with her last breath.

Determined not to be disadvantaged again, she feinted back and forth, up and down, looking beyond and in between the seething body of imposing disreputables looming far too close, hoping to locate someone responsible. An escape path. Anything she could use—

But nothing. Not a single empty table that she could see—though that might be in part that despite her efforts, she could not look *through* the jackanapes that persisted in hounding her.

The toothless one she'd named Toothy in her mind, just to be brassy—something Mr. Mitchell would have punished there towards the end—sidled so close she could smell the rot of his breath as it blasted hot and fetid across her face. "Our chickadee desires a room of 'er own, she does!"

That prompted laughter and leers—and from more than just the men aggrieving her now. Two others, seated not far away, plunked the tankards they'd been holding, now drained, on the table and stood to join the circle surrounding her, closing it in even more. The size and number of men had gone from frightening to terrifying.

How quickly it had happened, too. From reckless adventure to dangerous jeopardy in a trice.

The cankered nasties grinned. Licked lips. Flexed fingers. Stripped her frozen form clear of clothes with their depraved gazes.

Even though her heart started beating faster and the taste of panic edged sharp and sour into her mouth, she held her ground, feigned outward calm. They had no idea, despite her terror, despite her past—mayhap *because* of it—that she knew how to deal with this sort of lecherous behavior. These types of base-minded brutes.

Trouble is oft afoot for those misfortunate enough to not be aware. Sarah, again. The London burnish gleaned from living and working in the city evident. Sarah, who *knew* things, had shared much in her missives over the years. Missives that had grown in length and frequency when Sarah's sister had begun ailing. *Dear heart, wherever too many idle hands—and minds—gather, the dregs tend to clump together, you see, and will make use of any opportunity to strike.*

Please, Susanna, Sarah had written in her most recent letter, *wait until I can join you or, at the very least, until we can secure your safe passage before venturing out beyond your village.*

But no. After nearly eight years tied to first a harmless but selfish man who then became an indifferent and sometimes rude one, and who eventually became a rather harmful one full of ill-disguised ill intent, Susanna no longer intended to wait for anything. Or anyone. No matter how well meaning.

To that end, she quit waiting for rescue, filled her lungs and roared, "Stay back! *Back*, I say, you miscreants!"

She swung her valise at the sinister, black-eyed one who prowled intimidatingly close. "This is a respectable inn," she told them, practically spitting now, more than a little incensed that not a single person wanted to involve themselves (even the singing family with the crying tot had gathered up their children and bustled to the far side of the room), "*not* a brothel! *Where* is the innkeeper?"

Toothy pulled her backside against his front and clamped his beefy fives over her breasts as the others only laughed and nudged elbows.

She swung again, only to have her bag snatched from her grasp by one of the biggest louts she'd ever seen, face beard obscured by a dead squirrel or three.

"Wot's in 'ere now?" Squirrel Beard growled at her, frowning as though miffed she'd clouted his stomach before he wrested both satchel and control from her. "'Eavy for a wee bird, it is."

"Give that back!" Lunging forward, grappling to

reach her possessions, she bucked and kicked. The constricting hold around her middle only tightened.

"Eh, play sweet, now." Putrid breath assailed her nose, the beginnings of true fear starting to burn where he touched—his clutching fingers now fighting hers which sought to pry his hold free. "We's not 'eartless bastards after all. Ye'll get yer coin, just as soon as we get a stab at yer crack—"

3

LEST YOU WANT THEM CRUSHED FOR CHRISTMAS

✧

<u>DO NOT POST!</u>
<u>DO NOT POST!</u>

September 10, 1815

Dearest Sarah,

Wonder of wonders. Can one be numb? Yet in alt? Still grieving a past loss yet...<u>exultant</u> over a fresh one?

I can hardly hold the pen, my entire body shakes so...but I must tell someone. Quickly, ere I go shouting through the streets and find myself assigned to Bedlam for my glee.

He's gone.

Gone, I say!

James Henry Mitchell is <u>dead</u>. And not by my hand, though I <u>could</u> confess to thoughts of such since his reprehensible actions July 5 resulted in my poor baby's precipitous arrival and graveside services three days later.

I will forever hate him for that, for the thoughts I had—

Nay. For even thinking such hate squeezes my heart again to the point of agony. Threatens to stifle my glee and I would not have that.

Will one reserve their place in Hell for the plea-sure taken in another's demise? I can only pray it isn't so, for now I am free.

Free of his vileness! Can you believe it? I scarce cannot!

He is gone. Gone, and with <u>nothing</u> to do with me.

Felled by his own folly! Met his end at the end of a saber last eve, when he and some of his friends, all in their altitudes of course, were "playing" around. (Though if he acted as borish with them, it wouldn't surprise me to learn that saber tip had met his gullet on purpose!)

The numbness has traveled from my chest and now reaches my fingers. How will I feign sorrow and distraughtness over losing not only my baby but husband too? How can my blissfulness be contained?

Oh, Sarah, no one, not even you, know the full trials that wretch has put me through. I did not wish to complain (feared, in truth, you might put him to waste if you knew all) and I could not burden you with that.

But no more!

My fingers are wet. From wiping my cheeks. Pen just slipped to the floor. Ink upon the rug. But for once, my hands do not tremble with fear of reprisals, for anything being a speck out of place within these walls. Tingling still, they are, but now saturated with the tears of relief that stream forth...

There was more, until the page reached the end with:

Still I chuckle! But for my father-in-law's sake, I shall find the strength to disguise mirth as devastation. Even if I have to reach through my pocket and pinch my thigh blue. For James's father has always been good to me, and I would not hurt him for the world.

Oh, Sarah. I miss you so! Now that Ellen is gone, I do not see you nearly often enough.

You were right! <u>Life can be what you make it</u>, you told me once. And before I find myself shackled anew, to another man who may turn on me after the vows and my choices are removed, I shall make a few <u>adventures</u> for myself. I think I am due, do you not?

Adventures! Just the thought lifts my heart every bit as much as the astonishing news I impart.

Now. Deep breaths. (Forty-seven of them to be honest.) Another sixteen more. All right.

I shall endeavor to compose myself. Compose <u>another, postable</u> letter to you, expressing a wee bit of sorrow, but one you can discern the truth through.

⎯⎯⎯⎯◜◟◝⎯⎯⎯⎯

THE, no doubt off-key, hashed holiday carols that grew randier with each verse. The yammered threats against a lady's virtue. The black-haired female's outraged protests.

Leo didn't need to hear a one of them for his conscience to prick painfully at him to hasten his steps. Not when his own desire quickened them well enough.

"... an...inn!" Leo thought she said in the fraction of a glance, when his sight of her wasn't blocked. "Not a brothel!" Which might have made him smile, if he hadn't been so intent on reaching her through the bustling throng.

Shoving his way past others too laze-about or soused to care, Leo's gaze briefly met that of one of the cobs thick around her. One of the two that had just abandoned their table and shoved their way closer. He almost hadn't recognized Benny earlier, not with that thick pelt on his face, as the two of them had made it a point to avoid any acknowledgment of each other all day. Poor Tim, between all that bristle and the recent, acquired, lack of bathing, the cove had to be miserable.

A minim incline of a chin, a single blink between them, and they were in accord, he and his gammoner, Timothy Benton, who'd been aiming to associate with these maggots for a spell now. But "Benny" could only embog the others for so long.

Leo needed to get her out of there before things turned any grimmer. But how to do it without bringing any undue notice upon himself?

He had the coins to hire a private room, if there had been one to spare. But the inn had been swarming since morning, and with irritable, fumish travelers to boot. Could he and Nelson take her to the next town? Find better lodgings? Safer for her at least.

Have your wits gone begging? Other than her broken

*stage, no one has arrived the last two hours or more.
There will be no more traveling tonight.*

As he stormed between tables, glancing at all
sides, weighing the different threats, noting the
limited exits and the single entrance, he sped
through his scant options. But when a gangling,
fangless wretch put his grubby, grasping blocks on
the spirited lass? Dared to fondle her protesting
form?

A scarlet haze covered Leo's vision, blood boiled
(silently) in his ears and he abandoned any efforts at
remaining unseen.

⸻◦⸻

"SHE'S MINE!" a new voice bellowed, silencing those
around her into stillness, as a behemoth shoved his
way inside the menacing circle tightening around
her. "Paws off! Lest you want them crushed for
Christmas."

She's mine.

Susanna's eyes widened. Stomach jumped into
her throat.

Shouldering his way past the others, the
newcomer blasted straight to her. Her nerve-scrambled senses could only think: *Big.* That and *Welcome.*

At first glance, her rescuer looked as though he
belonged with the soused tipplers, singing abused
carols interspersed with lewd villainous remarks.

"She don't look claimed to me," Bearded
Squirrel swooped in front of her and rasped, bran-

dishing her bag from one finger, as though to mock how heavy she knew it to be. And to emphasize who had control of it now.

The one who'd just named her as *his* aimed his steely gaze toward the fellow and practically growled, knocking Squirrel Man aside and glaring at each of the reprobates who would do her harm.

As rough and wild as the weather outside, the blue tempest of his narrowed eyes burned hot, every bit as threatening as the men around her—only his ire was directed *toward* those who would steal what she did not choose to give.

Did she want to align herself with this sandy-haired, bristling stranger?

Do you have a choice?

As tall as Bearded, only a couple inches shorter than Toothy but wider than both. Scowling as much as—or more than—any of them, he closed in with a roar, giving her no chance to inspect him further.

Brute strength elbowed Toothy's stench aside and hauled her up against a wall of warm chest. A strong arm banded across her back as a gentle hand brushed over her head, past the fallen bonnet that no longer strangled (or if it did, she no longer noticed). His warm touch feathered over her head again and came to rest upon her shoulder. Comforting.

"Got delayed by the bridge, same as me." As he spoke, he tightened his hold around her.

Unbidden, a sigh slipped free. Tension eased from her aching limbs. Her forehead tilted forward, met the wool of his coat. Seemed her body decided to trust and relax into him before her mind could question further.

"Wot you think yer—"

"I saw 'er first!"

"You canna just—"

"She's *mine.*" Louder than their grumbling, he repeated that startling statement, his voice full of certitude, rumbling over her head. She wasn't sure whether it was the words, the way he spoke them, or mayhap the surprisingly clean scent of him, but the sound of his confident claim soothed even as it sparked awareness. Long-forgotten tingles warmed her belly as he argued against their protests, insisting she belonged to him.

A far cry different than her former spouse. What with Mr. Mitchell, when he ran low on funds and lower on luck after a day of gambling, offering to share her with his friends, despite her protests and weakness those two—

None of that now.

Nay, no thoughts of the past. Simply the sheer wonder of the protective breadth of firm chest snug against hers, the gently fierce way this stranger continued to hold her. The way he braved the others as he began edging away from the quarrellous crew, taking her with him.

"My valise!" How could she have forgotten? For even a—warm-man distracted—moment? She spun within the protected haven he provided to retrieve it.

Only to see another knave now had hold around

the handle of her bag with one nicked hand. A beefy fellow whose other hand (also covered in old scars) menaced a long, wicked knife.

"Think yer lyin'." The abrasive, burly brute's words slurred as though he'd downed a river of whiskey. "An' wot if ye aren't? There's enough of us here to take what we want."

She growled. Raised her booted foot and leaned back into the solid bulk of her rescuer for balance. "You heard him." She kicked out, slammed the sole of her muddy, booted foot into Burly's groin. "I'm his!"

The others laughed as he dropped her valise to grab his crotch, nearly cutting his own wrist—as he bent over with a howled, "Ye whorin' bitch!"

"Have it, then. A bruised cock isn't worth any petticoat's crack." Squirrel Beard thrust the fallen bag into her middle so hard her breath *whooshed*. In a quieter voice, he spat, "Now clear out before he straightens and riles the others." His voice rose again. "Or you'll be wishin' you ain't never came to Crossin's."

Hugging her belongings tight, she gripped his fingers hard when the man at her back grappled for and clasped her hand. His callused flesh was as warm as ever.

Safety. His big presence wrapped her in a cloak of it instantly.

You trust him that much, do you?

Seems that she did indeed.

"Come on," she said swiftly, her heart beating so

fast the words came out high and airy, despite the bravado of only moments before. She yanked his arm toward the exit. "You heard him. We best heed the advice and vacate without delay."

But the stubborn (strong-as-an) ox refused to budge, seemed to be pulling her back *inside*. The perilous murmurings behind them grew louder the longer they dallied. "Men!" Exasperation now combined with both fear and relief. "You are more flummoxing than the weather."

Time paused as he glared down at her when she resisted. Despite the shadows surrounding them, his current position and the brightest lantern angled their direction gave Susanna her first good look at the man at her back.

Big. Solid. While that remained her overall impression, she couldn't stop the wayward attraction compelling her to catalog his every feature in the split second allowed.

His maturity attracted every bit as much as his actions. After a decade or more spent with someone her own age, someone who had betrayed her on so many levels, the allure of this seasoned man's instant protection beckoned with reckless abandon. As did he.

The color of pebbles she'd played with once as a child when her family visited a beach in Brighton, his disarrayed, wavy hair fell down over his ears, the edges just brushing his shoulders. The sandy hue was threaded in places with solitary strands of silver.

His features were blunt, saved from severity by

the grooves on either side of his mouth. He might not be smiling now, but he had, frequently she suspected, once upon a time.

And his eyes—sharp, piercing, never still, taking everything in and somehow finding it all wanting—except when he turned that thunderous, grey-blue stare back to her with resolute focus.

That stormy gaze of his that made her stomach dip anew. That heated much, much more than just her cold fingers.

***

POSITIVELY *RIPPING*.

Bloody *damn* ripping.

He had to go and get involved. *Do you not have enough trouble on your already heavy plate?*

If he didn't get her out of here and find a way to disappear, trouble would be that hellion's knife to Leo's gut and one—or more—of these miscreants' daggers to her sheath.

At the thought, a chill colder than the temperatures outside shuddered through him.

Clasping her near-frozen fingers—had the woman no gloves? No muff?—in one hand, he snagged her bag with the other. When she balked again, he jerked his head toward his corner, indicating their destination.

She resisted. Said something he couldn't make out, not in this light and with her lips flapping frantically as she pulled *him*—not her hand, to free it, some masculine part of him was pleased to note—but tried to haul him the opposite direction. Back *out* the door she'd entered only moments before trouble bit him on the arse.

He gave his head a quick shake and lifted their joined hands to point. *There.* How much plainer could he make it?

She stood her ground, scowling at him as though he'd dared pull a pigtail or two.

Enough.

Feeling the pointed blades of anger directed toward his back, he swooped in and snared her waist, pressed her along his side and barreled toward his corner and *his* battered travel bag—assuming it still remained. Wouldn't surprise him a lick if a savvy conveyancer hadn't noted his distraction and disappeared with it.

In his haste, he'd failed to instruct Reaver on whether to remain or follow, and knew not if the dog had sided with his belongings or waited for him outside by now.

"Stop wiggling about," he growled in her ear, hoping he wasn't overly loud. "Retrieving my things. *Then* we leave."

Absurd pleasure stormed through him when she stilled, nodded. Fair wrapped herself around him rather than push free, one arm clutching behind his neck as she gave a little jump and coiled her legs around him as well.

Well now.

The past years might have been fraught with sea

battles, blockades and hoping to outmaneuver the wily French or Spanish captain opposite, but it now appeared, significant danger aimed their direction or no, his mast hadn't forgotten how to respond to a sweetly scented bit of muslin after all.

Trouble, Leopold. Pure damn trouble.

4

AMISS OR NO, TIME FOR A KISS

GIVEN HER CURRENT POSITION, Susanna was beginning to think prizing safety over adventure may have been of overstated importance. Not that it escaped her—the potential (and realized) perils of journeying alone.

Route detours. Sodden, slippery slopes followed by slipping horses. Painful delivery into a ditch. A split axle.

Thoroughly soiled-through slippers. Destroyed gloves as she and the other passengers and coachman struggled first to free themselves from the broken coach, and then to free the panicked horses, all while aided by rain and sleet, mud and mire until they felt fortunate to escape intact, despite the frigid temperatures they also fought, lungs stinging from the frozen air.

But would she rather be back at home, snug in

her warm night-rail, fed on lackluster stew and reading one of her dozen books (for the dozenth time) with naught to look forward to enliven her week save church on Sunday and Wednesday's post? Hoping for another letter? From either her nieces or Sarah?

Or...

Would she rather be held tight against (to be true, wrapped tightly *around*) a broad-chested, rough-faced man with kind eyes that, in the brief time she'd glimpsed them, nevertheless conveyed a plethora more? Irritation. Dismay. *Interest.*

And he was carrying her! As though she weighed naught (which she knew to be false), choosing to align with her against the others if for no reason...

No reason...

Hmm. *Why* was he? What prompted him to intervene? To inconvenience—

A startled squeal slipped free when he leaned over to retrieve his travel case and her body topsy-turvied.

Then he straightened, bringing her upright again with a *whoosh* and a whirl to her head. He turned, surveyed those around them and barked some order or another that cleared a path to the door.

Had he "rescued" her because he might want what the others had threatened? Expect it, even?

What of it? She had traded her youth and her parents' respect to rebel and marry her youthful folly and had paid dearly for the mistake, both with her own suffering and that of—

Nay! Now that Mr. Mitchell is laid to rest (or rather to torment, one might guiltily hope) you promised yourself no more grieving for the past.

Promised yourself adventure. Freedom. Mayhap even a chance to experience life—and physical love—by choice before succumbing to another disastrous marriage. For what other option did she have? It wasn't as though she could burden herself upon her brother and his new wife, not with her three adorable nieces finally thriving again, after the death of their mother.

And though Sarah, the one other person Susanna could imagine imposing upon, lived happily and securely in London, there were secrets her sister-in-law had chosen not to share. Secrets Susanna suspected held things the opposite of *secure* and *happy*, things that her sister-in-law would not want made known.

For that very reason—to safeguard the happiness of those she loved—for right or wrong, Susanna had never confided the extent of her travails to either Sarah or her brother.

After all, with Nate off at sea until recent months, and Sarah, too, grieving her sister, Susanna had shouldered her own brought-about burdens in silence. Yet now, amazingly, someone was *shouldering* her.

The masculine scents of leather and horse, of spirits and something else... Something undefinable but vastly appealing tickled her nose when she buried her face in the skin above his casual neckcloth.

So what if this divine specimen of masculinity *did* want something from her. Want...*that*? Had she not craved adventure? The taste of another man's kisses? A man of her choosing.

And did this one not smell divinely likable? *Lickable* even?

For shame. For shame.

Nay, Susanna decided, trying to think beyond how intimately the private, womanly area between her spread legs had pressed itself to his solid bulk. *For pleasure.*

When he thumped past the tavern door and barged outside, back into the raging storm and gloom, her damp dress iced against her skin. But she felt it naught beyond a mere trifle.

Oddish how the biting wind no longer stung as it had earlier, not with her curled within his welcome embrace.

A dozen steps into the courtyard his sure strides paused. He shifted her weight more toward his front, one arm braced beneath her bottom; the other pleasantly firm across her waist.

He twitched, facing two or three directions as though debating.

"What?" she asked past a quick gulp of cold air. "Do you live nearby?"

Of course he doesn't, you ninny—not with his own travel bag.

"Do you not have a room either?"

A grunt was his only answer.

She ducked her head closer. "I am sorry to be so much trouble." She aimed her words at his ear, his longish hair brushing her lips. "If you have a safe place for the night, 'tis all I desire—"

Well, not *all*, the insistent pulse betwixt her legs nudged her toward admitting. Susanna bit down on her lips.

Reckless adventure was one thing. Acting a harlot with a perfect stranger, quite another.

"*Grrrrrr.*"

The deep, sinister rasp made her flinch. She scrambled for the source.

As if sensing her unease, his hold tightened. Legs resumed, stalking forward again with purpose.

She peered over his shoulder, back the way they'd come, squinting against the sleet.

Mouth back at his ear, she murmured, "There's a mongrel following us. A snarling, spit-riddled one."

Nothing. Did he not hear her over the howling wind? Or simply not care?

The gusts whipped through the yard, scattering fallen leaves and swirling about some poor woman's pale stocking.

Mayhap it scattered her words as well?

But the rangy, mean-looking canine stayed on their tail (she snickered silently at that) so she tapped the side of his neck, beneath his flying hair.

When he paused and looked at her, gave another grunt, this one of barely concealed impatience, she pointed. "Scary mongrel, on your heels."

He gestured to the dog who then ran ahead. "That's Reaver. I'm his."

Then he took off again without waiting for her reply, but giving her something new to ponder.

I'm his. Curious phrasing, that. But then meaning of *reaver* filtered through... A marauder. A plunderer.

Gulp. Exactly how safe was she with someone who would name their dog thus?

———◦◦◦———

HIS *THINGS*. What a lark.

He'd given her a good dose of terror, going back for them.

Not considering the boyhood items saved by his mama and packed away in a trunk ("Someday, if you ever bring home a bride, you shall thank me, mark my words," she assured on the rare occasions Leo was home and the not-so-rare ones when he told her to toss the lot), his possessions were few:

> -a change of clothes including two shirts, one additional trousers, and clean socks and smalls
> -evening slippers for inside, on the infre-quent occasions he commanded a private room
> -a worn New Testament that came to Leo

when one of his enlisted men had fallen; a
man who had no family to speak of or return
his cherished Bible to (so Leo chose to
cherish it for him)

-a well-thumbed book of ribald poetry (purchased with intent)

-an old pair of peepers that had belonged to
his father, kept unbroken by the hinged
wooden case he'd procured. "You shall
appreciate these, too," claimed his mama,
"when the time comes you need them."

Well, he hadn't needed them yet, by damn. Could still see just fine, even through the wet and windy onslaught pummeling his vision and body now. Half his body, at least.

Because it seemed, in addition to the scant items filling his haversack, he had also acquired one new possession, for the short-term immediate future: the tempting-smelling lass plastered to his front.

When was the last time a fine female held on to him without expecting a coin after? Years and years.

And none of those ever smelled so...confound-ingly sweet. Like a cinnamon-butter tart straight from his grandmother's oven, filled with unexpected treats and spices...

Made a man salivate, it did. For what he didn't have.

But you could, I wager.

She spoke into his ear again, the soft, unheard husk of her words taunting him with silence. Yet filling him with wonder, too, as the innocent puff of her breath sped from his ear and neck, past his shoulder, his chest and stomach to land—

Ker-thump in his groin.

Frustration at not knowing what she said warred with the delight of her solid presence in his arms.

Keep her safe. Think about her lush figure and your unexpected responses to her later.

The expansive stable and connected carriage house loomed as he strode forth with purpose. Where else could he take her? Nowhere until morn, and even that came without certainty. With the continuing rains, 'twas doubtful the bridge could yet be repaired, certainly not overnight, which meant little chance the stage would be running. Nor would it know to stop here, until word got back to the line.

In the thirty or so minutes before she burst in and capsized his world, he'd seen enough conversations between the wearied, sodden arrivals and the others to discern a full coach had met with a rather nasty accident. But no one save her had arrived alone. Unaccompanied. And been the target for further nasties.

In truth, sometimes 'twas easier to let people know he could not hear a word, made it a simple thing to sit close without arousing suspicions, but it also made him stand out in a way he would rather not. Not here in East Crossings, where the rotten crew they trailed had a tendency to congregate. Not because of some foolish sense of pride, but because among certain dregs, noticed men—*especially* noticed men nosing about—could get themselves killed.

And you certainly just got yourself noticed, jolterpate!

He crossed the inn yard, reluctantly enjoying the weight of warm—if chilled to the bone—woman in his arms.

He was cold enough, and still had his coat on. Her cloak was missing and the dress saturated through—likely part of the problem. The nipples on her chest practically arrived through the door before she had. If the hard points had been enough to catch his attention, no wonder the others pounced. Considered her prey.

Just as he reached the stable, crowded with mounts of both holiday goers and stranded travelers within its walls, she wriggled free. Disappointed—how very absurd!—he waited for her to gain her feet. The moment she did, her jaws flapped a jumble of words with *ignore* in there somewhere. (Several times, in fact, which is the only reason he caught it.)

Shrugging in answer, he used bending to give Reaver's head a quick scratch as an excuse to avoid her gaze and try to regain some measure of equilibrium. He'd grown hard as a pike since leaving the tavern. What was he, fifteen?

Forty, you lout, but she's been pressing herself all over you. Be glad you can still respond, aren't heading for a metting with ye olde Mr. Grim quite yet.

Harder than necessary, he shoved the barn door wide, then gestured her through after the dog. A scowl toward him accompanied her steps. He liked her spirit. Despite what had nearly befallen her only minutes prior, the saucebox held her own. Would that he could hear whatever complaints she might be heaping upon his broad shoulders now...

Smiling to himself, he clasped both their bags in one hand and took up her chilled fingers with his other once he secured the door behind them, keeping the storm—and brawlers, he hoped— at bay.

The interior was darker than he expected, horses and stable hands bedded early for the miserable night, until he caught sight of the saddle room at the far end, lanterns bright, worn cards flying across a makeshift table. Visible laughter. One groom doffing his hat to swipe his leg, smile beaming as he counted a note trading hands his direction.

Guiding *her*—he needed to learn her name—to the stall where Nelson resided, Leo stroked the long nose when his good-natured steed rambled forth.

"This one's mine," he told her making an effort to speak softly. No sense letting anyone overhear their business. "Name's Nelson Rambler. She'll lick your palm—even without a treat—but won't bite. Stay put. I aim to gain us a measure of safety."

She replied.

He saw the vague outline of her lips forming words. Couldn't make out a one. But then she grasped his hand and tugged their bags free. He hadn't realized he still held them.

Trouble, Tucker. T-R-O-U-B-L-E. Another distraction like that could see you both in harm's way.

After placing their travel cases at her feet, she clasped his hands, bare like hers because his gloves were stuffed deep in his coat pocket. But unlike hers —which were feminine and delicate and had him entertaining wicked thoughts of where he'd like to place them upon his anatomy—his broad fives were big and rough, scarred long ago from Knife Nick, a stupid game he'd played as a lad, and more recently from the same blast that damaged his ear. But here she was, damn near cradling them in the warm burrow of hers.

More swiftly mouthed words he remained ignorant of. Then a squeeze of his hands and, "Thank you," plain as day.

She released him and went up on her toes to wrap her arms about his neck. A hug of thanks? An embrace of relief?

He might never know because the fierce grip, the guiding tug on his nape, his own curiosity driving him to taste...

He ducked his head. Found her lips. And kissed her.

5

HER GRUFF GALLANT

BLAZING SUNSETS!

The wretched, icy day of travel evaporated, replaced by giddy excitement from the deliberate glide of his mouth over hers.

Desperate hands clutched at the soft hair at his nape, and for the first time in hours, her fingers no longer felt numb. Not with the silky strands sifting through them.

Her throat—or was that his?—hummed in satisfaction as he pressed his lips against hers. Retreated. Returned.

A swipe of tongue and she opened her mouth for him. Her eager, curious body for what his might provide.

Pleasure? Dare she hope?

Somewhere outside, tippled carolers struck up a

tune. True carolers this time, or was that just joy sparking along her veins? Singing in her ears?

When he dragged his tongue free and would have halted (or so she feared), she pushed up toward him, drew his tongue back to her mouth, back inside, and sucked on it. Tasted the tang of ale. The hint of true desire and his masculine flavor.

A loud whimper escaped—definitely hers— when the ache hit hard and fast. The twitchy, hungry ache of passion. The one felt a multitude of times *before* her marriage, and only a handful after. The one yet to be satisfied by anything other than her stroking fingers—ever.

So fast, Susanna? So soon?

She jerked back. Stunned at herself.

Shocked, but not ashamed. Never would she be made to feel shame again. Never.

More intense than earlier even, his eyes gleamed at her through the shadowy barn—stable? mews?— she knew not and cared even less.

Her lips compressed. Already missing the pressure of his. She forced them apart. "Go. Talk to the stable master. I will wait."

For where else would she go? Certainly not inside the tavern. Nor outside in the storm. "Wait for your return, quite contentedly I admit."

Towering over her, he made no response. Simply held her gaze. Then tilted his head to look at her mouth.

Aye, he was appealing. Appealing in an earthy, slightly older, mature way, the complete opposite of

James Henry Mitchell, who had been her age. Who had *never* matured, even after marriage, and had, in fact, fallen in with the wrong sort of crowd and *embraced* the depraved folly. Either Mitchell hadn't possessed the wherewithal to remain true to himself and their upbringing, or mayhap he'd never had much substance to begin with, and she'd been too blinded by the idea of starting her own home to see the lack.

What she had learned, far more than anyone might wish, was that from shouting at her if his food wasn't on the table when he expected it, to shoving her around these last two years, to even trading time with her for a couple of his worst gambling debts, his reprehensible actions had soured every childish dream she had surrounding the two of them.

Had left a wise woman in their wake. One of keen discernment. One who, though she had experienced far more from others, now reacted in the most pleasurable, welcome way to this particular man, and how he studied her...her face, her mouth.

The focused attention made her lips tremble. Her heart, and the accompanying throb down lower, pulsed faster. Then he lifted his eyes to meet hers again and a slow, but definite, smile sprawled across his face, softening jagged edges. Causing her breath to catch.

SLIP OF A YOUNG, pretty thing, like her? Leo couldn't decide if the way she stared up at him made him feel ancient as Methuselah or as valiant as the Knights of Yore and as strong as a team of oxen.

Of a certainty, it made him want things he had no business imagining with her.

She wasn't a doxy. The hardened, over-used sort found trawling the docks the world over. Her teeth were too fine, her scent too fresh. Nor was she some lucky bastard's kept piece—her clothes weren't fine enough.

Add to that how her embrace was a bit overly keen for a woman who knew how to practice the art of allure and demure. The art of deny and delay... for pay.

Nay, for whatever reason, Leo had stumbled across a curious mix of innocence and determination. Of hesitance and eagerness.

And just what are you going to do about it? Do with her?

He knew not.

But two things he did know with conviction:

Never would he erase from his mind how back in the tavern she'd gripped his forearm and reared back to land a vehement (surprisingly satisfying—to Leo's thinking, at least) *thwack* to her would-be attacker's ballocks and bauble. A bauble that was likely blazing still, heh heh.

Nor had he missed how she'd flinched, cowed a trice before recalling herself when Benny closed in and ripped the bag from her grasp. Likely trying to protect her from another—who would have grabbed more than just her valise—but she would not have known that, not with the glowering, abrupt advance.

Her reaction had told him much.

Took a man a far piece denser than Leo to not realize the lass had been hurt before.

Given everything else he'd seen from her, the question that plagued him was not *how badly*. But rather *who* and *how long ago*?

Was she running? Trying to escape?

Nay...for would she not have shown more distraction? More attention—behind her? He'd not noticed her looking over her shoulder even once. If she worried about being followed or caught, would she not have attempted a quiet resolution? To stay out of sight and notice?

As you were tasked?

Instead, she'd braved her way inside and confronted the lobcocks. Shouting for the out-of-sight proprietor. The strain of her neck muscles above the green ribbon affixed to her droopy bonnet had shown her volume clear as any unheard bell.

Unable to resist her allure, he ignored Reaver when the dog brushed against his leg and traced his fingertips over the quivering seam of her lips.

"You are not the least bit afraid of me, are you?" he murmured, being mindful with his volume. "You know I will not harm you, correct? Will not do anything not fully agreed upon? I will do nothing that might cause you fear."

She gave a brief shake of her head and tugged him back down to whisper in his ear. The warm puffs of breath caressing the damaged shell reached far beyond the slight tickle caused in the center, raced through him like a shiver and arrived—thick and hot—in his burgeoning groin.

Now what, mate? No inkling what she just said.

You bufflehead came through as well.

But he could guess. Or make an attempt.

With one thumb beneath her chin, he turned her head to speak directly into *her* ear. To see whether he could create shivers that danced through her body as well? "You aren't, or we would not be doing this, I know. But—"

She said something else. He felt it in the subtle shift of her frame.

Just tell her.

"I..." Damn. Why was this hard?

Because you haven't been with a woman since?

He hadn't wanted one like this either. Not so swiftly. Since, or before.

He cupped her shoulders. Reluctantly leaned back. "Let me go check with Ol' Mikey. I should be able to safeguard you tonight, regardless of what that crew may pursue the deeper into their cups they dive. Ah—food?" Was she hungry?

Another shake. More words. Damn. He needed a lantern.

She yawned.

His fingers moved over her shoulders and down her slim arms, angling her until the light behind him fell upon her face. "Damn me, here you are likely dead on your feet, near frozen through, and I'm jawing. Wait here. Anyone comes in—yell." Yell? As if he'd hear. "Aim for the ballocks like you did before to Haggart."

She laughed, the delighted expression on her face twisting something hard in his gut.

A true quandary, she was.

Clothing and manner not that of a servant (pity he could not hear her speech to confirm), but nor did she conduct herself with the airs and uppish graces of someone used to ordering servants about.

"Are you truly here alone?" Because servant or no, he couldn't quite fathom that. Someone this young, this appealing...

She isn't that young. Looks near your sisters' age.

Hmmm. Not sisters, plural. More like his *youngest* sister. But his sibling of five and twenty, one of three still living, had a husband of six years and three boisterous children.

Trouble, Tucker.

Aye, for now he imagined her as a mother. Carrying a babe, and couldn't decide if the image attracted or repelled.

Depends upon whose babe she carries...

"Yes, I am," and a litany of other words and sentences he had no chance of unraveling, not given the speed with which she spoke.

And poked—

Him in the chest when she sensed his attention wandering, but who could blame him? He'd positioned her to where the light from the saddle room would reach her face, but it was nowhere near bright. And she smelled so...well, *bright* herself.

That clean, fresh-baking sort of scent that made a man just want to sink his teeth into—

"What of it?" Her finger met his chest again, her chin tilted at a defiant angle. "*You* are here alone...... no one eats for me..." Eats? *Eats?* Treats? Speaks? Ah. No one *speaks* for her. "...I please..."

He captured that defiantly flailing frozen finger —before it could poke or prod again. Held it easily. "But I am not a fetching woman traveling—"

"You......fetching? Me?" Her countenance fairly glowed at him. She sped through more words, even gave him a wink and a shy smile in the middle, having made a jest he remained ignorant of?

Should have kept your mouth shut, let her keep poking.

He swallowed a growl at the thought of *being* the one doing the poking, with his tongue and other things, forced himself to relinquish her finger.

Standing here, bantering about—*you mean contemplating your attraction?*—wasn't getting her either warm or safe.

Are you quite certain about that? She looks plenty warm to me...

Argh! Trouble did like to bite him on the arse.

So he escaped before he made a bigger fool of himself.

. . .

SSUSANNA GULPED. Though she couldn't quite decipher his expression, every moment he stayed near like this made foreign, near-forgotten things simmer and sizzle along every inch of skin.

He touched one finger to her bottom lip, stroked the side of her face, leaned down to grant her lips one more gentle kiss, and then left.

Spun about and prowled the opposite direction. His dog following after a single, curious glance toward Susanna.

Her blood raged in her ears.

Legs straightened and tensed. Thighs clamped together.

His horse, Nelson Rambler (she couldn't help but chuckle at such a contrary name for a female horse who stood placidly nearby), fluttered her big lips in a snorted greeting. Bumped Susanna's shoulder. *Where's my carrot?* the equine wanted to know.

But Susanna had no answer, not with her riotous thoughts firmly engaged.

What had just occurred?

A chance encounter with a rumbly, intense stranger and she was ready to behave the trollop? In a barn?

Why...

After the misery of her marriage bed?

After the fiery joy of the unexpected kiss just shared between her and her rescuer?

Why, yes.

Yes, she most certainly was.

She would take hold with both hands, with lips

and other parts too, and welcome whatever this night might bring between her and this compelling stranger.

You aren't afraid of me. His dark, smoky voice, the timbre like a warm, calloused caress over the bare skin of her back—her breasts—had sounded so gobsmacked.

He—

She snickered at herself. For they had not introduced themselves. What was his name?

No matter. He would tell her soon enough and she would see what else they might share.

He's brawny and rough-edged; you ought to be afraid.

Pah. She knew full well a fine face and form could hide any number of ugly aspects.

She rather liked the strong, not-quite jagged planes of his weathered face. He was very interestingly configured, this former navy man who had appointed himself her gallant.

She had deduced that much by the knot around the handles of his bag. Her brother had taught her that very knot years ago. Said it was a favorite—strong and hard to untie swiftly, ideal if you needed to secure something and had no locks on hand.

And at the moment, Susanna wanted nothing more than to secure another kiss.

"KEEP AN EYE OUT TONIGHT." Leo greeted his superior in a low voice after he caught the other man's notice and was able to separate him from the card game. "I just ran afoul of the wrong crowd."

"You?" The man, a few years his senior, made it a point to stand with the lantern's light on his face. Though his words were seen and not heard, Leo knew they were barely audible, definitely not discernible to anything, or anyone, other than nearby horseflesh. "What...going unremarked?"

He jabbed one thumb over his shoulder, into the darker environs deeper into the stable, pointing back the way he'd come. "A female. One who drew their notice."

"And what? You appointed yourself...protector?" His commanding officer frowned, before his expression cleared. "Ah. She's to warm you this cold night—"

"Nay!" Leo swiftly interrupted just barely managing to keep his volume subdued.

The slightly shorter man only chuckled. Raised both hands—dirty, grimy ones—as though he were the one surrendering. "'Tis nothing off my back... you...get your prick wet this eve—"

"It isn't like that," he nearly growled.

'Tis exactly like that. And snarling at your boss? You're getting as bad as Reaver.

"She isn't that sort." Which was true. Very true, more's the pity. "Was traveling, alone, on that broken stage. I need a safe place for her to sleep tonight.

Somewhere they won't stumble across her—or me, now that they might be looking—before morning."

He didn't even want to think what might happen if she went outside to use the privy house and was discovered by one of the scurrilous sorts they'd been tracking. The sort who would as soon steal what they wanted *off* her person, *of* her person and either leave her bleeding out or vanished...

A kick to his gut at the thought.

And come morning? What then?

Well then, likely she will be on her way while he would try to repair whatever damage his vehement defense of her had caused. But for tonight? A stall might do for him at night, but not a lady. "Some place that isn't filled with horse shit."

Mikey jerked a nod. "That's easy. Use the carriage."

"Your carriage?" Now that offer stunned. The most Leo had dared hope for was one of the stable lads narrow bunks in the back. He knew Mikey had sent two of them home ahead of the storm, not realizing how long it would continue nor quite how many journeyers it would heap upon their unprepared heads.

"You said she wasn't from around here? Isn't a three penny looking for a coin, to knife you in the gullet after and steal your purse?"

A prostitute? "Not even close."

"Cannot offer the bunks...caught...stealing..." He thought *occupied* was in there somewhere. Mikey finished by repeating, "Use the carriage. No one will bother you there."

Leo whistled his appreciation. At the same time, he reached down, his fingertips seeking and finding the top of Reaver's head just as the dog leaned against his leg. "And Reave?"

Mikey aimed one elbow behind him. "...fine with me. Learn anything?"

"Aye. My arse wasn't made for sitting on a wooden bench upwards of eight hours."

Mikey just laughed, showing off the gap where he'd blackened several teeth, made them look rotten as hell. Between that and the grime he'd let settle in his sun-weathered skin since coming out here instead of staying in London, he appeared exactly like the stable master he sought to portray.

"Benton arrived earlier, with another I haven't seen," he added, knowing this was the type of information he was there to glean. "Big fellow, scar down the side of his face. Younger though, not as hardened as the others. So he's back from wherever they sent him. And before it got too crowded to take a damn breath, I caught several complaints about not getting paid timely. I think that's part of what had them so riled up, ready to attack the lass."

"Trouble in smuggler paradise?" his boss concluded after Leo shared a few more observations. "...can use that. Wait here."

6

CONFRONT THE RUDESBY?

THE ABSENCE of rain spitting upon the mud-slicked ground; the *suck* and *squelch* of his boots beating a hasty retreat against the same. The steady snarl the dog emitted when strangers came too close (or when Leo ordered the dog to stay behind). The lass's litany of language—likely not too foul—directed his way.

He may not have heard any of them, but he knew, sure as certain, every one buffeted his blind ears.

Sneaking out the stable from the saddle room, not in sight of the tavern and refusing to acknowledge how good her small hand felt tucked within his, if still dreadfully cold, Leo led her toward the old, abandoned carriage house as quickly as he dared over the slippery terrain. No sense lingering.

He barely acknowledged the fluffy flakes that now swirled about, keeping his attention focused beyond their narrow path. Ensuring no one took note of their destination.

His gab with Ol' Mikey proved valuable. Leo had secured their safe—albeit unusual—accommodations for tonight. A jug of ale. Some nuts and a thick, aromatic meat pasty. Best of all? A lantern.

But when he returned, though not excessive time had lapsed, his wildflower had wilted. Propped up by the railing, the little lady blinked wildly, fighting to keep her eyes open. Nelson Rambler already returned to her corner, slumbering more steadily on her feet (hooves) than his "guest" for the night, as the female he sought to protect fair wavered on her feet (no hooves in sight beneath the mucked dress).

"Long day of travel?" he had greeted.

Another yawn, a single nod. A shy smile, as her gaze dropped to his lips.

Shy. Because they'd kissed.

Absurdly, that made him smile. He held up his booty. "I dare not lay these down or the mice will march forth. Follow me and I shall see you undangered for the night."

He wanted to do so much more—pick her up, carry her again. Ask fifty or more questions. Dance with her in the newly falling snow—

Addle-pate.

You dance about as well as Nelson back there.

UPON LEAVING the stable with her newly appointed provider, Susanna saw that the rain and sleet had shifted into snow which she took as a good thing. Mayhap the fury of the storm had blown through and would calm overnight. Would permit the repairs tomorrow that would see her safely on her way.

And your intriguing rescuer as well? She rubbed her no-longer-frozen fingers against the warmth of his. *See you both off in different directions? What then?*

She couldn't stop her sigh of regret.

No need to feel the least bit cheated. The least saddened, silly goose, she consoled herself. *For then, would you not have the recollection of adventure craved?*

That thought, aided by the enticing, salivary scents of cooked meat spiced to perfection perked her up more than a full night's sleep. Susanna squeezed the hand wrapped securely about hers as her energized steps shadowed his through the falling snow, out behind the stable and onto a less traveled path. The lantern he held illuminated the slightly overgrown road that led to a smaller, much more disreputable, rough-planked building. Mayhap the original homestead or barn? Before the inn opened?

She looked behind them and saw no four-footed straggler. "What of Reaver?" Nothing.

She refused to vent her frustration at his continued rudeness. Why, if he kept this up, perhaps she would decide she did not like his kiss after all. Wasn't oft running her tongue against the back of her teeth, tasting him still...

Dare she confront his uncivil behavior?

Or should she swallow her protests and retreat as soon as he delivered her to their destination?

Did you not stifle your protests these last years? Retreat any time Mitchell returned home, soused or accompanied by his contemptible cronies?

Aye, and I promised myself freedom henceforth.

"Your *dog*," she prompted, giving vent to her ire. "The one you belong to, or have you forgotten him already, along with your manners?"

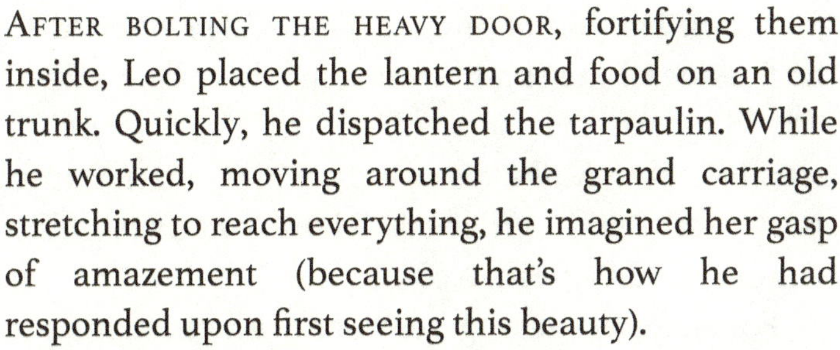

AFTER BOLTING THE HEAVY DOOR, fortifying them inside, Leo placed the lantern and food on an old trunk. Quickly, he dispatched the tarpaulin. While he worked, moving around the grand carriage, stretching to reach everything, he imagined her gasp of amazement (because that's how he had responded upon first seeing this beauty).

After folding the tarred canvas and tucking it out of the way, he lowered the carriage steps and turned, his arm outstretched to hand her up.

No simple gasp here. His lady *gawped*. Eyes wide, cheeks flushed, bedraggled bonnet and all. Looking adorably young. Devastatingly appealing. Imminently friskable. "Your carriage for the night, milady."

"We—we cannot..." She gestured, hands windmilling. "There!"

"Aye, we can. This is the very fine equipage of a

friend. I swear to you that we may use it tonight, a safe place to sleep. Nothing more."

Her face did not just fall at that. Did it? Nay, for she could not, had not... Didn't think he expected more?

After that kiss, you can lie to yourself thus?

Brimstone would be too good for him if he attributed desires to her she had not, only because he wished them so.

Fervently did he wish them.

"Friend?" Her look said she disbelieved *that* claim. "...certain?"

"I am. Up you go, now... There." He pointed to the far side of the shadowy bench where he'd aimed her. "Beneath that seat, off to the right, there's a chamber pot. Make use of it and I shall return shortly to see it emptied. Then you may sleep without disturbance... No?"

For she was shaking her head with enough force to dislodge some brain matter. She said something he could not make out, not with her in the darkened interior.

"'Tis all right," he attempted to comfort, hoping he wasn't making a hash of her protest as he retrieved the lantern, trying to illuminate her evening accommodations. "I have sisters. No need for any embarrassment—"

She thrust her head out—the bonnet already gone, leaving the drying straggles of her glorious black mane to tempt his fingers. "Where are you..."

"Where am I sleeping?" he hazarded when she paused.

She nodded. Frowned when he hesitated, so he tried again. "Right here, of course."

He pointed to the area in front of the carriage.

It wasn't overly crowded in here, even given the size of the majestic carriage, as it was the only item, aside from the trunk, on the dirt floor. The loft above, now? That was a stash and more, decades' worth of accumulation. But down here, the impressive carriage took up all but a few feet around on three sides, and then there was the five feet or so of space along the narrow edge that made up the door. If he shoved the trunk over—

Something prickled his back, and he glanced over to find her talking again. "You can relax your guard." He gestured her back inside. "Sleep."

She only stared, a slight pinch between her brows.

Said something too fast.

So he tried again. Pointing to the open ground, between the carriage steps and wall, he repeated. "I shall sleep out here. You... You are exhausted."

Are you attempting to convince her or yourself?

The lass is willing to entertain more between you. Do not be a fool.

He'd be a fool to imagine—or want—anything more than the kisses already granted. "Take off your wet clothing, will you? I will leave you in peace." *Damn me.* "You may retire in comfort."

※

A few moments prior...

SUSANNA BLINKED. Tried not to swoon.

The carriage being revealed before her, hidden away beneath tattered canvas blankets (and possibly an old sails?) looked like something the prince regent would jaunt about London in—if he could fit through the doorway and gain entrance, that was.

She turned astonished eyes to her companion who was busy folding the coverings. "Are you cracked in the head? We cannot make use of this, not unless we want to dangle from a hangman's noose upon being discovered here. In there!"

Once again, he ignored her, only opened the narrow door, its edge surrounded by some of the most detailed, intricate carpentership she had ever seen, and then let down the steps and gestured her inside.

"'Tis wrong, claiming this for the night." She was adamant. "What if the owner returns?"

Of course, widgeon, because on a night like tonight, everyone is eager to have the horses slip into a ditch.

While she indulged in fanciful wool-gathering (What might it be like to travel, to sleep in such a thing? Had she, ever, seen a carriage so splendiferous?), he dared assert this was the coach of a friend.

"A friend? Ha! As if I am befuddled enough to believe that! Convince me, if you dare. For until you do, I shall not believe another word."

"Up you go now," he said, not answering her concerns. He held the lantern aloft, illuminating the interior she could not help but approach.

She might think what they were doing was wrong, be apprehensive over reprisals, but other than binding her life with Mr. Mitchell's, Susanna had never considered herself foolhardy. *Oh no, what would you call* this *adventure?*

Opportunity. And she wasn't about to ignore a chance to experience such a majestic coach, if only for a few moments.

Afraid to sit, to besmirch the velvety interior with her dirty dress, she knelt on her knees, betwixt the two long benches on either side of the door and gazed in wonder as she worked the knotted ribbon of her bonnet free.

Gleaming mahogany (possibly rosewood—she didn't really know her woods) framed the corners and rooftop; thick velvet upholstery covering everything, walls and seats, in a beautiful greyish mauve known as stone (recognized from an old copy of *La Belle Assemblée* she'd perused with her nieces shortly before they'd concocted the scheme that ended up finding their father, and her brother, his new wife).

Why, the trampled way the building itself looked, not to mention the thick, raggedy coverings he'd gathered, one would think the carriage would possess an air of neglect, but nothing of the sort. The dark, reddish wood shone. Even the pliable leather window coverings tied down tight, to inhibit dust and dirt during travel, looked new and had not loosened from their moorings.

She listened half-heartedly as he told her of the chamber pot, offered to empty it.

"You, sir, are totally cracked if you think I am soiling a chamber pot in here. A veritable loon, you are!" She laughed and shook her head at him before turning back to continue her awed perusal wherever the lantern alit.

Pull-out drawers with golden knobs had been built beneath the squabs. If she couldn't lie full out across one side, surely she could on a slight diagonal, the plush seating so very deep.

And when she gained her feet, sodden skirts be damned, for she needed to test the height, she could nearly stand upright! Only needed the slightest of bend to her knees or neck to avoid bumping her head. And oh my, she put her hand over her head, palm up, dirty or no she had to test the soft cushion above. My, oh my. No bumping anything hard in here.

She couldn't stop her excited squeal. "This is a veritable plush palace you have brought me to!"

She turned to face the man who had shown her such wonders, standing there with a look of consternation on his face, one she quickly sought to wipe free. "This is, I vow, the most unique, amazing, ripping, *sparkish* carriage or coach I have ever, *ever* had the fortune to behold. Thank you for this! Now really, where are we sleeping for the night?"

Ducked just inside, she aimed her eyes upward,

past the carriage's roof, and indicated the loft above. "Up there?" It looked woefully packed with things. Old things. Bits and pieces of chairs, scraps of lumber, untold crates and more, all stacked higgledy-piggledy. But mayhap...mayhap there was room? "Is that where you have been bedding down?"

Then she looked back to him. "Or shall we just make a pallet down here?" She pointed to the ground. "This would be fine for me."

Fine? When not fifteen minutes ago you were clear frozen through!

Pah. She didn't notice the chill from her dress anymore, not since he'd taken up her hand and brought her *here*.

While the building itself might appear more disreputable than most, the few windows having long since been boarded over or blackened by years of weather (and lack of scrubbing she easily surmised), the inside proved as neat as any outbuilding she had entered. Someone took care of things here. Which meant someone would be returning to find them.

"Take off your wet clothing, retire in comfort."

"Comfort?" she asked incredulously. "What would you have me do? Be stript to skin when we are discovered? Exchange one wet dress for another? Everything in my bag is soaked clear through." She knew because she had checked when he and his dog had gone to speak with the stable master.

But the wretch ignored her protest, only encouraged her back inside. "I will protect you through the night. Sleep now."

"Arghhh!" she cried, frustration finally having its way with her. "Why do you keep doing that? I do not believe you to be rude, but you keep proving me wrong. There are things I would *rather* do than sleep. Like eat." And other things too, but she wouldn't—or couldn't—say more out loud. Not yet. "That is beef I smell, dinner you procured?"

Why did he persist in ignoring her? Try to shuffle her off to Nod, then stare at her so raptly? As though he would commit her features to memory. The way in which he waxed and waned, from considerate and kind to abrupt and not even civil? It made no sense at all to her storm-sluggard brain.

One moment he was comforting her, the next turning to shove the trunk in front of the already bolted door—and giving no indication he heard her question.

His tousled, overly long hair fell over his ear, hiding his face, when he knelt, to tuck the coverings inside.

As she thought back to his speech, her aggravation with him eased. Had not his every word to her been an even, steady husk? The deep syllables careful in volume? Every single thing since his bellowed claim...

"What is your name?" she called out.

Nothing.

She clapped twice.

Nothing again.

"Snake!"

No surprise—no response.

Pushing off from the narrow doorway, she jumped from the coach, startled him when she landed—for he swung back to face her, body tensed as though ready to defend—or attack?

He had not heard her. But he'd felt her land. Sensed it, either through his feet or from the slight *whoomph* of air.

"What? What is it?" His eyes darted around them—seeking danger? Surveying their quiet surroundings, before focusing back on her with every bit of the intensity he'd shown each time he'd faced her. "Did you hear something?"

"Nay, I did not." She spoke clearly, slower than she usually did. "And nor did you, I wager."

He only frowned, the horizontal grooves in his brow furrowing when he narrowed his eyes at her.

"Can you hear me? At all?"

A wave of relief—and regret—rolled over those strong, compelling features.

A sharp shake of his head. A definite scowl to his lips. A tinge of embarrassment entering his eyes and she *knew*. Knew with utter certainty.

"Oh, you dear man."

7

FROM TROUBLE TO TEMPTING

Dear man.

Whatever else she may have mouthed was lost when she launched herself at him.

Oof.

He caught her. Barely.

And then she was half hugging, half hanging off by the tight grip over his shoulders and behind his neck before he commanded the wherewithal to return the embrace, arms around her waist. Legs firming beneath.

Asinine, how his eyes watered. Had to be the smoke—

From where, you dolt? From what? You know *better.*

Couldn't be the tenderness mixed with compassion, but more than both, the grasp of *understanding* that lit her features right before she hauled off and jumped into his arms.

She deduces you are deaf as the dead and hugs you for it?

Keep hold of this one, Leo.

The avid sweep of her fingers down the side of his face, over his jaw and back up toward his ear approached a level of intimacy that made him squirm. But from anticipated *mental* discomfort, not physical. There were a litany of reasons why he'd grown his hair out to cover the ghastly sight. Several inches of them, in truth.

When the pressure from her questing encountered his destroyed ear, she hesitated, seemed to catch her breath, and then brushed his hair back only to kiss the damaged flesh. It was still numb. Had no feeling around it, not where she kissed, but he felt her touch. Felt it deep. In his heart? His soul? Mayhap, but definitely between his legs.

He wanted nothing more than to lose himself for a few blissful moments in the caring that she offered.

Nay. You ensure her safety for the night. Her honor.

Honor? Would he not honor them both with pleasures far beyond—

The press of her body against his sent thoughts spinning. The damp caress of her tongue—her keen, open-mouth kisses—all below first one ear and then the other, with a quick smattering across his jaw and lips in between, bade him to think he'd been knifed in the gullet after all.

Conked on the head.

Breaths against his cheek. More words?

Definitely more attention to the scarred, roughened skin around one ear. A tighter hug. And desire screamed at him.

Then it mattered not—his mixed, confusing array of emotions, her eagerness to comfort... The delay to his mission...

For the hands that petted him, stroked his nape, molded to the back of his head were naught but icicles.

"Gloves," he rumbled, pulling her arms away from his shoulders with a clasp to her wrists.

She eased to her feet, still chattering away, no hint of her earlier exhaustion in evidence while he stripped off his coat and swung it about her shoulders.

She beamed at him, sallied forth more sentences he remained oblivious to, as she scrambled to get her hands to peek out the long arms. The generous fit swamped her more than adequate figure. Made her appear even more appealing, knowing the lined wool, warm from his body, now comforted hers.

"Shhh, now." She stilled at his request, allowed him to gather her chilled fingers again.

"Gloves, I say." He pressed her palms together and surrounded her hands with his. "Why have you none?"

He made sure to stare at her mouth when he finished.

She hesitated, her fingers fluttering within his grasp.

"Speak without haste and face me. I can usually discern enough in most situations."

She bit both her lips at once and gave a nod. When he squeezed her hands and released them, she used her newly freed arms to gesture, depicting her words. Words she prefaced with a swift swipe of her tongue across the inviting mouth he stared at so intently. "When the horses slid...ice, we...the coach and passengers ended up in a ditch."

That much, she spoke slowly, but he could tell by the tension growing in her frame the memory affected her. "Broke...loud...outs..." Outs? *Shouts.* "......clambered to......mud...sucked..." Her words flew fast enough they soared right past him. "...others...hurt..."

There was more but that was enough.

Climbing free of a side-tipped carriage was difficult enough in any weather. But with everything drenched and frozen? 'Twas a wonder both she and her things had fared as well as they had.

Speaking of things, he retrieved both their bags, tucked his just inside the door on one bench and leaned in to plop hers solidly in the farthest corner on the opposite side.

Another shiver wracked her limbs.

"Up," he told her, turning her about to assist. "Inside. Time to get you warm."

She resisted, clutching at his forearms.

"Both of us," he assured, for after that unexpected embrace, only a man with no sense at all would sleep outside the carriage, upon the dirt floor. "We will continue this inside."

Continue what, exactly? Seduction? Explanations? *Introductions?*

When she made no move to climb the steps, he subdued a growl and told her earnestly, "I vow to you, with regards to the use of this carriage tonight, we may remain without any hint of discovery or discipline if we shutter ourselves and the lantern inside." He pointed to the single biggest crack in one of the planks, where a noticeable waft of cold air entered. "I will patch that with whatever I can crowd in to keep out the worst of the cold, but mainly, I do not want our presence in here known, not if I can help it. And not to those who would have done you harm."

If the weather could get in, so could their light get out. Not till he had her wrapped up tight in the carriage, lantern on or off, could he relax his tense vigil.

And what about wet clothing? Do you bid that on or off?

As he swallowed a groan, she gave a single nod, interest—and excitement?—writ upon her features. Yet again, a shudder, slight but apparent, shook through her frame but she gave no awareness of it, only motioned for him to continue. Shockingly, with her mouth closed.

He almost smiled, but couldn't, as awe trembled through him.

It was as though, upon realizing he could not

share in typical conversation—and that he hadn't *intentionally* behaved the unmannered brute—she all but invited *his* chatterings to blather forth.

As though she trusted him to decide, and guide, them both for the better.

'Twas a heady feeling, the faith she placed in him. There on December 22—edging toward the 23rd—in this ramshackle part of English countryside known for naught but its ill-kept bridge and less-than-savory sorts, Leopold Michael Tucker felt, for the first time since he last captained the *HMS Restless* in open waters, with hearing and command still intact, *in charge* again.

Responsible for making the right choices to secure the safety of those under him. Of those dependent—

Aye, and you desire the sweet, trusting ballocks-breaking lass under *you too, do you not?*

He choked on a snarl. Of course he did. If for naught else than to warm her chilled skin.

Right. Tell yourself that.

Did he retreat from this strange mix of arousal and awareness? Of passion and protectiveness? Remove himself from temptation? *Do you not mean trouble?* Did he commit only to seeing her safe harbored for the night, and then go on about his business as he had been the last months?

Or years? Lonely years...

Or did he surrender to the inexplicable spark that burned bright enough between them to illuminate those dark patches hidden in his soul since

Ann-Marie? Since he loved and lost, and resisted trying again?

Love? Tucker, you really were clouted on the head.

"Right," he said, lungs and midriff expanding fully on a deep breath. Right. *You wanted to be in command again? Take responsibility for her.* "You have yet to stop shivering. Please. Remove your wet things, change into dry clothing. Use the chamber pot as you need, and let us both retreat inside."

Again, her lips danced, waltzing out words he was completely oblivious to. But still, he stood there and stared at her mouth, feeling it do things to him he'd thought would never occur again. Not when he decided years ago that love wasn't in the cards for him.

"I wish I could hear your voice." He hadn't meant to admit such a thing.

She made a dismissive gesture. Contorted her facial muscles. Then relaxed them back into the mischievous expression he was coming to know as her playful side. "No, you do not," pronounced very clearly. "Wretch-ed. I am—it..." She pointed to her mouth, those sweet lips he already needed to capture again. "Reach."

What? "Reach?"

"Nay. Sk-sk-sk-*reech*. Screech."

"Ah. You would have me believe you sound as a screecher?"

"Aye. Off-ten. I am a sore—" She punched one fist (lightly but unmistakably) into the fleshy area above her opposite elbow and exaggerated a wince. "Sore. Try-al. Trial."

His smile broke free. "As if I will believe anything of the kind."

She rose up and nuzzled his ear—the bottom of it, not the top—where he still had some sensation, warm puffs of breath, the only testament to her continuing communication.

"You realize I have no idea what you are saying —er *screeching*."

She pulled back, eyes alight. "Simply cat-er-wall-ing." The lass winked at him. "You miss not."

Not?

Naught.

Ah.

'Twas the most entertaining conversation— evening—he'd had with anyone since the blast.

And the realization that it was exactly that—a *conversation*, give and take between two people, wonder of wonders!—between him and another, and about something other than lurking round cutthroats made *him* wonder...

Had he too quickly abandoned his mother's efforts to see him returned home? Might he still "converse" at the big family gatherings he had been purposefully avoiding ever since? The ones brimming with his three sisters and their spouses and the sundry dozen or more younglings running about?

Had he been too embarrassed to even try?

Aye, you beetle-brain. 'Tis your pride that has kept you alone these last two winters, away from the Tucker household and hearth, waiting full of love and open arms.

Hmmm. This winter was not yet over. The holiday gathering likely about to commence for the year...

Yet, when he now imagined returning to the bustling abode where he'd grown up, it was not a halting, gesture-filled coze with one of his brothers-in-law he saw. Nay, 'twas the delighted smile plumping his mama's cheeks and brightening her eyes as the adorable lass only met this eve entertained with one tale or another.

'Twas the way *she*—the woman easing from his arms, not the one who reared him—looked over, caught his eye, and *winked*.

"Inside now," he ordered in his best commander's voice, flicking his head and hair, trying to dislodge the disturbing—*Do you not mean enticing?*—vision.

"Posthaste and with pleasure," he thought she said, before leaping back up while he took a careful moment to pack dirt and straw along the rogue plank (and to gather his flown senses).

Only to have her approach from the side as he finished, returning his coat and, red-faced, indicating the chamber pot she'd placed at the door. He smiled after her retreating form as he pulled on his coat. She still wore her wet dress. Must be waiting for him to make himself scarce before exchanging it for something dry.

Scant minutes later, he'd emptied the night-tub

outside, taken care of his needs, and scrubbed himself free of dirt and the day. Returning to their haven, he secured the iron bar across the door, hauled the trunk in front of it and greeted her inquisitive face at the open coach door. "May I hand up dinner?"

She acceded with a smile and scrambled to the far corner, making room for his bulk. Before ascending, he gave over the wrapped food and ale, and moved the lantern to the floor of the carriage. With the leather flaps drawn tight, and keeping down low, he had no concern the soft glow might betray their presence.

Outside, the snow had sailed downward so thickly it had obscured his boot marks before he could gather a branch and do the same. He swiped at the moisture melting about his hair, the shoulders and arms of his coat before taking it off.

The sinister circumstances of the last hours had one unexpected boon. For, thanks to them, seemed he had finally unearthed a night's recompense for himself. For the first time in days, he could allow a tranquil breath and release the constant cognizance for mischief that kept his muscles taut and his mind suspicious. He could be at ease for once. And mayhap sleep deeply as well.

The very thought settled through his limbs like a wave full of peace.

He climbed in, sat opposite and tucked his coat out of the way (a pillow, perhaps? for later). Then gained his first full look at her. "Your dress," he all but accused. "You still have it on. Please, quickly now, change into something dry," he counseled, attempting to smooth his tone. "My eyes will remain closed."

She immediately tapped fingers to his knee and he focused on her lips.

"All...wet through." She motioned with her hands, encompassing what she wore and her bag, then twisted them at the wrists, as though wringing out.

Egad. "You have *nothing* dry? Warm?"

"...clothing...other things..."

"No dry clothing?" he confirmed.

Even before her head shook *nay*, he reached for his bag, untying the rope securing his haversack. He foraged for his spare shirt and raised it between them. "'Tis clean, but not fancy."

"Yours?" She brushed his fingers when she claimed it. "'Tis...perfect."

Again, he closed his eyes. This time turned his body and his head away, for why tempt his peepers to peek?

He waited in agonized silence. But, for once, not agonizing because he felt alone. Somewhat discarded, or as useless as an afterthought. Nay, the only agonizing thing prodding him at the moment was the *anticipation* of seeing her attired thus: in his shirt.

And naught else?

Too soon, and yet not nearly soon enough, she tapped again. Only this time on his jaw.

He swallowed past the tingles constricting his throat and opened his eyes.

He soaked her in, the light flush huing her cheeks, the black strands a muddle of damp hanks and finer, drying strands, the heart-wrenching, staff-stiffening sight of her in—damn them both—naught but his large linen shirt, tugged over her head and gaping at the neck, more off one shoulder than on, extending past the discernible swell of her breasts and covering only the top portion of her thighs.

Her milk-white, beckoning-his-hands-to-grasp-stroke-and-*plunder* thighs.

Feet bare and legs—

"Stockings!" The syllables gurgled up from his starving lips. Starving for the taste of that milky skin. "Wait but a moment."

Three seconds later he handed her his clean pair of socks. The thick ones. But then, like the veriest of jolterheads, he watched as she eased the first over pretty white toes and drew it up past her ankle and—

"Beef!" he strangled out, wresting his attention to the packet of food. "Are you hungry?"

She glowed at that. Nodded. And stared at his hands as they revealed the packet of nuts and displayed the pasty. Made him think, mayhap, she wanted them plundering too.

8

SOMETHING IMPRESSIVE

"GO ON, now. It's time we both got to Nod." Reaver the Impressive turned his no doubt doleful expression toward the man who spoke. "Dawn comes early enough, sun or snowstorm."

Mikey was using his Midlands-middling voice, as Reaver had named it. 'Twas the one "stable master" tended to use each evening, but only *after* the hour grew ever later, the coins and cards flying across the rough table had first slowed and then stopped, and any visiting coachmen, various grooms and the inn's two stable boys had drifted off.

'Twas the voice the man used when it was the two of them, or occasionally the human and one of two others, either Reaver's man, Tucker, or ol' Benny Wrath.

It was a far cry different from the street-bumpkin-lout voice Mikey reserved for *guests* of The Filthy Pig, and travelers who stopped only long enough for a change of horses.

A far, far cry different from the priggy, officious one the man employed in London.

Looking longingly past the long (but not impressive) rows of stalls, past the sleeping, snuffling and, occasionally, stomping (often snoring or snorting) horses, Reaver gave a single whine.

"I know, boy. You want to go to work at Tucker's side. He will be back for you come morning. Now go curl up next to my bunk."

Reaver swung his head, long snout impressive (but not as emphatically so as the tongue it housed), and aimed himself toward the even smaller room off to the side where Mikey had stowed some stray he'd caught thieving from guests earlier.

A two-legged youngling, now slumbering, who hailed from somewhere along the coast, given the scents of ocean and brine Reaver had picked up from the lad's clothing.

But more importantly? What caused his impressively large paws to pad forward without excessive delay? 'Twas the scent of juicy meat his impressive nose had picked up as well....

***

Laughter. Tranquility.

Tingling lips and a riotous belly from kisses given—not taken.

"Not expecting a cuff to the shoulder or a sharp curse every moment Mr. Mitchell was at home?" As her wearied muscles loosened from the well-guarded, well-remembered anguished clutch, so did her mouth.

Susanna rambled. Knew it was so, spoke more to the incredible beef pasty wrapped in a bit of waxed paper making its way back to her chattering lips after that first bite that had near sent her into rapture. "Not counting the reprieves I had helping first Ellen and my nieces, and then caring for the girls at their house those last months before Nate returned home, why, I cannot count myself having a more splendid meal."

Another swiftly chewed, vastly appreciated bite of the thick savory pasty he'd insisted she have the larger portion of and she was hieing off again, filling the comfortable silence between them—because she could.

"I had not realized how very dowd I had become, in spirit if not in person." She flicked her gaze from the remaining pasty to his countenance. His stormy eyes stirred, alit, as though her chatter amused him. Didn't frustrate or anger. How refreshing, that!

Not that she was typically overly loquacious, not since long before the reality of her marriage crashed down upon her. But now? In this unique moment that felt heavy with anticipation yet light with possibilities, across from this man who intrigued her like no other? Whose protective nature mingled with his physical allure?

Well, despite more than one poor experience in the sexual realm, all Susanna could think was, *Let my adventure begin!*

"I vow, I had quite forgotten the sheer joy to be felt in the presence of a handsome man."

She knew he couldn't hear her. Couldn't understand anything, but the circus in her belly jumped about, exquisitely so, and bade her lips to somehow release her joy.

Knowing that she could ramble whatever she wanted and he would remain mostly unaware made her sad. And yet relieved as well, because she could admit out loud things that would ordinarily remain stifled. "I may not have known you long, sir, but I like what I know. I like it very, very much."

Tucking a bit of beef past her bottom lip with the back of one finger, she chewed, swallowed, and met his rapt gaze. Finding all that intensity focused on her, admiringly so, the acrobats in her middle turned even more fervent flips. "Aye. I find you very pleasing."

She took another bite, the savories meeting her tongue nothing close to warm but no less wondrous, and smiled at him, laughing at the slightly crinkled forehead, the perplexion his half-bemused frown, half-curious smile couldn't hide.

This close, she saw the short stubble covering his lower cheeks and jaw. A shade lighter than his hair thanks to the smattering of white hairs among the darker blond. Her palms itched to stroke the firm jaw beneath. How prickly might *his* facial hair be? How soft?

She swallowed past a delightfully tight throat—tight with attraction, not anxiety for once—and gestured to her mouth and then her ear, her fingers flying as raptly as her words. "I know. You have not a single notion of what I prattle. It is all right, for I can hear well enough for the both of us this eve."

Pasty gone, nuts and ale still beckoning, she wiped her hands on the paper, and then firmed both palms flat on the squabs and faced him squarely.

The puzzled expression had eased, once he realized she didn't expect him to acknowledge or respond to her words. If anything, his intriguing face had relaxed. Yet still he studied her in a way that showed he saw past the surface.

Uncomfortable at what he might glean, she stared back. Pleased when, despite the tumblers in her stomach, she continued to meet his gaze.

"You." She pointed to his chest, spoke slower, on purpose, and then motioned to his face. "Are quite handsome." Laughed outright when his sandy eyebrows arched upward, disbelief writ across his sun-weathered features.

"Aye." She gave an emphatic nod. "You heard. Hand." She opened hers right in front of his eyes. Then lowered it so he could see her mouth. "Some. Handsome."

There! I said it and I am not going to apologize for thinking it.

'Twas a mature face. One of experience. Of, mayhap, a dozen or so winters more than she claimed. Perhaps a couple fingers more. But nowhere near old.

And those lips—

Had she seen a man's mouth so lush before? Not pursed in anger nor pinched in irritation?

You have not.

Hers tingled the more she stared. She wanted to touch those lips again.

Wanted to experience his unique blend of intense yet gentle passion, and she vowed to do it before she slept.

"How long were you out in the storm?" His words rumbled quietly into the space between them, bringing forth more heat than she had any right to feel beneath the soft linen of his shirt. "I fear your wits have yet to thaw."

"You jest!" She nearly choked on a nut, coughed into her hand, smiling widely, breathing in his clean, masculine scent from the long sleeve that fell about her palm. But before she could assure him of her sincerity, he spoke again.

"What made you travel by yourself? Without anyone to accompany you? Are you evading the one who hurt you? Escaping him?"

Her mirth faltered. Smile fell.

Bastard! Look what you did.

Leo hated how he'd stolen the joy from her face. Replaced it, not with fear thank God, but with a look of mulish determination. To resist his efforts at inquiry? Or perhaps, someone else's efforts to return her where she did not choose to go?

"Will you tell me why you are traveling? Or where you are headed?"

"...my brother...family...holidays. And you?"

What did he tell her that wasn't a lie without revealing overly much? "Work brought me here."

"Work." Her eyes narrowed, flicked toward his haversack. "Not...navy work, surely? ...far inland?"

Damn. Perceptive little puss. Too bad he could not enlist her aid in his search for information.

"A favor for my superior who..." He wasn't in a position to explain. "Ah..."

"You...dither." At least he thought the last word was *dither*. She held up her hand, palm out. "I... enough. Were you strangled here too?"

Strangled? Strangled... Stranded!

"Aye, in part."

"And you travel...only your dog and Nelson Rambler?"

"Correct. 'Tis only the three of us."

Her soft smile bloomed again as she turned her attention back to unwrapping the nuts, and it was as though the sun burst forth, illuminating all the shadows he had become adept at hiding among.

That quickly, he had returned contentment to her features? Eased her heart? And as to his pathetic explanation, she did not feel the need to press for more? Was appeased with his minim explanation, as to why he was here? A rare woman indeed.

REAVER'S LONG (IMPRESSIVELY LONG, he knew) canine tongue swept up and out, over his muzzle, gleaning every bit of grease that clung to his fur and short whiskers.

He'd already cleaned the empty waxed papers to a shine. After wolfing down (*wolfing*, heh-heh) the remaining portion the young and clueless simpleton had left unguarded.

"Hey ho, old man. I'm alone."

"Benton!" Mikey moved faster than his stooped posture of late might indicate, scuttling to stash away the mirror and tooth black he used to keep his smile offensively grimy. "What are you doing out here?"

Licking at front paws (the ones also impressive in size) with pre-nap thoroughness, Reaver glanced over at the newcomer Mikey spoke to, giving his own, single "*Wrrooof!*" of welcome.

"Hey ho, Reaves." Bearded Timothy Benton, who in London went by Lord Wrothington, ambled over in his somewhat ragged country attire and placed fingers on the dog's neck, giving an appreciated scratch before heading to the "old" stable master, where the two conversed in hushed voices that Reaver could nevertheless hear with ease.

Because, aye, his auditory skills were impressive indeed.

Was that not why "Old" Mikey had chosen him —Reaver the Impressive—to work so closely with Captain Leo Tucker?

Speaking of Tucker, Reaver missed his man's

foot. Or palm. In the months they had traveled together, Reaver had grown used to Tucker's light, comforting touch any time he slept.

Being here—in the equine-crowded, straw-filled (equine-*excrement*-straw-filled) place—without his person to look after set Reaver's fur on edge. His whiskers to twitching.

Tucker might have told him to *Remain in the stable, good boy*, but that didn't mean Reaver had to like it.

"What prompted you to risk coming out here?" Mikey whispered so low no one else would overhear. No human, that was.

"You see Tucker? That filly he rescued?"

Mikey grunted in agreement. "They're safe for the night."

"Keep them hid," Wrath, as he was called in London society, said. "Beyond riled Haggart and Bowyer and their cringers. Every minute that's passed got them to fuming hotter over not taking Tucker down and claiming her. Did what I could to stall and detour, but now Haggart aims to make an example of them both. Went out blustering a few moments ago, gunning for their trail. Idiots. Why can their liquored brains not give it a rest for one god-damn night?" Wrath's hands went to his falls. "Claimed I was heading out for a shit. Just need to piss, but need to get to it and back in there. Tucker get anything yet?"

"Have you?" Mikey countered rather than waste time answering.

"Rumblings. Nothing worth spending Christmas in this godforsaken place for."

"Storm has made everyone batty."

"Booze did that. They're all pissed as a newt, they are."

"Snow will help. Still coming down?"

"In sheets."

"Good. They'll give up soon enough."

Good, indeed. Grand, in fact. Anything was better than the incessant rain that persisted in muddying his impressive paws.

Reaver flexed one in front of him. His thick brown fur shone in the lantern light.

A soft snort, followed by a *plopping-squish* hit his ears seconds before the awful offal smacked his nose.

Blasted horses.

Smelled up the stable something fierce.

When could he retrieve his human and leave?

9

BECAUSE LENGTH MATTERS

FOR THE NEXT several hundred heartbeats, they ate silently, sharing the small bounty. Their mouths busy chewing, savoring or sipping ale, all the while speaking all sorts of things with their eyes. Things Leo could not help but hope he heard aright.

When his last bite of beef disappeared and he declined the last few nuts, telling her to take pleasure in filling her belly, she alternated between eating a couple and feeding him a time or three. Did her fingers linger that last time?

Feeling strangely out of his depths, he licked his bottom lip—where she'd touched him—and remarked, "Memorable picnic, eh?"

She beamed at him. "The. Absolute. Best."

"Tell me your name?"

She did, but far too fast.

"Once more?"

Slower didn't do any better. With no context or other, readily familiar syllables and mouth movements to aid him, he remained at a loss.

"Do not frown."

He discerned that clear enough and chuckled. "Forgive me, but I cannot make it out."

"Nothing to forgive. Oh!" A quick smile and swift actions saw her rummaging through her travel bag, only to emerge triumphant with a hastily bundled parcel that appeared impervious to the day's travails. From it, she revealed several smaller (wrapped with more care) packages—gifts, he surmised—and a small case tucked alongside. From this, she liberated a thick stack of folded letters and a pencil, an excited look on her face.

She opened one of the letters and scribbled hurriedly upon an empty space.

He studied her as she wrote. Her chills had abated. While not hot by any means, the ambient temperature in the carriage had risen, with them both in proximity. The lantern aided as well.

She finished with a flourish. Only instead of handing him the paper she'd written on, she crossed to his seat—his side—close enough that the peaceful breath he'd enjoyed moments ago riled back up to not peaceful at all, for now she was close enough to smell. To hold.

To kiss again.

.   .   .

"HERE." Cuddling next to his brawny warmth, Susanna held out the old letter she'd written months ago, a silly, nonsensical talisman of sorts she kept with her as a reminder that hoped-for miracles were possible.

If not always for herself (though she did count finally being rid of Mitchell somewhat of her own personal triumph, if not outright miracle), then for those she loved and prayed for.

How fortunate that she had it, and a couple others, with her now to write upon. How fortuitous that she'd stashed these with the gifts for her nieces when the storm refused to abate.

She tapped the edge of the page against his fingers but didn't let go. So they both held it as he read where she pointed.

Susanna Oliver Mitchell.

Then she lowered her fingertip to the one word she'd penciled below:

Yours?

"Captain Leopold Tucker, but I go by Leo now."

"Leo." A strong name for a strong man.

This close to him? Both his heat and scent wrapped her in such a conundrum of comfort and yet unease.

Unease because, for the first time in ages, she wanted a man. Desperately so. Ached to rise up and claim his mouth again, to press her flesh against his, and have him take over.

Somehow, even in his passion, she knew he wouldn't harm her. Wouldn't take more than she wanted to give. And at the moment? Reckless Susanna wanted to give all.

He was so different from any man she had ever spent alone time with. Aye, Captain Leo Tucker was appealing.

Captain, she scribbled, beyond pleased with herself. <u>*Knew*</u> *you were navy.*

"You did," he confirmed. "I was. Am. But not... Not..."

"Shhhh." Though she knew he couldn't hear her, she said it as she squeezed the fingers of his nearest hand.

Whatever he was doing, here, had some element of clandestine to it, but not in a nefarious way, she could not believe. Not given how he had rescued her, how he spoke to her with an earnest, steady quality she found beyond attractive.

She sensed his hesitance to say anything untruthful, and after the deception she had lived with for years, she would take far less, information she could rely upon, than rubbish-filled volumes of insincerity.

"Mrs. Mitchell. I..."

Hearing those words leave his mouth, being addressed as such, threatened every modicum of ease she'd gained in his presence thus far.

· · ·

"Mrs. Mitchell. I—"

From a tender squeeze to sharp talons in an instant, her nails bit into the back of his hand. The piercing panic he sensed halted him as he released his hold on the note they jointly held. He angled his body to watch her face. Which had puckered as though she'd licked the hind end of a goat.

She shook her head in an exaggerated fashion.

Hmm. "You *were* married? *Were* Mrs. Mitchell?" An abrupt nod, further puckering. "But no more?" Another nod, an unmistakable look of relief. "Mr. Mitchell treated you poorly."

Not a question.

Her features froze, no acknowledgment of his words. No denial either.

Her gaze fell to the side.

"Then I shall call you Lady Susan—"

"Nay." Her eyes flew back to his. "Susanna...no lady."

He knew that, for she'd arrived alone, not chaperoned nor surrounded by servants. "You seem young to have been married." The frozen expression remained. "And widowed?"

There was the relief again.

That Mitchell fellow was a bastard. Good thing he was gone—or Leo would have traced the man to ground for behavior unbecoming.

"Children?" Though he thought not given how she wasn't surrounded by any.

To his dismay, her eyes immediately filled with tears. She dashed them away and shook *no* again.

"You are sad because of the lack or..." He waned as the silent tears blame near punched a hole in his middle. "And you do not have to answer this old fellow's prying, busy-headed curiosity—"

She covered his mouth with her fingers. He kissed them without thinking.

Her watery eyes grew luminous.

"He—James Mitchell"—she spoke slowly and clearly—"was selfish...uncaring..." There was more, *a lot more* he suspected, beyond "uncaring". He shoved down the thought and concentrated on her lips forming syllables and words he needed to grasp. "...lose the baby..."

"Oh, Susanna." He dropped the folded square and drew her into his arms—and onto his lap. So much he could say. Wanted to say.

But somehow, didn't need to, for the woman simply ducked her head beneath his chin, delved her fingers under the hem of the shirt he hadn't bothered to tuck in after taking care of things outside and fluttered her fingers beneath his shirt until they came to rest on the skin of his torso. Pressing lightly at the top of his stomach, her thumb alone grazing upward toward his chest. She stilled, just like that, resting her fingers and palm not quite against his thudding heart and it seemed, sure as certain, miraculously too, that she managed to "hear" all he hadn't voiced.

The aching wrench of compassion. Of frustration on her behalf. For what she'd endured.

Curiosity about her; curiosity that flared like a bonfire.

After a few moments, she withdrew her fingers, bent to retrieve the paper, then floundered by his outer thigh until locating her pencil.

Married?

"Me? No. Never." Which was far and away peculiar for any navy man in his position. "Almost, though," something compelled him to add. "Twice."

Which explained much, how a man of eight and thirty (his age when he officially stopped commanding the *Restless*) could have been captaining a ship without a wife. Was beyond unusual, he knew, the navy preferring its officers married and "settled".

Her pencil hovered... Hesitated. Trembled as she glanced up at him.

"You wish to know more?" he asked.

A nod her answer.

"'Twill likely bore you to Bedlam."

Never.

Underlined *twice.*

"Ahhhh. Let me see..." *Let me dither, more like.* Never had he spoken to another about his two lost amours. Far easier to pretend he remained single, alone, first by choice, and then by necessity, because of his injury. (*How long might you lie to yourself on that front?*) Far easier than to confess it was fear. Fear that had kept him single nearly the past decade or more. Fear of more pain that bade him to keep to himself?

Admitting it now, he frowned. For it seemed a weak excuse at best.

She stirred against him, scribbled, then shoved the page in front of his eyes.

Chuckling, he grasped her wrist and lowered it a few inches. *Need those peepers of your papa's after all?*

Smothering a growl, he read.

You need not tell me.

She squirmed upon his lap.

Anxious? Or... "Are you uncomfortable?" he asked, tensing his already clenched thighs; for every muscle he possessed—certainly the enlarged one centered between them—had grown taut from her proximity.

Her scent.

Her compassion and curiosity over his unre-markable life.

Not <u>un</u>comfortable. Uncomfortably <u>curious</u>.

That made two of them.

"I was young," he rumbled, thinking of his hushed voice reaching her in the quiet, after stretching to adjust the lantern as dim as it would go. Did the snow still swarm beyond their carriage-made cocoon? Did the cold night still seep past the straw and mud he'd packed in the plank? Was she truly comfortable?

And there you go, dithering yet again.

"Younger than you are now, I wager. Loved Ann-Marie with everything in me. But we both knew a navy man had to earn his way to a wife." 'Twas foolhardy to marry before his rank warranted it.

"So we wrote and spent every moment together when I was on liberty. Time passed. I gained promotions. Enough so that I proposed—by letter, but I was so excited. Did not want to wait. Knew she would want to join me at the earliest opportunity."

He shifted, curved his arms about her waist and held on. Because he knew what was coming. "Only when her letter finally reached me, brimming with acceptance and delight, it was accompanied by six others. A veritable tome of letters: my mother, two closest sisters, Ann-Marie's parents each wrote, as well as her younger brother. All filled with sorrow and condolences, as she'd fallen from her brother's horse during a mad gallop directly after penning her acceptance, racing to my house, to share the news with my sisters—" He broke off, coughed into his fist. "And damn me if I didn't just tell you far, far too many words. She died."

And for the first time, ever, in the telling of it, in thinking of it, he didn't die inside at the memory.

He hugged the still figure in his arms, rested his chin against her temple. "And there you have it, a once-broken heart makes for a poor suitor."

She held up two fingers, lifted them high, right

in front of his face, easily discernible even with the lamp dimmed. She slowly bent one, leaving only the other upraised.

"You wish the rest? The other 'almost'?"

Her head nudged his chin.

"Shorter in the sharing, I promise. Some years later, I courted a fellow officer's daughter, because she was pleasant enough." And because Leo should have been married by then, according to his superior, the very woman's father. "Courted her for nearly seven months, applied myself to that end, to securing her hand, all the while attempting not to compare her to my love, until one day, I realized how very much I did enjoy her company. Looked forward to the time we spent together. Could actually envision a life together and was ready to propose. No longer out of duty, but from desire—only to have her cast me aside." He could chuckle about it now, but at the time, his heart had ached anew. "She'd fallen for someone else, long before we met, a younger man her father did *not* endorse and had used my slow advance of a courtship to give her time with him, until they both disappeared in the night.

"'Twas a while before I realized her actions broke my pride, mayhap injured my self-confidence, but affected not my heart. After that? Nay. Nothing. No interest in pursuing another." Not beyond fleeting pleasures of the moment.

Not until tonight. Until you.

<hr>

"Reaver."

Mikey lowered a bowl. "Fresh water for you, boy. Just melted enough to drink."

Neither of them had been able to sleep. Malease hung in the air. (Or mayhap that was simply the horse stench.)

The canine trotted across the dirt floor and allowed the agile length of his tongue to slurp the cold treat with sloppy abandon, uncaring if clean droplets splattered his face or the floor surrounding.

Was *water* not used to clean nearly *everything*? Why, his impressive tongue was doing the humans a boon! They should thank him for his efforts.

Be appreciative he cared enough to share his water with the dirty floor. And a bit of the wall beyond.

Be impressed that his superiorly long tongue could do so much—and with so little effort on his part.

After drinking—and splattering—his fill, he brushed up against Mikey in thanks and approached the lesser-used exit, the one that led deeper into the woods, ready to keep watch for Tucker's return.

Turning in a circle before settling, Reaver swiped his tongue over his wet, glistening muzzle, gathering up a few remaining drops. Highly satisfied with himself.

Because length really did matter.

10

A DEEPER CHILL

❦

<u>DO NOT POST! DO NOT POST</u>

September 7, 1815

Dearest Olivia,

Never can I thank you enough for this summer. The few weeks spent with you outside of Duffield proved a balm over and above what I so desper- ately needed after birthing little Philip, only to never see him open his eyes, never hear him cry... nor feel his warm, breathing

smudges here made the ink blur

breathing little body suckling at my breast, protected against my heart.

I did not realize, until those solemn summer days, after Sarah returned to London and you sat peacefully with me outside, content to hold my hand or brush yours down my hair or do nothing at all except <u>be near</u> me, in silence, as we watched Nate and Faith digging out the over-grown gardens or listened to the welcome chatter of Charity ordering Hope about in the kitchens, while the two baked treats or prepared lemonade (and Hope hollered orders at her growing kittens to get <u>off</u> the counters before they got caught by <u>grown-ups</u>), how much I longed for female companionship.

<u>How much I missed my mother.</u>

Thinking I was to become one myself, in the months prior, had so many thoughts of my own maternal parent hovering about.

I defied them, you know, her and Papa both, to marry James. Refused to entertain a word against him.

'Twas years after Nate left for the sea, and shortly after Ellen birthed Faith. Our parents seemed <u>so old</u> once Papa retired, and I felt so very misprized by them. Our village sorely lacked in amusements. I had known James forever, it seemed, and the time spent with him burst with fun and adventure. And kisses, welcome ones.

I persisted, nagging my parents till Papa gave his consent "against my best judgment, missy" and, I suspect, because neither he nor Mama knew what else to do with me. (Nor were there a glut of marriageable men clamoring around, so many in our area having either moved to bustling Birmingham, gone off to war, or simply not of an age, slumberous little village that we inhabited.)

But while I took to housewifery with a quiet joy that saw me maturing (I would like to think, well beyond my young years), eager to become a mother, James...

Well, I could not tell you this last summer, not with him waiting impatiently for my return, but he has proved a most wretched spouse. Simply put, without the stabilizing influence of his father's hand, James took to drinking in excess, to seeking idle entertainments beyond our quaint town and spending <u>all</u> his time with others disreputable in nature (or should I confess <u>nefarious</u> in nature?).

He fell to gambling and grumbling—and were it not for the financial wherewithal from his family, I know not how we would maintain our home and James his stable.

It wasn't until spending those weeks with you and Nate, watching how you conducted your-

selves toward each other that stark realization slammed into my soul with all the force of a fist to my stomach. I believe it made me grieve even harder, not only for the babe buried, but also for the innocence lost after choosing the wrong sort of man to bind my life with.

Papa was right, I had realized shortly after his heart gave out and we saw him buried not long after my marriage. Accurate in his assessment that James lacked strength of character—something Papa had seen beneath the veneer of charm that had blinded me.

But when Mama followed to the grave not twenty months later and with Ellen's health beginning to fail and England still at war, I could not trouble Nate. Had nowhere to turn, save to endure the marriage bed I'd made, no matter how unpalatable.

And you know what I am beginning to think? As the hour grows ever later, and my jar of ink and the lamp both run low? That here I am, seeking to console myself through another unending night... Awake. And alone. Awaiting the return of my spouse, wondering if he will be soused enough to sleep or just bosky enough to rile at me instead...

In truth, apprehensive over whether he will

arrive alone, or with a mate in tow, one he lost monies to, one expecting—

I realize now what I thought would be a simple _thank you_ has turned into a rather maudlin ramble, has it not? As I bare my soul, not so much _to you_, I suspect, _but to myself_.

My guilt.

For I did _not_ want a babe born into this union. This mockery of a marriage. One that has more trials than I will commit to the page.

My secret shame?

Is that no matter how fervently I wished to be a mother, I wished this babe away from me with even more fervor. I prayed this babe gone because I could not fathom bringing an innocent soul into the not-innocent-at-all environs of the hateful, artificious abode James has "provided". Nearly imprisoned me within.

Olivia, Mama, Papa, Nate, Ellen, Sarah: I confess to you all. 'Tis my evil thoughts and lack of strength to leave while I still could that killed my precious baby, and I will suffer that burden, that scar upon my soul forever.

Dear Lord...

Dear sweet, innocent Philip, please forgive me for acting the monster and not protecting you as a mother should.

———————————

STIFLING SILENT GIGGLES, amusement that shook their entire bodies, like misbehaving sinners during the Sunday-morning sermon, with Susanna again wrapped in his coat, secure in his arms, they peeked out the carriage house door Leo edged open.

"You were right," he whispered, lips to her ear. "The storm has moved on."

She claimed it was so moments ago, and the validity now presented itself before his eyes.

The snow had stopped, the moon high enough and clouds retreated sufficiently to allow the reflection to beam over the blanket of white that cloaked *everything*, giving a blue glow to the still landscape.

The fresh inches of snow subdued the muddy sludge of the past two days, bathed the land with new beginnings. And without the rain and wind to interfere, smoke from the inn's chimneys greeted his nose.

As did the frosty nip in the air.

"Told you I do not mind emptying the chamber pot should you wish to use it again." She squirmed against him and pointed—outside.

Please, she'd written only moments ago, a shy smile partnering the request. *Now that we are <u>more</u> than strangers, I— Please. Outside will do.*

So outside it was, he'd agreed, not allowing himself to beg her clarification on exactly what *more* they might be. But he would not take her to the inn's outer "office", not when that increased the chances of them chancing across anyone. The opposite direction it would be, deeper into the woods. No sense courting the danger of discovery.

Once his eyes accustomed to the night, he secured the door behind them and journeyed forth a few cautious steps, keeping keen watch all around. When all remained still, including the warm woman bundled against his chest, and idly wondering whether Reaver might disobey and join them, Leo took up a brisker pace, mindful to take a criss-cross, meandering path, one that would avoid leading directly to their haven.

By his estimation, nearly two hours had passed as they exchanged tidbits and confidences both. Surprisingly blissful ones.

Oh, the desire was still there, floating just beneath the surface like a good portion of the hull on a great hulking ship, but 'twas the sails *sailing* said ship that commanded his attention: conversing with her.

Though his body lodged its impatience, he was enthralled. Her mind, her personality, he had learned, drew him, lulled forth his interest in her with every shared laugh. Every suspected sorrow.

Through gestures, words—many written, some spoken and mouthed—he'd gleaned much of her recent past.

A deeper chill settled in his limbs, far worse than anything mere temperatures could cause, thinking of all she'd told him as he worked his way over the snow-covered paths and further into the trees.

Of her less-than-satisfactory marriage and overly controlling spouse.

She'd confided of a wild plan to sneak out when she learned she was pregnant, her goal of escaping to London to seek refuge with her sister-in-law. But when Mitchell discovered her sewing men's garments (ones made with seams she'd intended to let out as the babe grew, not knowing exactly when she might realize her escape), she'd fabricated a tale about sewing them for her brother and, eventually, abandoned the idea of leaving as too risky. Too adventuresome, now that she had *a growing life within me to think of.*

By the time he knew of her protective sister-in-law, the London Sarah, Susanna had scribbled across three worn letters, front and back both, started on a fourth and he'd feared that at any second their light might wane to nothing. Without exception, it had been the most unique, artless time he could remember ever spending with a female.

The restrictive nature of her spouse, the confines of her marriage, explained her restless need for adventure.

He'd shared a few memories of his time aboard the *Restless,* teasing her that with the day's events— or yesterday's events, as it were—she had gone well beyond restless adventure to her own *reckless* one.

And then came, to him at least, the most shocking revelation of all—

When he noticed the top three words on the next page she drew forth to write upon.

"Dear *Lady Scandal*? Whatever have you to do with *that*?" Only someone buried beneath a rock had not heard of the infamous female daring enough to advertise for a spouse not quite a year past.

What did this fierce little puss who kissed like his every dream have to do with Lady Scandal? For even Leo, who practically *did* have his head buried under a rock (outside of his work for Farnsworth) knew of the mysterious woman who had put advertisements in every paper that would run them, requesting only inordinately wealthy men, those with superabundant pockets, apply for the position of being her husband.

"Wait. 'Tis very forward of me to demand," he'd said, "even to request, explanations from you. You need not say more. I shall pinch my curiosity to nothing and you may decide what we discuss next."

The pencil flew.

Good man. Polite.

He snorted at that. "Ha. Tell that to my mama and sisters. They would call me many things, doubtful *polite* among them."

He found it all too natural to rest his chin on her shoulder as she again put pencil to paper.

Brother. Navy. Nathaniel Oliv—

"Nate?" he burst out, straightening in shock. "Captain Nathaniel Oliver is your brother? Miracle of miracles. We served together before he received his own ship." Then he remembered. "Oh, Susanna, I am dreadfully sorry. I recall now. He left the navy, returned to land when his wife died, to care for his daughters." Her nieces. Little girls he'd heard a few lively stories about, but their aunt? Very little...

Married now, she wrote.

"He is? Found himself another wife? That scoundrel. Did not take him long. Good for him. Hope he's happy."

going <u>there</u>

"There? To visit Oliver?"

And did he dare tell her he knew her brother sufficient to receive his own invitation to visit for the holidays? Or would such knowledge halt every bit of the ease with which she had been confiding in him?

A small mark, indicating affirmative, had him laughing. "If only all my conversations could be so succinctly resolved.

"But wait, I cannot help but ask again. What does your *brother* have to do with Lady Scandal? *He* married her?"

Nooooo. Nate wasn't one for anything so outlandish. Leo couldn't fathom it. "Answering an advertisement for an obscenely wealthy spouse? Does not sound like him at all."

Not the sort of thing captains in the navy would ever qualify for.

Not unless Captain Nathaniel Oliver led some sort of secret life...

As you do yourself? Pretending the life of a roofless roamer?

With fingers to his cheek, she directed his startled gaze to her lips. "Nay. 'Twas her, Lady Scandal's, com-pan-ion, *companion*...wed...his lady..."

"Repeat the last."

"Im. Post. Ter. Imposter."

"Nate wed his very own *Lady Imposter*?" She beamed at him and he knew he had it aright. Dismay bellowed up from his chest. "*That* sounds like him now. Exactly what he needed."

She was nodding, eyes bright with excitement that made her look even younger. "I helped. My nieces...letters...solicitor..." He made a circular motion with his hand, inviting her to share more. Given the hour, and the waning oil, gathering her words took more effort and he feared he missed more than he gleaned.

"Tomorrow?" she said after he'd bent to check the lantern, measure the weight of the remaining oil. "...share more...the morrow?"

"Absolutely." Because how could he imagine not seeing her after tonight?

. . .

LEO WAS A SAILOR, roughened by sea and by life. Now surrounded by darkness more often than not. By silence—always. Yet he wanted her with every cell of his being. Craved her light. Wanted to be the one to see her smile, to make her laugh. Wanted to banish those shadows even her mischievous nature could not hide.

Trouble, it appeared, hounded others beyond himself. Much like dogs and soldiers, smugglers too, it traveled in packs.

He knew the precise instant her brain cobbled everything together.

He knew her older brother. And she had just bared secrets to Leo that he'd wager his randy prick she had not voiced so fully to another.

Mortification swept over her, painting her cheeks and forehead pink as she skittered away, crossing back to the opposite seat, tucking her spine into the corner and damn near shrinking in on herself.

He waited for her to face him again. Her eyes shadowed with that wounded look—one he never wanted to be the cause of again.

"No, sweetheart, nay. Whatever you may be thinking, please halt." The carriage may have been grand, large by coach standards, but he was a big man and could easily reach between them. He brushed the dark hair from her face and behind one ear. "Please, trust me. Do not try and hide.

"Aye, I count Oliver a friend. A good friend. That does not mean I would ever betray your trust. *Ever.*

"Know that anything you have shared with me this eve will remain on these broad shoulders and in this thick head." He indicated each with a light slap, the same hand still tingling from touching her cheek after tucking her hair back connecting with first his opposite shoulder and then above one ear. "With ease, yet with sorrows for all you have endured, I will carry your secrets to my grave. Happily, will I shoulder them for you..." He trailed off when she started scribbling again.

do not talk of your <u>grave</u>, you wretch

But her embarrassment had abated, in part, an impish glint brimming in her gaze as she glanced up at him before looking down to write again.

Exactly <u>how</u> close are you and my brother?

Close enough, he and his new lady extended an invitation to join them for the holidays through Twelfth Night... But Leo couldn't tell her that, not yet. Not until he smoothed away any hint of lingering apprehension.

If he were to count on fingers the number of friends not family, easily would Nate Oliver be among them. "Close enough that I'm more than a little astonished he had *anything* at all to do with Lady Scandal." She didn't seem mollified by that answer, so he blurted, "I've certainly never spent hours straight sharing confidences with him. Never kissed him."

Which made her laugh. And Leo feel powerful again. In charge. Because *he* was the one to return the lightness to her spirit.

And if his reckless, wondrous lady desired a spot of privacy in the bracing outdoors before they both retired for the night, he was blame well going to provide it.

11

GOLDEN GIRDLES AND GROWLING GNARLERS

"Be abused of the notion I do not know exactly what you did earlier—stealing the rest of that boy's victuals."

Feeling no remorse whatsoever, Reaver panted through a bit of a head toss that had his lovely, if tattered, ear flapping up against his thick neck.

Victuals. When *dinner* or *food* would have done just as well.

Aye. This deep in the night, this *alone*, Mikey was back to using his priggy tone to express displeasure.

Pah. The stable master had already stuffed the unlodged lad so full, 'twas a wonder the bantling could sleep.

Reaver allowed a good amount of his agile tongue to loll out the side of his mouth, past his bottom jaw (so Mikey could admire its impressive proportions) and gave a halfhearted whine. A single *woof*.

"Nay, he doesn't seem to have any people of his own," Mikey answered, astute man that he was. One did not gain the various positions in life he held, regardless of their birth, without talent and skill to see them advance. "Aye, I shall see he finds someone before I hie back to London."

Mikey pulled out a tin of some thick, oily substance. Reaver had seen him do it before, so didn't need to bestir himself to investigate. 'Twas of the sort typically used to keep saddles and other leather supple. The man scooped some out and slicked it between his fingers. Then he slapped his hands against his scalp, keeping his hair good and greasy. Keeping his disguise in place. "Never you fear, Reaves. Just keep an ear out for *trouble*. For Tucker."

Another single bark.

Another swipe of his tongue, and Reaver set himself to doze, with one ear cocked toward the night.

***

Susanna shifted rhythmically against Captain Tucker's broad chest. The damp scent of his wool great coat he'd insisted she wear rose up to tickle her nose. But this close to him, nothing could outshine his personal scent, the one that comforted and aroused in equal measure.

I will carry your secrets to my grave. Happily, will I shoulder them for you...

To have secured her complete confidence in him, and so swiftly? How did he manage that?

But he had it. Commanded her unwavering faith in him, even before he'd astonished her so, mere minutes ago, by confiding his own secrets in return...

"You have entrusted me with much," he'd told her when the confines of the carriage prevented her escape from the mortifying knowledge that Captain Tucker was no stranger to her brother. Nate, who would take her guilt upon his head the moment he learned how Mitchell had treated her. Who would, with vehemence, castigate himself, assume responsibilities for things that happened without his knowledge, and more often than not, occurred when he wasn't even on English soil. Nate would—

"Susanna." The soothing way Leo had uttered her name paused the circuitous mental tirade.

She braved facing him, afraid of what she might see. Only to be met with yet another surprise from the brawny, mature seaman taking up his half of the carriage and then some.

"You have entrusted me with much," he repeated. "Shall I return the favor? Tell you why I am here, what I remained quiet on earlier? Myself and others are investigating the very crew that would have done you harm."

"Others?"

"Two men who are near at this time, who pretend, same as me."

Pretend? In secret? With disguises, mayhap?

"You pretend to be someone you are not?" To be able to hear? A vagabond sailor?

"We seek to gather information from those unsavories. To discern their next move or meeting. The tall one? The younger tall one, with all his teeth, he's with me."

The one who had forced his way into the already threatening circle? She wrote:

He is <u>not</u> a rotten lout? Squirrel Beard?

He laughed. "That is not far off, but Benton would be mortified to hear you describe him thus. Aye, he is on the side of right."

"Then why..."

"Why did he grab your bag, thrust himself in the middle? To keep another from doing worse."

"And the other who works alongside you both?"

"Not someone you have met." Which she deduced meant someone whose identity truly needed to remain concealed.

"And you feign hearing to avoid attention?" She spoke with care, *over*pronouncing, if that were a thing, repeating some syllables and phrases she thought might prove a challenge. Quickly writing others. He never exhibited impatience, no irritation, simply studied her mouth or her hands with focused intent, snaring quick glances at her eyes, making her more aware of herself—of her responses to him—than she could recall ever being with another. "Watch them from afar as they speak?"

"What makes you say that?"

"Because of the loud, forceful way you blustered your way through their circle to reach my side." He had barked and bellowed his claim to stave off challenges before they could be uttered.

A calculating light entered his gaze. As though he, too, recalled that moment. "I believe we need you to join our team. You are very astute."

"Were that the case I would not have bound myself to Mr. Mitchell."

"And had that not been the case, you might not be here with me now."

First the unexpected compliment (had anyone, ever, described her as *astute*?), now words to console? "And I would not exchange this night for another, not even if offered all the regent's golden girdles." She winked at him.

"Does he have a girdle of gold?" Leo had reared back in mock shock, heart and lips alight with laughter, for all in the land had heard tales of the difficulty their eventual king experienced, being laced into his straining whale bone stays and girdle.

"I confess I have not seen that," he said, voice somber, belying the twinkle in his eyes.

For which I am quite relieved to learn, she'd written to his obvious delight.

And now they had ended up here, outside, two pair of his socks on her feet, covered by *his* huge slippers (routed from his haversack, only to keep her feet dry), with her wrapped in his great coat and held against his chest as he made his way through several inches of thick, fluffy snow working deeper into the woods.

While cold, 'twas not the blustery, blistery damp mire that had soaked the land through the last couple of days. The very stillness in the air, the moonlight sparkling off the pale, snowy scape, encurtained the two of them in their own private world. Were it not for the soft crunch of his boots as he trod through the snow—alternating betwixt regular forward paces and sliding, sidelong ones—and the sounds of his breaths, she could, almost, imagine the silence he endured so very stoically.

And here he carried her, without complaint, to what amounted a privy run? In this glistening, snowy oasis she never would have seen at night, much less savored the silence sufficiently to appreciate, for he'd cautioned they must remain quiet and alert.

Yet even that, knowing danger lurked beyond, could not dampen her delight with this moment. With this man.

Benevolent stars shone down beyond the moon's bright orbit, as though blessing this beautiful night so close to Christmas. As though blessing them, Susanna and her valiant savior of the day.

FOR ONCE, sounds buffeted Leo, doused him from all

sides, no matter that he *needed* to concentrate. On disguising his trail. On keeping her safe.

Yet his thoughts *rat-a-tat-tat-tatted* his garret. *Can I keep her? Not only keep her safe, but* keep *her?*

Right, you leatherhead, because after marriage to that miscreant Mitchell she'll want to be shackled to another.

His heart *thump-pounded* louder than ever, despite the minim of effort it took to carry her.

Blood rushed through his head like a river crashing over rocks, pulsing in time to the dance her fingers did, feathering through his hair at the back of his nape where she held to him.

Where her light touch damn near destroyed whatever composure he typically claimed.

Because sure as skit, he may have spoken first, but with every word exchanged between them, every look, every kiss, the lass now held sway over him. Claimed him, did she but know it. Him, Leopold Michael Tucker, who had thought to die alone and in silence (not for a few decades, but still)... He now *wanted* to fight for her. More than that, he *needed* what was best for her, and he wasn't yet convinced that meant him.

How did one young female bring so much sound and light into his world? A world where, for once, he wasn't on his own. And it wasn't just holding her that made it so.

It was *all* that had been shared between them since the moment her fiery spirit drew him forth. It was the way she tugged on his hair and stifled chuckles against his chest when he pretended to stumble and nearly drop her.

Then did it again several paces later, as he intentionally dragged his boots, shuffling sideways through the snow every bit as much as he took a few regular steps. Making a hash of his path, making it so easy to tease her, even as he reveled in her slight weight against his chest.

The way she lightly pinched his neck as though in silent admonishment and then caught his eye and winked before leaning in to kiss that very spot.

It was the way being with her recalled to mind how he'd conducted himself the first eight and thirty years of his life, before silence surrounded him and took him apart from everyone else. *Stop blaming your hearing. Has she not shown you that removing yourself was, in effect, your choice?*

A choice he could not regret, not given how 'twas his very choices that had brought him here, working with Farnsworth and the others, hoping to dismantle the degenerates smuggling not only French brandy but English flesh as well.

He turned a circle, glancing back the way he'd come, pleased to note the slightly circuitous route he'd taken also intersected with a deer or fox trail, creating a myriad prints and places where the snow had been disturbed, not making his route easily discernible.

And then on the return amble, after they had both, privately, tended to business and then together formed a snowball or two to throw (actually, that was all her; he had grinningly endured), after traversing not quite half the way back toward their destination, she pinched the flesh between his neck and shoulder *hard*. Stilled his feet instantly.

Put the rest of him on guard as he swallowed any protest. What was she trying to tell him?

Before he could ask, she shifted in his arms and tapped his opposite shoulder then held up two fingers in front of his face, pointed off to the side.

He tugged her higher, placed his lips at her ear, allowed only a wisp of sound to emerge. "You hear two people?"

It was a guess and an accurate one, her slight nod confirmed. "Coming closer?"

She gave a light shrug, but then clasped her full hand against the side of his neck and squeezed gently, a comforting, solid motion. "Stay here?"

Another light nod.

Then she held up a third finger. *Three.* So someone had joined them? A new voice? Was it the people he was after? *Who else might you expect? Who else would be skulking about in the woods, closer to dawn than not?*

Well, he was, for one; *they* were, for two.

And at least three others were near enough to hear? Dread tightened his muscles.

"Listen," he told her as softly as he dared, moving lips against her ear and praying nothing that could carry escaped. "Pay attention to their words. Should they approach, tap my cheek twice. And hold on." For at that point, he would either be fighting or fleeing.

Another nod. Her body had gone tense against his.

He heard his breath, maybe not with his ears, but with his head, heard the measured silence as he worked to keep his frustration and excitement under control.

It hadn't been that many breaths—somewhere between forty and sixty-four (he lost count twice)— when she clasped the side of his neck and used her thumb to turn his chin toward the carriage house.

"Are they moving?"

A nod.

Another, *frantic* nod, before he could ask anything more.

Damn. He wasn't sure *what* the gentle pressure on his jaw meant. Did she tell him to stay? Retreat? Or, damn it, to run?

⸻⊷◉⊶⸻

"Stupid cur! Would have me some fun with those new loads if I ain't left my pistol inside."

More like if you knew how to shoot something other than your jaws.

Catching scent of his man beyond the clearing where the idiots chittered, Reaver baited the others the opposite direction. Finally! After hours of inactivity, he could go to work. Be useful. Pay for pilfering portions of pork and other pleasant sundries.

For unlike dinner, evil gave off a stench. One as nauseating as a decaying corpse, and though it clung not to all of the men with Haggart, on him? Haggart reeked of it. Likely bathed in—

No. Wait. Given the stink that surrounded him, likely that sloven scavenger hadn't met bath water since months that didn't end in B-E-R.

"*Brrr! Grrr!*" Reaver gave a good, saliva-filled snarl, keeping his impressive tongue in check, so as to let his long, sharp teeth braggart a bit. Intimidate Haggart.

(Heh. Heh. Braggart Haggart.)

One of the men landed a booted kick near enough, Reaver let out a howl. Then rounded on him, all fang and growl that had two of them stumbling back. "Wait! Ain't that the cove's dog? Maybe they stayed after all. Looked for his horse, the one he whinged about this morn, but the stable was too dark to find my arse, much less someone else's nag."

"That dog? Thought he belonged to the inn." That was good old Benny Wrath. "Saw him out in the stables when I rode in."

More grunts. Definitely more grumbling. (Theirs.) A few more growls (his) and the laggards eventually dispersed. But not before both Reaver *and* his man's new lady heard a few choice bits...

FROM SNOWBALLS TO SNABBLED

"Your friend," she gasped, the second Leo turned from bolting the door after the mad, circuitous dash toward safety he'd made the moment she'd pointed and tapped his cheek twice, mouthing, "Go!"

Wild-eyed and woefully out of breath, even though he'd been the one running, she grabbed up the lantern and held it near her face. "Friend," she repeated, more terror lining her features than he'd seen all evening, even when *she* had been the one under attack.

"Take a couple breaths. Talk soft," he instructed, telling his own thundering heart to calm. "Tell me, what friend?"

"Squirrel Beard." Exaggerated circular motions in front of her face made it clear.

"Benton. What about him?"

"Danger...no..." Or was it *know*? "...suspect... not..."

"All right. Deep breath, little one." She did as bade, lungs heaving as she looked to him for reassurance. "They know—or suspect," he hazarded, "that he is not who he seems?"

"I do not know!" Another breath that blew against his chest. "Mad." She scrunched her face in anger. Then relaxed it to finish in a rush, "...he... enter rupted..." Interrupted. "...said whore it..."

Whore it? Lost, Leo motioned for her to repeat. "Whore-if-ick. Whore-it. Id."

Whoreifick...? Whore-id? He kept sounding them out in his head until... Ah!

Horrifically horrid. Not good. "Do you hear them now? Were we pursued?"

"No. Nay...distance...barking...shouts...not..."

"Not coming near?"

She aimed her palm toward the door he'd heaved to and motioned it forward several times.

Going away? "The sounds. They are receding?"

A nod.

"What else? Tell me all you remember."

A quick grapple for her pencil and another hastily unfolded letter. She balanced it against the carriage's exterior as he held the lantern aloft while she scribbled phrases around and in between the inked lines, occasionally pausing before writing with fury again.

"Good. Good girl," he murmured as he praised, not wanting to distract her, to crowd or hover, but more and more impressed with every word she recalled, every phrase she jotted.

Not four minutes later, she looked up, almost seemed lost. "Here." She handed him the page, took the lantern from him. "...everything. All I heard."

In his grip now, he scanned her words. "Susanna, you are a jewel. Still no sounds? Beyond us?"

"A wine, I think." She pretended to drink, pointed to the bolted door. Then held two fingers up high on either side of her head...like ears? Ah, a *whine*?

"Reaver? That you?" The dog must have answered because she sped past him to the door.

He was on her just as fast. "Hold up, now."

Hands to her waist, he lifted her to the side. "Stay put a moment, hmm?"

He eased the bolt aside and slid the door open a thumb's width, ready to brace it against intruders if need be. But when he peeked out, he was met with a welcome sight indeed.

Reaver's tail fanned out in the snow, wagging a welcome and obliterating any obvious prints they might have left.

In fact, the entire area was littered with so much zigzaggery that any human trail had been long obliterated. Instead, slushy indentations hashed the grounds going from north to south, east to west, and every direction in between, such that no one would be able to make heads nor fairy tales of the direction most recently traveled.

With a happy hop, the dog burst through as Leo

widened the door before securing it behind the canine.

Who promptly jumped up and landed huge, muddy paws on the front of his shirt. "You big galoot." Quick hands made short work checking the damp coat and body beneath for damage, then lingering to scratch behind the ears, one upright and the other, torn one slouched. "You know better than to jump. Have you met our lady, Susanna?"

Shite. *Our lady.* He'd not meant to introduce her as *theirs,* but the words tumbled out before he thought to stop them.

Flushed—from the excitement? The race to safety? Or his claim?—she dropped to her knees, uncaring of soiling either his other shirt or her own pristine self (which made him smile for some reason) as she gave Reaver an enthusiastic embrace, no hesitation whatsoever despite his dirty fur and fearsome appearance. No notion what she told the dog, lips buried against Reaver's coat, but the sight of them together, of her instant acceptance, did something to him. Something that felt peculiarly... *permanent?*

"WHAT A WONDERFUL PUPPY YOU ARE, saving your master and me." Holding the wet yet warm body against her own proved remarkably comforting. She'd never had a pet of her own and, other than Faith's kittens this past summer, had spent little time with animal companions. "Even though you stink."

She laughed when the dog took one step back, cocked his head and angled one ear as if to say, *Well, human, mayhap you do not smell so inviting yourself.*

Could one be fraught yet exhilarated too?

Gripping tight to Leo, listening with all her might over the savage rampage of her heart, aiming to commit to memory anything at all the captain and his partners might find useful, she had concentrated beyond her fear. Because aye, she recognized the contempt in Haggart's speech. Along with two others, and then for a short while, Leo's friend Benny as well.

She knew not what to listen for, so made notes mentally, counted on her fingers anything that might be of interest to tell him as soon as she could.

But when Reaver burst into the throng, growling and snarling, distracting the men away from them, and she'd caught one last sentence, terror had shredded composure and she could not return them to safety and light fast enough.

But now she had shared what she needed to. So 'twas time for the energy clogging her limbs and riling her heart and stuttering her lungs to quiet before she breathed herself into a faint. Hugging the dog helped. His long wet tongue licking her cheek? Not so much, but it did make her laugh. "Shall I bathe in bacon grease for you, hmm? Would that—"

"Susanna."

The rumbled timbre snared her full attention and she rose, keeping the tips of her fingers on the dog's neck as he sat on his haunches now, glancing between the humans who stood over him.

Holding the words she'd written toward the light, her captain took up her free hand in his, threading their fingers and giving hers a light clasp as he studied the page.

She leaned into him and glanced again at what she'd written. Was it helpful at all?

Haggart and 2 others (not Toothy) + S.B. for part; one spoke with more refinement than the others (not S.B.)
-Lord (never named that I could discern)
-"sparring match" (Boxing Day?)
-Lady Diamond or Diamond's Lady
-Portsmouth
-"2 more" (of what, I do not know)
-London
-hairy (or Harry?)
-bitch from earlier (me?)
-damn bridge
-cart
-more trouble than worth
-plans to demand more money (did not hear who from)
-"time to snabble S.B., too g— d— peery" doesn't like face
-17 or 17th (uncertain if number or date or £ or ?)

SHE WAS BRILLIANT. Bloody brilliant.

Leo tightened his hand around hers before releasing her to fold the page and snug it in a pocket. "Can I keep this? Give it over to—"

Had her nod been any more fervent, he feared she might flail her head from her neck.

"I need to share what you learned. Will you be all right?"

A calmer nod. A swift look at the bolted door, then she pretended to lift a watch face from the nonexistent ribbon at her waist, where ladies often carried their timepieces.

"How long?" he surmised. "Ten minutes." She appeared relieved. "Barring trouble." Then scowled at him.

She flashed five fingers at him, her hand going from fist to wide and back again, three separate times, then indicated racing after him, head down, both arms bent and powering at her sides. "You will grant me fifteen minutes and then come after?"

A brisk nod, hands on hips now. Eyes determined. Chin defiant.

Why did that warm his lonely soul? The idea that this young female, so recently met, standing there, facing him down in naught but his shirt and coat would chase after his hide if she deemed it tardy? "Have you a watch?"

She frowned at him. "No."

He chuckled. "Me neither.

"Give me twenty, twenty-five. I will scout our surroundings before venturing afield. Ensure no one is near. Reaver will keep guard and set up a cacophony if anyone but me tries to enter."

He paused, but rather than reply, she slid her arms from the voluminous great coat that swallowed her and rose up onto her toes to swing it about his shoulders.

Without a word (he knew, because he kept sight of her mouth), she flew round to his side and held up the shoulder, so he could easily tuck his fist and arm inside. Once the effort had been duplicated and he wore his coat for the first time since it had graced her body, she leaned in and hugged arms about his waist, then stepped back with a decisive nod.

Feeling strangely bereft, he wrapped one hand about her nape and tugged her forward to place his lips against her forehead. "Go ahead and sleep. You have endured enough excitement for the day. I shall return soon. Watch over you till morn."

Watch over me till morn?

Go ahead and sleep?

Pesky, attractive, annoying, glorious man.

Sleep was not what she wanted to do with him.

Nor could she fathom anything of the sort: bedding down, alone and oblivious to whether he had returned safely; not with him gone—outside—where danger lurked, as well she knew.

Her thoughts much too heated at the moment for her to take chill, she tidied their surroundings, first outside the carriage, and then taking better care with her wet things, draping her damp dress and stays, shift and stockings over the carriage wheels and across whatever she could find so they had at least a modicum chance of drying—rather that than wadded as they had been, with no chance at all.

She then put the inside of the carriage in order (which did not occupy her nearly long enough, taking all of ninety seconds), encouraged Reaver to jump up and dispatch a couple of crumbs she saw on the floor between the squabs, and collected all the pages she'd written over—

Stopped to pet the dog who watched her humming-accompanied activities with a curious sort of pleasant expression hinting a curve upon his doggish lips until she just *knew* it had to be over eighteen minutes—

Didn't it?

Where was Captain Tucker?

Was she being impatient? Had it really been nearly twenty minutes? Why, it felt like two hundred. But what if it had only been twelve? What if it had been twenty-five and he needed her help? What if—

The infernal lantern sputtered to fumes.

Leaving her in utter darkness. And the seconds passing slower than ever.

13

TIT FOR TAT

———◦◦———

MORE THAN ANYTHING, Leo missed hearing the wind.

From soft to fearsome, he'd loved the near constant sounds of it whipping or whisping past.

On land, a slight breeze singing through the trees, setting the leaves to dancing.

At sea, the power of great howling gales, heralding an epic storm that comes up of a sudden. Ordering the flapping, wind-spanked sails lowered well ahead of the fury.

The way the air, all but invisible itself, would whisper a greeting. Buffet his cheek. Curve around the shell of his ear... Whistle lightly or echo deep.

How he missed hearing that: the ever-present, completely overlooked sound of wind.

Yet, if offered the ability to experience its comforting refrain again, he'd trade that miracle, easily, for one minute of her voice.

Susanna's. How did her words sound?

Were they the soft, freshly appealing tone equating to her youthful face and mischievous smile? Or, mayhap, did those lips produce a lower pitch, rich like molasses, hinting at the hurts in her eyes?

Hurts he wanted to vanquish.

Starting with sharing how very pleased his superior had been with the knowledge she'd captured. Returning to the carriage house with both stealth and subdued eagerness (that's where the stealth came in), he rolled over parts of his conversation with his commanding officer.

Inside the stable's smallest room, away from prying eyes—and ears—Leo had shared her list, summing up with a concise, "So, if her guess is right, and the 'sparring match' she heard of is instead the twenty-sixth, then Boxing Day. As to Lady Diamond or Diamond's Lady? A ship name, I'm thinking. Especially if Portsmouth is correct."

His boss had concurred, expressing dismay. Evidently knew a ship matching that description and didn't want to believe its owner might be involved in the wicked happenings they had traced to this crew and the village of East Crossings.

Knowing this latest direction was thanks to the brave, spirited lass waiting for him, a peculiar sort of pride puffed his chest. Well, that, and also at satisfying Ol' Mikey's quest for knowledge.

Aye, Ol' Mikey, of the stench-filled garments,

dirt-encrusted face, callused hands and sharpest mind Leo had ever known. The man recognized in other circles—when he wasn't in the back of beyond impersonating a stable master—as Farnswobble in much of London society, a name he both detested and yet cultivated on occasion, appearing weak and indecisive; or, as he was known to most, the venerable Duke of Farnsworth.

"Oliver's sister? Sister…" the duke, currently aliased as Mikey, had repeated, as dazed at the news as Leo had been once he'd imparted *select* details about the female he'd rescued. (Much of what he'd gleaned, the things of a personal nature, would go no further than himself—ever.)

"Indeed. Journeying to his abode for the holidays. And Oliver himself got married earlier this year, he did." Succinctly, but with relish at divulging something so outlandish, Leo handed over what Susanna had shared about her brother.

"Caught up in that scandal business?" Mikey spoke without haste, still swallowing the unexpected treat. "You are bamming me."

"God's honest truth. Wed her companion or some such."

He saw the other man give a low whistle. Then grunt, imagined the *Huh* that issued forth, before, "So she does…had started…a hum, to sell more rags and scandal sheets."

"That too, I'm sure, but no, 'tis based in truth. She exists; Lady Scandal is real."

Leo knew the "real" Mikey was a slightly older resembler of the duke's. That the two met in the navy well over twenty years ago, but beyond that? Very little of the stable master the duke had ordered away for a few days.

Though Farnsworth could play many a role, including the rigid, high-toned prig he was rumored to be in elevated London circles, it hadn't been difficult to conclude that his boss was most comfortable away from town trappings and the somewhat weak-of-character image he inhabited there, beyond from his naval office.

"The bridge...out but another stage...coming through...that direction or...another by noon."

Leo grunted, perversely not thrilled with the news that jostled him back to the conundrum at hand. "Whenever it arrives, we cannot send her on unaccompanied."

"Escort her," Mikey said. "'Tis Christmas. None of us...working through the holidays."

"You are."

"...crimes against England to solve." And his own personal ones as well, Leo knew.

Ones from the duke's, and even Leo's, past.

But as Mikey had again perused the list Leo gave over to his care, despite the dimness, he'd seen the satisfaction at closing in on their quarry fill Mikey's glittering eyes.

Time to put work aside.

With every step through the snow-dampened night, the darkness that accompanied thoughts of the prey they were after melted from his shoulders, his movements lighter, faster as anticipation prodded him onward.

After confirming the perimeter remained clear, he approached the door, softly alerted Reaver to his presence and then silently—as far as he knew—let himself in before barricading the door behind him.

The carriage house was naught but a pit of black. He refused to acknowledge the shred of disappointment that flared, instead, allowed satisfaction to thrum through him. *Good.* She'd doused the lantern and now slept.

"All right, Reaves, you and I shall bed down for the night," he thought more than spoke, unwilling to risk waking her, as he turned.

Only to have a soft yet hard wall of femininity crash into him.

Moments ago

Inside the stable's smallest room, far away from prying eyes, the "ol'" stable master kept his sharp gaze on the cautious exit of Tucker. Though his keenness to return to the female waiting for him was apparent, Tucker didn't fail to register his surroundings before venturing forth. Good man.

Given the way he spoke about the woman who had knocked him off his assignment? Wouldn't surprise "Mikey" any, when he and Tucker met in

London for their informance next month, if, instead of the Duke of Farnsworth handing out another assignment based on their latest findings, Tucker handed in his resignation. Announcing he was ready to leave the navy altogether and become a landsman.

Ah well. Tucker was more than due.

Captain Leopold Tucker, a noble giant with a heart of gold. A man Mikey had once thought to call son-in-law.

A pang of grief hit hard, a boot stomping into the hollow where his heart belonged. His willful daughter, the only female issue blessed to him, before his wife died birthing their son some years later, remained missing. Her whereabouts, her very presence still on this earth, a mystery since she'd run off with that knave who would forever remain unnamed and dishonored.

For a true man did not take flight with a duke's daughter... Only to "lose" her in the countryside.

Before the familiar, long-held rage could warp his judgment, Mikey forced his attention back to the boy.

The boy sleeping, filth and all, in the narrow bunk usually reserved for the stable master himself. The little imp he'd rescued from the vitriolic female who had suffered the lad's thieving paws earlier. A young lady he had quite recognized but who he had no doubt had not done the same, his disguise, both to the eyes and the senses, complete.

Of everything he did when personating

another...changing his hair, facial expressions, gestures, 'twas maintaining another's bearing that proved, if not the most difficult, at least the most troublous. Sustaining the somewhat stooped posture the real Mikey possessed, thanks to an old shipboard injury, had made Farnsworth's spine yell at him even more than the dark memories.

Though not everyone had the same demons riding their soul that kept them in teeth-black and hair grease a few times a year, when they weren't suffering the *ton* as an inept, slightly imbecilic duke, he did it, willingly. All with the hopes of discovering the whereabouts of the few still missing females, the ones not accounted for when Lord Blakely and his men splintered that abomination of a lordling's estate and evil society a couple years back. Now that Napoleon had been truly defeated this past summer, that was his sole purpose—finding the women who had vanished. That, and preventing the disappearance of any others.

And, confoundedly, it wasn't only females now. Males had started vanishing as well...

So quietly that it had been going on for nigh on two years before it caught their attention. *His* attention. Ah well, they were doing what they could. And would continue on until rummaging out the mystery and putting a stop to it for good.

Stretching his arms overhead despite the discomfort, he anchored his thoughts back round.

The boy. *How can I use him yet provide for him too?* For no near-starving child was found hours from home thieving days before Christmas if they had suitable conditions elsewhere.

How can I use him best?

What might be seen as either callous disregard, or shameless ill use was, in fact, a well-laid gamble.

A service for a reward. Tit for tat.

Was that not how commerce, how very countries even, worked?

Seemed after rescuing a guest of note from the little wag's snaffling, he now needed to put the lad to work. Hopefully aim him on a path better than thievery, an act which could see him hanged if caught by the wrong person.

But not before he studied again the list just delivered.

And read past the hasty scribbles meant for him.

Was he not in the business of information? Of saving lives?

And something at the uppermost of this particular page demanded his full attention.

Stanton House, London, September 27, 1815

My dearest Susanna,

*Your recent missive, surmising <u>beyond</u> words put
to the page, both calms my worries, and yet
heaps concern and regret both heavily upon my
head.*

I confess to utter shame, dismay over my <u>igno-rance</u>, for not perceiving the depths of despair <u>he</u> put you through.

When I think of the months, the years, you so valiantly gave of yourself to assist Ellen and the girls, why, contrition cuts like a ragged blade.

Shall we come to an accord, my dear? You grant yourself however long you wish to heal, grieve how you need to (or not) over this latest loss, and when you express a readiness to move on, I shall do all within my ability to see you securely, and contentedly, settled. Now, worry not, sweet Sus, for I consider myself a most modern sort of woman and have come to know <u>much</u> about the ways of men since locating to London.

Should you desire another spouse, one we would research with scrutinous care, we shall apply ourselves that direction. Should you not...

Well, my dear, in truth, men can be the most satisfying, flattering, confidence-building crea-tures. And yet, as we have both learned to the detriment of our personal safety, they can also prove the most ruinous, untrusty, vexatious of wretches.

If you wish to remain independent, we will lay our heads together and, however challenging it may prove, find a way to amass some sort of financial wherewithal for you to do so.

Should you (and this might be worth your strong consideration, but only if you are feeling currently stifled and rather bold, or mayhap only curious over how a more reliable, <u>gentlemanly</u> gentleman might treat you in intimate realms) wish to sample a few, before making any commitments, that would be understandable as well.

Sample? A few... Men? Who in blazes was this... this brassy *female* who dared spout such preposterous drivel to the lass Captain Tucker had taken a fancy to?

Just because you choose to keep your falls closed and your flapper to yourself does not mean others agree.

With a growl toward the pesky reminder of all he'd chosen to do without, for it had been a *choice*, he wrenched his attention back to the remaining few sentences.

Wherever your heart or head may lie at the moment, do nothing in haste that cannot be undone.

Remain strong and true, dear heart, and cele-

brate your fortuitous freedom for however long it may last.

With all my stunned and aching heart,

Yours always,
–S–

P.S. You will note my current direction above; please inscribe your next missive to me here.

Here, this unknown female had written.

Here. At *Stanton House*.

The unusual abode he, along with his brother-in-law, jointly owned?

Who in the blazes was this female?

–S–

–S–, of the brazenly ludicrous advice.

–S–, of the... He had to reluctantly admit, forthright and (somewhat) reasonable counsel.

The mysterious *–S–*... Whose writing, he also conceded, he rather admired. 'Twas not overly flowery as some of the females of his acquaintance. Nor was it an illegible scrawl. But something in the middle. Feminine, with a flourish or two, yet somehow still... Bold.

–S–, who he was suddenly desperate to meet the next time he was in London.

–S–, damn this secretive female, who currently resided in *his* London home. The one housing not only his sister, but his nieces as well.

How the devil had *–S–* managed to beguile her way into living there?

Of vital more importance, regardless of whether he admired anything about her, what sort of devilishly inappropriate advice was she dispensing to his *unmarried* nieces?

14

ALAS, ASLEEP BUT NOT ALONE

A FEW MOMENTS PRIOR

HAVING NEVER BEEN PARTICULARLY afraid of the dark before, 'twas a revelation—an unwelcome one—to realize how, when one anticipated the arrival of another with not dread but instead with growing glee, being faced with interminable darkness made the minutes crawl slower than a broken carriage through frozen sludge.

The blackened windows Susanna had noticed upon their arrival let in not a shred of light. Protected her from discovery every bit as much as they vexed beyond belief.

Even Reaver had more patience than she, the audacious canine daring to intervene the one time she'd approached the door, thinking to look out.

Oh no you don't, young female who my man has

taken a swift liking to, the barely vocalized lingering growl seemed to say.

Hands on hips (completely ludicrous, as the dog couldn't see her any better than she could see him—or could he?) she glared down toward the sound. "Really, now. You would stop me from assuring us both of his safety?"

Aye, I would. Another rumbled growl (sounding much like his master) that Susanna deciphered clear as day. *As he tasked me with yours, or did you not hear his parting directive?*

Stroking her fingers through the dog's thick, drying fur was a simple matter of reaching out a few inches, as Reaver's head met her outstretched hand. "Parting directive? Mighty high in the instep for a canine, are you not? Did your, no doubt impressive, hearing pick up something mine failed to? For all I heard was 'Go to sleep, pretty Susanna'—yes, I might be annotating a bit there—'you shall sleep. And I shall stand guard.'"

Her stroking fingers became vigorously scratching ones as she knelt to hug the comforting bulk to her. "Bah, I say. Upon his return, I shall let my hitherto reckless side roam free." *While I allow myself to roam all over your master.*

Hitherto? Funny human! (Forget the dark, 'twas vastly more frightening how her mind insisted upon attributing articulate rebuttals to a rough-looking cur she would have likely run from if she had crossed him on the road.) *Has not this entire journey of yours been one grand and reckless adventure?*

"All right, I shall grant you that." Could hounds purr? For she would swear the one panting near her shoulder practically did. "But it wasn't until your man decided to claim me and fairly turned me topsy-turvy that I began to *enjoy* it—"

"Reaves?" The hushed voice reached her ears a second after the dog strained in her grasp. "Coming in, boy. Don't piss your excitement."

As if I would! Affronted at the very thought, the dog's long snout nudged her chin, to Susanna's giggle.

Not two seconds later, Captain Tucker slipped quickly through the door. Gave her a trice to admire the twinkling stars overhead, the glistening snow scape behind and the welcome breadth of his strong form in silhouette before he heaved it to and bolted it behind him. She gave him a scant second to turn—

And launched herself into his arms

"You're back," she cried, relieved, pleased, breathing in his crisp, comforting scent while checking hair and scalp, shoulders and arms for any new injuries. "Whatever took you so long? I imagined all sorts of tragedies that might have befallen you, kept you away. But you are here, solid. So very welcome."

She cared naught that he couldn't hear her, the only thing that mattered was that he'd returned. That his hands went first to her waist and then to her bottom as she clutched and climbed up his brawny mass.

That his scent, now filtered through a light waft of stable and outdoors, comforted as much as it titillated.

What mattered was that she could not seem to stop the cravings riding her. The need to taste him. To lick her tongue into his mouth, revel in the slow glide and fast thrust of his against hers when her hunger finally reached him.

Carriage. Inside. Now. Please, she either said or thought. Perhaps only wished. But Captain Tucker, good man that he was, knew how to discern orders —and yearnings.

With a minimum of grappling, he found the carriage and pushed her inside the narrow opening. He followed, the coat she shoved from his shoulders falling behind them, to a single *woof* of welcome and a *thump-drag.*

I hope your dog doesn't chew wool. But she wasn't concerned enough to stop. Not when Leo's broad-fingered hands met the bare skin of her thighs as she tugged him farther inside and brought him with her as her back met the squab.

"Ah, sweet Susanna." His voice was a deep husk in the darkness. "Am I dreaming? I have fancied you —this—for hours."

His breath, warm and moist against her neck, thrilled every bit as much as his words.

Silly man. If naught but a dream, 'tis one we both share, she answered with her heart, her lips busy attacking his again, her fingers fumbling with his falls, needing to release him. To feel him.

Needing to ride him.

I have craved you from that first kiss, when you expressed wonder that I did not fear you.

For she knew what it was to fear. Earlier this night and back home, in what should have been her *safe* abode.

But with Leo? Her brave and caring Captain Tucker? *Never will I fear you, good man, not when what bursts between us is like dawn spilling across the sky... Giving light to places within me I had not realized had grown so very dark.*

As though she had spoken out loud, he wrenched his mouth away from hers. "Tonight, though, here in the darkness, we kiss." The words were a promise. But one he threatened to break when he stilled her questing fingers. Wrapped his hand snug about her wrist and halted her efforts.

"You cannot hear me"—but Susanna certainly heard her frustrated whimper clear enough—"but *kissing* is not all I want to do this eve."

"Ah, my restless Lady Reckless, calm now." His lips nudged her jaw as he spoke. His grip moved her fingers away from his falls and to his back as his other hand skimmed past her shoulder to curve over the top of her head. Upon realizing she had wedged herself against the wall of the carriage, he lifted his glorious weight from her to tug her an inch or two downward. "I'm not finished yet, lass. Not nearly."

She wrinkled the fabric of his clothing within those restless fingers he accurately accused her of, unable to stop the tilt of her abdomen as it sought out his hard length. "Either speak or kiss, dear knave, else I shall strum myself and act a true trollop before you now."

The breadth of his chest and shoulders swamped her like an ocean wave, made her giddy because her body fair floated against his. He didn't push her down; he didn't drown her. Though she feared her raging desire, her internal dampening for him took her further and further away from the steady shore she'd clung to in her mind these last difficult years.

And then she gripped his flesh. Granted, 'twas the flesh of his back, firm and hot beneath her hands where she'd delved beneath his shirt. His skin against hers was softness over hard muscle. She hugged him to her, ran one foot over the back of his leg, the action opening her to the decadent press of his affair right where she wanted him. She gave another whimper. Turned her face and encountered the gentle fingers he'd placed along her cheek. Sucked one inside, ran her tongue past the tip all the way down to the base, where she let the tip of her tongue linger until that wasn't quite enough.

Her lower body rising now, she wiggled her head until she could suckle his finger in earnest. His surprised moan brought further dampness to her core.

He swore. A single *damn*. And then, "Aye, all over, I vow. We kiss. From here..." He pulled his finger free, trailing the wet of her saliva on her chin and neck before encountering his shirt she still wore and yet his finger continued downward...

Downward...

Until he reached right where she needed him. Desperately so, it seemed to her. Odd, for one who had learned to appreciate being ignored.

Yet now? With him? Her throat gave a strangled, self-muffled keening sound when his fingers encountered flesh that felt heavier, more swollen than ever before. She arched toward his gossamer touch.

But then the fingers holding her scalp sifted through her hair, gave the lightest of tugs. "You nod," he said on one of those rumbling snarls that stroked her ears. "You nod, and I lick you to completion tonight."

She gasped. Tightened.

Lick? Aye, that please.

She gave a whimper when he, her invisible watchman in the night—*her protector*—feathered fingers through her aching core. Would that she could see him! Witness his body above hers, see his head between her thighs.

Would his eyes be heavy lidded? The hunger in his gaze difficult to glimpse? Or would the heat she felt be mirrored back? The unquenched craving only deepening at his look of desire?

She blinked, cast her gaze around them, saw utterly nothing. Not with the light out and naught to encroach upon their haven. Even the dog had gone silent, no sounds beyond the carriage, beyond her own accelerated breaths and the intense thrumming of her heartbeat.

The darkness heightened everything. No sight. No sounds—not for him, only her.

She would have to devise several touches that had meaning. Mayhap a hand curved about his neck, *I'm falling for you.* A kiss upon his jaw, *I think you are the most handsome man I have ever beheld.* The squeeze of her feminine muscles around his masculine ones, she thought on a gasp as one finger dared enter...

Give me all of you. Hard. Fast. ...Forever?

"COME MORNING," Leo promised, speaking past the saliva moistening his mouth, "when I can see your face, when you can communicate words and I can read your expression and am not completely blinded..." Because he could not fathom the ultimate intimacy with her, not this first time, where he could neither hear nor see...

Not after the hints she'd revealed about her past. What if he did aught that reminded her of her husband? Her expressive eyes, quick-to-smile (or pinched) lips would tell him before he trod too far the wrong direction.

"Come morning," he vowed, his heart hammering so fast 'twas a wonder he wasn't light-headed as his exploring fingers met the beckoning heat between her legs, slick with dew, desire he could not wait to taste. He tightened his hold on her scalp. "Then I shall take you fully as we both crave." *If that is still what you want.*

But tonight? Now? He needn't have worried.

For her head didn't simply nod. It jerked in such a frenzy that he was chuckling against her belly as he made his way unerringly past the linen of his shirt. His adventuress remained pliant, open beneath him, one foot on his shoulder, the other propped on the squab, as he scooted to kneel on the floor of the carriage.

Brushing her hair one last time, he brought his arm down, parted her folds just enough to inhale. To be greeted by the velvet welcome of pure passion. "You smell both sweet and wicked, lass."

He couldn't stop his fingertips from feathering over her silky heat. Nor his head from lowering. Couldn't stop his thumb from seeking out the hard knot at the top of her treasure. Knew, if he could have seen, she'd be pink, flushed, glistening. Knew, if he could have heard, she'd be panting—the fast breaths lifted and lowered her stomach, her abdomen, where he rested one hand.

"I do anything you like not, tap my head twice." *As if that would get your attention.* "Or hell, kick me." He chuckled when she reached forth to run her nail tips through his unkept hair. The surprisingly sharp caress tied him in knots all the way to his weighted ballocks.

His thumb circled, then retreated, his wet fingers sliding along her cleft, testing her entrance. Gauging her response. "And I shall stop." But when she arched into his hand, nudging her hollow against his fingers, bidding him to enter, he had to admit, "Though you may have to kick hard, Susanna, to claim my attention away from *this*."

One lick of his tongue made his meaning clear. One early taste that had every muscle in his loins straining. He brought his tongue fully into his mouth, swallowed. Figured parts of him started glowing. "Hold on, now."

That last was more to himself as his hand left her stomach to part her plump folds for his mouth. His other hand, answering her entreaty, and sliding forth a finger past the wet satin to snug inside her passage.

Where she gripped him, hard. Hard and eager. Hips tilted. Nails grazing above his ears.

He leaned forward, ever so slightly, and touched his tongue to her flesh. Swallowed a satisfied growl as the musky luster of her met his mouth.

He slid another finger alongside the first, relishing the tight clasp of her inner muscles. The faster arches of her hips, the less languid caresses through his hair.

Aye, Leo, like that, he could practically hear, *only faster, please. More.*

Which was easy. Was what he needed too. So he kissed her, full on. Mouth against her quim, lips laving her swollen flesh, tongue circling her pearl. And he sucked. And licked. And moaned. His fingers moved faster when she strained toward him. Clutched his head now. Threatened to swallow his hand. His tongue. His blame heart, if he wasn't careful.

Yet he could not help but wonder, what sort of sounds did she make? *Any?* As his fingers thrust deep and his tongue painted over her pearled knot, as her physical responses grew wetter and more wild, did she only pant? Did she curse? Or did she mayhap speak with naughty abandon? All things he could not wait to learn tomorrow.

And then there were no more thoughts. No more questions, for the lass arched against his mouth, legs straining, fingers pulling on his hair, hips thrashing...

He imagined a deep and throaty groan as she peaked, but had no time to debate, no time to do more than pull back, after one soft lick, his tongue swiping over his glistening lips, as he swallowed and smiled. His shoulders rolled back as pride puffed his chest. Only to have her clamber up to push against his chest, push hard, as Leo allowed himself to be shoved backward against the opposite bench, as her fingers fumbled in truth, scrabbling to open his falls.

But this time, she knelt between the squabs. This time, she didn't straddle him, only liberated him—to his definite groan—and proceeded to curve her dainty yet strong fingers around his length. Another groan and he encircled her hands with one of his, rode the startling sensation of the pressure she created, the friction beneath those delicate fingers that frigged him with such innocent enthusiasm, there in the silent dark, that Leo found himself laughing even as she fetched his mettle in such a way he felt both unmanned and yet more potent and powerful than he ever had after an act of intimacy.

"What a fine kettle you have brought me to," he admitted, knowing he had to be hoarse, when he thought he could speak without singing hallelujah to the heavens after that most miraculous of releases, using the long length of the shirt he still wore to soak up his spend before shoving it to the side and finding her in the darkness, to pull her on top of him. "Finesse vanishes every bit as much as our light, I fear."

But her lips upon his, her tongue stroking his, the unheard words that brushed by his cheek, his ear, the fierceness of the embrace she gave him before settling across his chest, one leg tucked between his, the other between his bulk and the seat, her fingers resting against the pound of his heart, told him without words that aye, they had both been humbled.

What the morrow would bring he did not know. Travel was most likely a certainty. Evading Haggart and Bowyer and the others ever more important. Sleep should have been impossible. There were... what, only another two—if he were lucky—hours remaining till dawn?

But unlike these last few months, where the black silence of night shrouded him in aloneness, pleasant remembrances of the last few hours buffeted his brain with every bit of solace as the longed-for sounds of the wind...

Sounds...

The little catch in Susanna's throat—a moan? a whimper?—each time she'd caught him staring at her mouth and her words had faltered beneath a shy smile.

The sigh of delight when she beamed at him each time he'd correctly surmised her meaning.

The sound—a squeal? a gasp? (Dare he hope, *his name?*)—she made when he'd strummed his tongue over her pearl, his fingers nestled deep inside to the welcome squeeze of her body, and she reached her pinnacle.

What she might have said when they both stroked him to the same? (His name, again, mayhap?)

Deciding to imagine *all* of them, for once Leo slipped into slumber with a smile...

15

A-COUNTING WE SHALL GO

MIKEY'S THUMB NAIL, intentionally jagged and lined with dirt, worried the edge of the letter.

–S– of Stanton House continued to mightily pique his interest.

'Twas an annoying, rather welcome, realization as so little did these days beyond work.

Alas, I still must destroy your words. Forgive me.

After committing the handwriting of the brazen saucebox to memory—and everything she had penned to Susanna Oliver—he further infixed the list the younger woman had recently provided, locking its contents in his mind before touching flame to the page and allowing it to burn to ash before approaching the stirring lad.

"Wake now, boy." He gave the child's shoulder a slight shake, tamping down the reluctance to enlist the little thief's aid. In addition to recalling damn near everything he had ever read with startling precision, he knew to make the most of every situation—and person. "I have a job for you, lad."

Bleary eyes gazed up at him, clearing after quick darts around the room reminded the urchin where he was.

He pushed off the covering Mikey had drawn over him and sat up. His legs swung off the bunk, small feet in deplorable excuses for shoes dangling inches above the floor. "Job? Doin' what?" he asked with more than a glimmer of suspicion.

Mikey intentionally remained on his feet, leaning against the open doorway that led to the larger saddle room and not coming forward to kneel and meet the boykin eye to eye. They were not equals nor peers. "Mikey" held the status, the power in any exchange they might make. Best the laddie respected him from the start.

But none of that prevented his hardened heart nudging toward an ache at the distrustful yet hopeful expression the youngling hadn't had completely beat out of him.

When he'd caught the boy pilfering belongings from passengers exiting detoured coaches the prior morn, his instant anger had melted upon seeing the old bruises beneath the too-short sleeve of the ratty coat and low on his neck where a scarf should have been but wasn't. "Shall we come to an agreement, you and I?"

"What sort o' agree-ment?"

"The kind where I trust you to deliver a parcel and a message, and in exchange, I pay you for your efforts." The little whelp narrowed his eyes, a smart brain behind the untrimmed mop of dirty hair.

"No, you don't—I can see it in your eyes. You nip out with the package? Without sharing the message? You shall wind up with less than you would otherwise have."

"How do I know you ain't lying?"

"That, my boy, is twofold."

"Eh?"

Mikey subdued his grin. Wouldn't do to have the lad think he was laughing at his ignorance. But there was something surprisingly pleasing about a stubborn seven-year-old standing up to a man with forty years and 150 pounds on him. "It means there are *two* different ways you will know I speak the truth. The first is *trust*. Trust me and what I say. Did I not honor my word earlier? With both food and a safe, warm place to sleep? Asking nothing in return."

"Did so ask for something in return. Made me give back what I'd nipped."

It took more effort to keep his humor from showing at that. "Those things weren't yours to begin with. So I shall ask again. Did I not grant you what I promised?"

He waited until the boy gave a grudging nod before continuing.

"All right. You deliver the package and message

for me. Come back with the coded word in response and receive your reward. Your payment."

"Coded word?"

"A watchword, a signal, a token between mates so the one you deliver the message to knows that it came from me, and what he tells you allows me to know he received it."

A small grubby hand rubbed a chin, as the child evaluated both Mikey and the empty waxed paper on the floor. Evidence of Reaver's own theft. He turned curious eyes back to Mikey. "And the second way? You said there was two."

"Go wash your face, visit the office and come back. We will count out your reward together. You will know what coins are waiting for you upon your return."

"Upon my return with your watchword?"

"Correct."

Belligerence. Embarrassment. Both of those filled the boy's gaze, each vying for dominance. "I cannot do that. The counting part. I do not know my numbers."

He had assumed as much. "Which is why we shall do it together."

⸻◦⸻

MONIED COVES WERE rum as a two-headed beetle. He'd only ever seen *one* of those (and suspected his cousin had pasted on one of the heads). *So* out-of-the-way!

The "parcel" Nipper (what his mama had called him before she died) was to deliver was just as peculiar, to his way of thinking, made up of:

-coins (counted, together with the odd stable master, *twice*—ugh!)
-the lone remaining stocking (one of two) he (Nipper) had nipped off the pretty lady earlier the day before, and
-a tin of boot blacking
-a 3-item "spoken message" Mikey had made Nipper repeat *thrice*.

(Oy. So much counting, his head was going to blast open like a grenade.)

After repeating the message that third time, glaring at the stable master all the while (because he had knowed it just fine after the second time and the man had the swagger to tack on a *fourth* item), Mikey sent him to find the "Second-*tallest*, *hairiest*-faced fellow among the *loudest* group of men in the tavern. Sorrel-colored hair, like a squirrel. Name's Benny."

Easy enough.

But double *oy*. And not just because he'd had to repeat *that* three times back as well. Nay, *triple* oy. Because he suspected which group he was being sent to siddle alongside...

Upon making his way to East Crossings and the tavern, Nipper had seen which louts were the *meanest*. Had taken pains to avoid them earlier when their voices got louder and louder with every ale or gin or shouted, lewd verse worthy of the raff. When his pater drank to loudness (or lewdness), Papa's fives came out. And Nipper knew to hide.

With the winter weather huddling everyone inside, The Filthy Pig was thronged. 'Twas toilless enough to flit between the women's skirts and men's backs until locating the buck he sought.

Just to make certain sure he winnowed out the right cove, he ran up to the table, crying, "Uncle Benny!"

Aye, the fellow he'd picked out jerked sharply toward him, striving to keep the surprisal off his face. He needn't have worried none, well-nigh half of it was hidden by whiskers.

The dumbfoundering erased as soon as it had flashed, the man whisked his chair back, making room. "What the devil are you doing here?" he asked, all thundering outrage.

This Benny was a clever whipster, latching on fast.

"Mum sent me," Nipper trembled his lip, thinking to do this right. Had that fat reward waiting for him and all. "Och, Uncle Benny, I thought I'd lost ya in the storms."

"Pardon me." The shaggy-faced man said, speaking to the gruff, scarred-up fellow next to him. Then he rose to his feet causing Nip's eyes to go wide. Gore. He was big.

The tall, hairy "uncle" grabbed hold of his shoulders and aimed Nipper toward the kitchen, speaking clamorously. "Your mum knows better than to send you out after me when I'm off an' working. You best…"

His words drifted quiet as soon as and they were out of the others' sight. His hard hold gentled some too.

Pulling Nipper around to the far side of the big stove sticking out from the wall, Benny dropped to his knees. Green eyes—brighter than Nipper had ever seen—swept him up and down. "So, Nephew. Explain."

"Got a message for you. And this."

Nipper pulled the package from deep in his pocket and thrust it over. "Hide that. And listen good."

Shifting to one foot, but keeping the other knee on the ground, Benny pocketed the parcel and nodded.

Puffing out his chest, determined to get this nonsensical list right, Nipper counted off on his fingers.

"One. Mikey says get shackled and get out—no dallying."

"Shackled?" Those green eyes grew wider than a wheel.

"Two. The one with the crying tot. Second floor. Middle room, fracted window lookin' out at the stable."

"Tot?"

"Three. Hide your face. They know you ain't being candid. Knows you're crooked."

"Crooked?"

Nipper nodded, finally expelling a hard breath, now that his official package and messages had been dispatched. "He didn't *say* it, but me? I'm thinking those uglies in there—they want you gone."

"Gone?"

"Dead." Nipper huffed. And he'd thought the gent was nimble minded? Oy, not with these one-word grunts this bufflehead kept giving him. "Now gimme the coded word so I can get me reward."

"Coded word?"

"Are you a simpleton? Guess I was wrong 'bout ya, Professor. 'Cause you ain't saying much o' sense at all."

N*AY*, he wasn't.

Because Timothy Benton, currently heir to his father's marquisate (and not speaking to the man after a decided difference of opinion), known in London by his courtesy title of Lord Wrothington (or "Wrath" after his temper earned him the rights to that), reeled.

Reeled, the "buffled" head he'd just been accused of spinning like a top.

This little bugger, looking half starved and so earnest Tim's arms ached to reach out and hug him —because the little ladkin reminded him of his two favorite nephews, boys he missed like he would a severed arm—had just delivered some of the most startling news to cross his awareness in months. Ever since portraying someone he wasn't.

Though he'd tried, more out of spite than desire, living the life of a vagabond wasteling obviously wasn't something he excelled at, not if those he sought to spy on had figured him out, now planned to exscind him.

He had a bounty on his head? Dashed inconvenient.

The coins he had just pocketed were more than a little. Easily enough for several days' hard travel. But the rest of this? 'Twas the words that pitchkettled his stomach... Get *shackled* to the lady with the *tot*?

His commander had gone daft, undoubtedly from inhaling too much horse shit. Farnsworth wanted him to pretend to be married to some female with a baby? Had his superior drunk himself under the table and hit his head on the way down?

"A lady with a baby?"

"Ain't that what I just said? Told you? Second floor. Middle room. Broke window. Stables. Watchword? What is it?"

He didn't have an inkling what sort of "word" Farnsworth expected. Wagered that was something between him and the youngling, to ensure the bag of coins didn't disappear into the night. "Do you know the female? Is she single? Alone?"

Smashing. He'd have an irate husband challenging him to a duel come noon. Yet another reason for his father to deride his choices.

"Course she ain't alone, Professor, you addlepate. Did I not tell you she was here with a *baby*?"

Both of them spoke in hushed whispers, and had since retreating to the empty kitchens. Empty in every way possible. The pitiful inn, after being besieged with unexpected guests, had been depleted far earlier that night, now many lay sprawled or propped up, sleeping or capsized. Unlike them, he was still sober. And awake, hoping to glean something useful.

So dashed tired of pretending to be uncaring whether he bathed or shaved, forcing himself to talk crude and coarse. Even worse, having to *listen* to the others. To laugh and join in even when what they said roiled his stomach. Least Tucker was spared that, didn't have his garret filled with the filth this crew spewed from daylight till dark and beyond.

As to Tim?

He just wanted a bath. And a bed. Preferably one *without* a "wife" and baby.

He bit back the urge to growl. "Tell me what you know of her, and I'll give you the word."

"Aye, I knows her." The boy gave him a boastful smile. "*Knows* what her stockings and shift looks like too."

Timothy wouldn't touch that one with a ten-foot rod. "Bolt out the rest, if you will. A description of her wouldn't be amiss. If your messages are to be believed, we should not dally."

"Don't question me messages. I might filch your shoes as soon as look at ya, but I ain't no liar. And I just 'membered *four*." The stripling held out four fingers—but not until counting off the first three again. "Four. You's to tell the lady that Liddy's daddy sent ya."

Oh, hell. Hell and the apocalypse.

Liddy? Lydia, Farnsworth's daughter who disappeared more than a decade ago? He knew about it. Everyone his generation did.

Above their own allure, dukes' daughters were sought after because of their proximity to such a title. He'd been on his Grand Tour, gadding about Italy or some such at the time. This was before he and Father nearly came to blows; before Timothy joined the navy. Rumor and rattletrap had it that Lydia had been more vivacious than her mother had been, more apt to enjoy parties and such. To keep her out of trouble, and after some rebellion since her mother had died, Farnsworth had taken his daughter in hand, and she traveled with him beyond London for several years.

Only to defy his wishes and succumb to the flattery of a lowly sailor without any exalted connections to recommend him, fleeing off to wed him over the anvil. And before a month had elapsed, he returned to Farnsworth, begging forgiveness because the man's only offspring had vanished under his care.

Liddy's daddy sent me.

And the "mother" he was to introduce himself to and convince her to portray his wife had been close enough to Lydia to understand that message?

Well now. If he hadn't been sufficiently riddled with nerves before—at the thought Bowyer or that bragout Haggard wanted his head on a pike—he was appropriately anxious now. One hand met his jaw, scratching through the thick beard he'd grown the last two months. Thicker than many could grow in two years. But at least that gave him an idea.

No time to waste, really, not with the lack of travel options tonight.

And he was supposed to disappear? Hide his face? Right. Six foot four and reddish hair that resembled a fox more than not? He was certainly noticeable.

And if the female upstairs had known Lydia, there was a good chance she would know him too. At least know of him.

Which should be true in the reverse, aye? If you and the female have a past acquaintance, should that not smooth things over? Grant yourself a safe haven in her room tonight? Wait for the others to clear out tomorrow...

He thrust his hand in the opposite pocket, where he knew a couple coins resided, pulled one out by feel and held it up between them. "Can you get me a sharp razor? Shaving equipment? Without anyone being the wiser? And bring it to me in her room?"

The boy all but chortled, a gleeful expression climbing over his wearied face. "Without question. You knows I can."

When the child reached for the coin, Timothy curled his fist around it. "When I see you upstairs. And I'll add another to it if you can find me a hat as well. Something at least halfway clean."

Appeared he had a "wife" to meet and convince to help him.

"And you will tell me the word then? So I can get my reward from Mikey?"

As soon as he deduced something that might work. "Absolutely."

16

A LETTER OF NOTE

DESPITE BEING alert and active most of the prior night, Leo woke long before dawn. A life at sea saw to that.

Even without the sun or the birds' songs (in the warmer months) to herald the day's beginnings, he came awake—and aware—in an instant.

Knew full well where he was and who lounged atop him. Slender in places, lush in others, the body that resided, with a delightful heft and presence, against his torso nestled between his thighs, along the spread of his legs.

Nothing would mar him savoring the next hour or so, while he waited for the day to begin, for her to stir.

Nothing.

After their hours of one-sided chattering (all his) that somehow, with Susanna Oliver (Nate Oliver's *sister*—how the mind still boggled over that) seemed to flow with such joyful relaxation he could scarcely believe it, expectancy brimming through him shouldn't have surprised.

But it did.

Had he become so benumb to joy that to bask in its presence near bewildered?

Excited by the lift to his typically troubled first-awareness thoughts (thanks to war and life), excited more by the presence of the woman snug atop him, Leo welcomed the rising sun with a foreign anticipation infusing his muscles.

Daytime. Which would give them opportunity to converse again, the bedamned lantern run to fumes stalling anything she might say to him. Stalling her words, but not her touches.

Her questing caresses, as she'd explored his face in the dark, the puckered scarring along his neck and sorely mottled the flesh of one ear.

Halt, Tucker. Think you more of her touches and the primed prick you woke with will only pain you further.

No clanker, that.

Soon enough, prodded forth by his impatience, the sun yawned awake. With it, daylight came, edging through the old roof, the split planks high on the walls.

Draggled weakly enough through the grimed-over windows and into the carriage where he'd reached over his head and rolled the leather covering up and away.

Allowed him enough light to skim again their early conversations from last night, the crowded words a hash of ink and pencil. The one he had sharpened thrice or more during the night for her with his ever-present penknife. Her precious hand and the lively chatter that issued from it thrilling him anew at the chance to savor every scribbled syllable again...

Susanna Oliver Mitchell.
Brother. Navy.
Charity Faith Hope

Her nieces, the mischievous ones who managed to wrangle an unexpected spouse for their father, thanks to Susanna's assistance as well.

25 come May

Her age.

Crisp bacon and roasted cabbage

Her favorite meal, which he'd twitted her over.

1815 Christmas Eve <u>Eve</u>

When he'd asked her favorite holiday—and written with a decided twinkle; one he'd returned, it not escaping his notice that she described that very moment, with him.

A shove. Into the table

When he questioned what happened around the tragic birth of her baby.

Sheer will alone—not the poor roads and weather nor the preposterousness of the notion—kept him from seeking out the grave and digging up her wretch of a spouse to carve his remains up as bait.

Now, as his gaze stroked over every word, his thumb caressing a few while his other arm curved about her waist, palm splayed—indecently comfortable, possessive even—over one buttock, he "saw", for the first time, the writing *beyond* the myriad penciled phrases. The ink alongside.

The letter beneath.

The one also in her hand. The slope and curve of her letters now as familiar to him as his own.

WANTED: For Matrimony

What the devil?

ONE KIND, *dependable man. Desirous of children a boon.*

Desirous of me? A prerequisite! (Dare I say <u>covetous</u> of me? Unwilling to share.)

TO SHARE? Leo's body stiffened.

Generous of nature but stingy with his fists.

Muscles strained.

EASY TO SMILE and willing to join in together on chores.

Not obsessed with drink nor cards nor gambling (nor gambling while drinking over cards).

Content to return home each evening alone. Not cause me to lose sleep worrying if his sorry hide will stumble in drunk and angry, or simply stumble in and pitch floorward before sleep overtakes.

FLOORWARD? Is that even a word?

At her self-mockery, her gentle humor, his screaming muscles slowly, ever so slowly, unfurled from the fury clenching them.

Bah. Stupidest list ever!

Nay, it wasn't. 'Twas the most informative list. Mayhap the most important one he had seen since leaving the war efforts—even before. Leo wasn't so nog-headed that he couldn't deduce this described the lass's late husband.

The next page, the second one abounding with her scribbles from last eve was even further packed with ink...

Desired: For Matrimonial Life

*One stalwart, kind man, in possession of both
manners and teeth,*

He had to subdue a laugh over that, grateful
when his tongue ran over his, satisfyingly, intact
chompers.

seeks a lady to share his life.

What, ho? Speaking of teeth and manners, what
manner of letter was this? His brows drew tight in a
frown as he roved eyes over the entire page.

Aye. All in *her* writing. Yet written from the
direction a man would pen. A man *also seeking a wife.*

A silent whistle circled his lips as he allowed his
surprised, astonished breath to feather from his
lungs. A measured, rolling inhale to calm the
uneven beat of his heart and he went back to the
top, reading with less haste...

*She need not be titled nor fanciful, filled with nonsen-
sical knowledge of fashion or the latest on dits about
town. She does need to desire me in return. To wish for a
life of love and joy and perhaps hope we might be blessed
with a child or two of our own. If God sees fit to provide.*

*Most importantly, she need be steadfast in both
manner and with her smiles.*

*In return, I shall hold her each night, laugh with her
each morning and love her throughout our years.*

The description heated the air about his face, for

did he not, deep down, also crave that very thing? Steadfastness of character, unlike Farnsworth's chit he'd nearly offered for? But of vastly more importance, the love and laughter? What he missed from his innocent, early years with Ann-Marie more than anything else. Did he not crave that most of all?

What of the desire the lass alludes to? his contrary side wanted to know.

So obvious between us it needs not stated! he argued back.

Very well. Carry on.

The page was littered with abrasive Xs, swirling loops and all manner of cross marks and scratch outs, but a few additional phrases remained legible:

> *Dear Lady Reckless*
> *Dear Lady Adventure,*
> *How daft can you be, Susanna?*
> *Lady Reckless? Adventure?*
> *Bah. More like Lady Clod-brain.*

He pried his fingers from their warm bed atop her flank and used both hands to fold the note along its creases with precision and care. Leo sighed. Then again. A long, thoughtful exhale, as he felt the welcome weight of Lady Reckless Clod-brain settling easily against his chest, his heart.

Steadfast of manner...

In possession of teeth.

Another smile cracked at that.

Desirous of children. Desirous *of me.*

Hmm. She had given him much to ponder this fresh, new morning.

SECONDS TICKED SILENTLY BY. Minutes that flew with the swiftness of a bird soaring overhead. Yet they crawled too... Crawled with the excruciating pace of a spider down the wall (when one was naked—in a hip bath, and the insect not easily within squashing distance).

Leo wasn't bathing.

Nor did arachnids dare well within the duke's carriage.

But the temptation to read more? The acute ache to know more about the cinnamon-sugary bundle still sleeping over him could not be quelled.

Temptation so easily within reach...

Another letter, this one open but not pencilled over nearly as much, with the top portion folded lazily forward, compelled him to risk the uncrinkling of it...

Are you not jumping far beyond propriety, crossing bounds and violating her privacy?

She's wearing my shirt and naught else.

Nay, her feet are covered.

Aye, with my *socks!*

Not anymore!

Granted, for she now had one trim, bare foot wedged against his calf.

She had also left the stack of open letters *right there*, on the opposite squab, and by blazes...

He would apologize when she awoke, but nay, he wouldn't—couldn't—stop. Not when the conviction of *her* penmanship greeted him once more...

Dear Lord Not At All,

I write to you as only a caring, wise and protective older brother could.

My sister is the sweetest, most stubbornly independent woman I know.

She is overly generous, overly giving, sometimes to her detriment. Overly forgiving too.

But after assisting my three outlandish daughters in securing a most un-sought-for yet perfect marriage and bedmate for myself, 'tis the least I can do to see her satisfyingly shackled as well.

Hmm. Written as though inked by her brother yet still in her hand as well.

A letter of recommendation? One in the same vein as those *imposterous* ones she and her nieces had provided that aided in Nate securing his wife?

In exchange for your (nonexistent) title, you shall receive an eager female of child-bearing age who would love nothing more than to take care of you and your home together.

Susanna is faithful, true and sincere in her statements. Unafraid of hard work, but would appreciate it be shared. She will love you to distraction, delight in your company and be most thankful for whatever attention you can spare.

Something hard and hot squeezed his chest.

In exchange, what she wishes, fervently so, from you:
Be true as well.
Come home at night, sober and alone, so she need not be anxious over escaping unwanted attentions, and after, should she not be successful—

Good God above. Further proof of what that brute had subjected her to.

...not be successful, spend hours crying into her pillow, vowing to resist with greater fervency the next time.

His hand shook with rage. The words wavered as the page trembled before his eyes.
Imbecile! 'Tis no more than you deserve.
Not what she deserved, though. The horrors her husband had put her through...
Nor does she deserve you abandoning all honor and continuing to read. You—
What she deserves is to be cherished the rest of her years!
She would tell you herself, part of him rejoined, *if you would but give her time.*
Time they had not. For who knew how soon the

bridge might be repaired? How soon the stage would charge through again?

The stage? Pfft! You know you have every intention of escorting her yourself.

True.

So be patient.

Patient? I have waited forty years for her, his mind snarled, yelling back, silencing his conscience for the nonce. As several still shaken, decidedly deep breaths steadied his hand and saw the gentle weight upon his chest lift and mayhap *hmmm* or sigh—felt, not heard—the rage toward her deceased spouse transformed from blind fury into fierce curiosity as Leo steeled himself to continue; to learn what she wished for...

Kisses, and many of them. (Invited ones, that is.)

Hugs too.

A two-room abode would be lovely.

An already sharpened axe for chopping wood come winter.

Pin money would be most appreciated as well.

Remember her birthday.

Remember to celebrate Christmas and retrieve mistletoe every year.

Attend services with her and

And the rest was so scratched over, marked through and inked beyond recognition that not a single letter shown through, much less a sensible word.

Angling the page, he devoured the rest, what she'd written along the bottom, perpendicular to the primary.

Susanna, you foolish spinner of air castles. Nate may have found his "lady" but you are a pitiful loon to expect the same.

No man worth having will ever accept a used bride. Not one <u>more</u> than husband-used, but used, on occasion, by his horrid cronies. A woman who felt relief equal to her sorrow when her sister-in-law sickened, giving her— me—an escape some days.

Though (I hope and pray daily) that our good and gracious God has forgiven me, no man walks this earth who will accept those sins and my other, greatest—

Good God, indeed. 'Twas a wonder her smiles and spirited nature had not been crushed beneath the boot of the knave she'd taken to husband.

But she was wrong.

Vastly so. To think no man would accept her, along with her past burdens, the "sins" alluded to— and, in particular, the one that, given the somewhat newness of this particular page (not nearly worn about the edges as the other two), still marred her present.

Troubled her so.

Well, Tucker, your affinity for trouble cannot be denied.

True.

Neither could his desire for the lass.

The one who had no inkling he now knew her secrets. Much of them, anyway. And remained desperate to learn the last: the one *unwritten*.

So he could purge from her conscience whatever guilt she still harbored. Blow it from her memory with a puff of his breath.

But what of the rest?

Her dream man, mayhap?

His eyes skimmed back over the legible lines. The simple wishes.

Kisses. Shared labor. Hugs. Church services together. The sharpened axe. Mistletoe.

He wanted to chuckle at that. Wanted to curse and cry too. What sort of devilish lout had brought her to yearn for such simple things?

The sort who would toss her to others for coin.

Too damn troublesome to contemplate.

There was not a thing on her list he could not provide. Not a single thing.

She asked naught of conversations, of hearing.

And had their scant hours together not already shown they could communicate far better than he had with any female not family? With any*one*?

A LONG, long, loooooong while later, as he continued to congratulate himself for resisting the lure of reading another, she stirred.

Awake at last?

Relief stormed through him.

Breath held, waiting...

Waiting...

Expelled in utter dismay.

For she turned on her side and cuddled closer, the fingers of one hand slipping past his shirt to curve over one pectoral, her slumberous breaths warming the skin all around.

He shifted to his side as well, his spine to the seat, long legs bent awkwardly as he held her to him, rested his jaw against her head. Tried to keep his eyes closed and return to sleep.

And tried.

And...tried.

And

...

tried.

Sincerely.

Attempted

...

to

sleep.

...

To

be

calm

...

and

still

and

settle

...

his

rampaging

thoughts.
...

To

be

silent

and

honorable

and

...

and

...

But then his restless gaze fell upon it.

Another letter, partially open. The new angle of his head propped upon his arm revealing what had been hidden before.

This one, emblazoned with **DO NOT POST** across the top.

And temptation proved stronger than patience.

... ...

...Olivia, Mama, Papa, Nate, Ellen, Sarah: I confess to you all that my evil thoughts and lack of strength to leave while I still could killed my precious baby and I will suffer that burden, that scar upon my soul forever.

Dear Lord... Dear sweet, innocent Philip, please forgive me for acting the monster and not protecting you as a mother should.

Leo's clenched hand shook anew. Blurred the words before his eyes. Pressure filled his jaw, a tooth may have dared crack, as sorrow burst, hard and heavy, across his heart.

This.

This explained the *unshared* secrets shading the soft hue in her eyes.

This *unposted* letter that he had dared to read.

17

GALLOPING GUILT

LEO KNEW the moment she awoke in truth.

'Twas all he could do to keep himself motionless. He needed to hug her so tightly to him with a vengeance that was a chore to tame.

But the slumberous form that had rested against him these last sparse hours so trustingly, so very welcome, had stiffened to the point of pain, he feared. Mayhap needing a moment to orient herself. "All is well," he assured, working to keep his voice even. "Glad you are ready to salute the day."

He knew it wasn't every morning she greeted atop a stranger, no matter how intimate things might have turned between them and the hours since he felt that word applied. The word of *stranger*.

For it didn't, not any longer.

Nor did he want to frighten her, never that.

His thoughts were still a rictus of mire given everything he'd learned.

So he schooled himself to reveal nothing of the riot blazing through him.

Forced his expression to be as neutral, as blank as he could. Didn't want her to glimpse the rage still firing his every limb.

Took strength in the way she slowly relaxed against him again, before pushing herself up on one arm, to glance down at him in sleepy wonder.

Took solace in the drowse-warmed scent that filtered through his nostrils like a benediction. Such a jewel, this one, who called to him on so many levels.

How could any man treat a female he had sworn to love and to cherish, according to God's holy ordinance, in such a way? And to do so with having escaped any just retribution?

Death? Do you not consider that sufficient and just retribution?

Not even close...

He bit back the rancor bristling to break free. Couldn't let the anger storming through him show. Couldn't frighten her, not when she had already braved so much. So he kept his emotions to himself. Worked to blanket the beast of his anger, lest his ire burn the tenuous, yet so very real, connection between them.

"Susanna." Susanna. A name he wanted to say now. Tonight. Tomorrow. Again and again...

A woman he wanted to cherish and protect for as long as she would let him.

It had taken weeks before Susanna could sleep through the night. Even longer before she could be startled awake without jumping through the roof or trying to flee.

It seemed, once the body was conditioned in certain responses, it took far longer to untrain it and keep oneself at ease.

Coming awake so swiftly, long after the sun rose, with her nose buried in a warm chest and a big hand resting over her thigh didn't send her scurrying for cover as it might have a mere three months prior. Nay, because her nose told her even before her mind realized the truth: that she was safe.

Safe, and within the amazing embrace of Captain Leo Tucker. She wanted to kiss his chest. Wanted to lift herself up over him and push him to his back. Wanted to straddle him and revel in all the sights that had been denied her last night.

She wanted him to make love to her fully, no matter that *love* was an impossibility at the moment. He could not feel for her anywhere near the depths her feelings approached for him, but she would satisfy herself with his strength and his presence and his big and brawny body for every minute that she could, until he sent her on her way.

"Good morning." Her words were a rasped husk

that took her a second or three to realize he could not hear. For she had not faced him.

Smiling, she shifted against his body on the narrow squab and rose to balance upon one arm, seeking his gaze—

Which looked at her as though she were an unwanted hair in his ale, the warm expression she had come to know the last few hours was gone, frozen into a mask of immobility.

No warmth to his narrowed, hard-held eyes. No inviting tilt to the lips showing smooth and inviting past the thicker stubble shading his jaw.

He looked so cold. So controlled.

His expression void of the caring and heat she had become accustomed to. No amusement now. No indulgent teasing over her reckless whims, only a hardness she didn't understand. Could not have imagined waking to.

"Susanna."

The rumble skittered past her ears and fluttered her belly.

Ah. He would explain now. Tell her what was wrong.

Smiling at him, if a bit uncertainly, she gathered herself (somewhat difficult to do wearing the man's shirt!) and scrabbled backward, gaining the opposite seat.

Only to crinkle something beneath her bare thigh. She darted to the side and glanced down.

DO NOT POST! DO NOT POST!

...no matter how fervently I wished to be a mother, I wished this babe gone from me...

Her letter. To Olivia. The one unsent. The one confessing the worst of her sins.

Her eyes flew to his for a single flicker. But that proved sufficient.

He had read this. Read them.

He knew...*everything*.

Time halted, heavy with the ever-present regret she could not shake. Only now, instead of occupying a small box where she tried to keep it locked tight, it overflowed, flooded her being.

Her face flamed. Lips numbed. Heart tried to pound away into the past as her frantic gaze took in the pages. The letters. Her secrets. Her shame. All revealed in the murky carriage light.

Her balance bobbled as she tried to blink. To lick her lips.

He was saying something, but she couldn't hear what. Ringing in her ears battered her brain.

It wasn't even a betrayal she could accuse him of. She had *handed* him the letters, time and again the prior eve. She had failed to secure them once done.

Now 'twas all her secrets and shames laid bare.

His stone-faced hatred was nothing less than she deserved.

Through the haze, he gripped her arms, brought her back to his lap. How could he bear to touch her?

Her head buzzed. Filled with screams of self-derision. She still couldn't hear him.

The screams turned tinny, higher in pitch, and she winced. Wavered in place. Tried to surface above the depths before she drowned.

Escape! Is that not what she'd told herself, when she'd learned she was pregnant? What Sarah would have counseled? *Escape while you can.*

The advice she had failed to heed that had ended in such unspeakable tragedy.

Escape.

Ignoring the new cracks forming around her fragile heart, she wrenched her unseeing gaze from his and clambered off him, all ungainly grace. She slapped aside his outstretched hand. Babbled over his entreaties, the ones demanding to be heard over the constant buzzing. "Still a moment... Listen, please. Nay, *talk* to me. I took liberties, should not have—"

"No." She shoved off him when he would have embraced her, used the impetus to skitter backward, out of the carriage. The noise and clamor disturbed Reaver, who gave a single bark, his confused attention swinging between her gawky retreat and the man who jumped smoothly down after her.

She still wore naught but his shirt. She'd toed off the socks during the short night, to rub her feet along his legs before slumber claimed her.

As he was supposed to this morn. Claim her, fully.

"Nay," she cried, arguing more with herself than the stalwart presence that had come to stand beside her, one full pace away as she stood in front of the big carriage wheel where she'd draped her dress. A single pace that loomed like a chasm as she stared at the wrinkled, mud-stained clothing she'd spread out in the most haphazard fashion.

You cannot arrive to your brother's wearing that!

What choice did she have?

Feeling as though she was tearing off skin, she ripped Leo's shirt over her head and ducked beneath the drying hem of her dress to draw it on.

Along with her composure, any claim to grace had gone flying out the window as she twisted this way and that, tugging the sides ruthlessly, trying to get the uncomfortable garment in place.

And without first donning shift or stays? For shame, young lady.

She wasn't sure who nudged her then—her mama's old teachings? Always beautifully polished Sarah? Or her own conscience which was rent asunder as sure as the broken coach from last night, a good part of her wanting to plop down and have a strong cry—in his arms, if he would let her, while the other, more familiar part, just needed to flee.

When the distraught raffle that was her hair got tangled in her fingers, she debated tying it in a knot or yanking it out by the roots. Surely that, at least, would distract from the pain centered in her chest, the one radiating from inane emotions she should *not* be having. *Not* so soon. Not with—

"May I?" He placed his fingers at her back, indicating the buttons she would have difficulty reaching, gently nudging her abrupt fingers aside.

Silently, still seething with shame and embarrassment, she nodded.

He did up three or four before speaking. "Susanna, I—"

She whirled on him, still not meeting his eyes. "Nay! I will not listen. Not now. Give me time—" She looked at him then, one fast second that for her, was fraught with so much emotion she wondered how she managed even that. "La-ter," she said, pointing to her nonexistent timepiece. Then her ear. "Will list-en. Listen later. Not now."

Her kiss-awoken lips wobbled. Eyes dared swim. She just needed a hug, drat him. Wanted to inhale him again, to rest against his strength.

But now he knew. Knew *everything*. Only evil monsters prayed their babies away. Let their husbands barter them as tender.

Captain Tucker will understand.

But that frantic flick of her head, flinging her disastrous hair from her face to glimpse his had only revealed his hard, clenched jaw. Even harder eyes.

He would not understand.

Nor could she blame him.

Only herself.

"Susanna. Please. Halt."

But she was torn, as torn as the stockings she abandoned for the shambling, not-quite-painful act of drawing on her walking boots—her feet sorely abused from the cold and excessive trudge of yesterday.

Lady Adventure? Pah. Lady Tragedy, more like, for she could not even keep her wicked secrets to herself upon such a short acquaintance with such a special man. And who would have thought that she would have been off her guard sufficiently to feel thus so quickly?

"You have me at a significant disadvantage, you know."

Despite the anger shading his features, his voice —that low and sensual ramble, called forth every feminine response she'd denied the last few years. Bade her to jump back into his arms, wrap hers about his neck and hold tight while he spoke, coaxed her back to peace.

"Leicester! Loughborough! Then on to Derby!"

The jingle of horses thundering by, the noisy arrival of the first coach to pass this way since she'd arrived—the hue and cry of her destination—for good or for ill, it made her decision for her.

She spun back to the carriage, half climbed in and took no care shoving her possessions back into her valise. The wrapped gifts for the girls went in first. The wretched letters crumpled as she stuffed them deep. When her grasping hand clasped one of his discarded socks by mistake, she shoved it in too.

Finished, she scrambled backward, stumbled down the daft steps, wrenched away when he offered aid and focused just below his neck as she dropped her bag to gather her disarrayed hair and worked to twist what she could into a tight coil at the back of her head.

Bonnet! Where was her bedraggled bonnet? She scoured high and low, damning her gaze when it persisted in flitting his direction time and again.

Reaver had come to lean against Leo, whose fingers absently stroked the dog's head; even sitting the canine came up to the man's thigh. After drying during the night, the dog looked slightly less disreputable. But the man? Even decently, if informally, attired, with his pants on, shirt untucked and without a neckcloth in place, he still made for a commanding presence, drat him.

'Twas the wide breadth of his chest that still drew her, compelled her arm to lift toward him before she ruthlessly forced it back, the muss of his overly long hair, thicker bristle along his cheeks and jaw... The hard jaw and soft lips she would never touch again.

Her recently healed heart cracked even more.

"Leicester! Loughborough!" Even muffled through the planks, the distance, the shouts reached through easily. Would that the rest of her morning had followed.

When has anything been easy, *since you persisted in throwing in with Mr. Mitchell?*

Last evening had been easy. The last hours, the most blessed she could remember. Until awaking to the hatred in his eyes. The anger. That brief reminder chilled her soul. One final spin refused to reveal her missing bonnet.

"What is it? You have gone frantic." Hands to her shoulders, he stopped her further retreat the second she swooped down and then back up, clutching her bag.

"The coach. 'Tis here. I must go." No inkling whether she spoke slow enough. How could she concentrate, when her heart thundered every bit as much as the hooves that had raced past?

"Stay. Please. We shall—"

She thrumbled past him. "Move, Reaver!" The dog refused, now standing sentry in front of the door, stupid thing.

So she went round, grappled with the heavy bar that bolted the inside—

Only to have it miraculously lifted.

Leo. Standing before her. Hand on the door. "I would escort you. Wherever you would go." That deep, comforting rumble. She couldn't let it entice her, not now that he knew.

Can you not? You may see anger in his face, but he has enacted no ire toward you.

"Susanna, please—"

"Leicester! Derby! Only two seats left!"

Derby. Where she would exit the stage and travel to the smaller village of Duffield.

Duffield, where she'd grieved and started healing this summer. With Nate and Olivia. With her nieces... Charity's baking and adorably imperious ways toward her younger sisters. Sweet Charity, who had grown up far faster than she should have, when her mother started ailing. Young Hope, Faith in the middle, the girls' mischievous youngling kittens so quickly scaling curtains and growing into cats.

Within the three-story ramshackle manor house and grounds that offered an escape once again...

But only if you can forgive yourself.

Reaver bumped against her leg, unbalancing her into Leo. A glance downward revealed the dog had her bonnet in his mouth! Muddied (dried mud, but still!) green ribbons trailing in the dirt. "Give me that."

You really ought to stay, the canine seemed to say, eyes wiser than they should have been, as she pried her battered bonnet free of his teeth. *Stay and listen.*

"No, you naughty dog!"

"Susanna. Please, wait but a moment. Let me—"

Aye, the dog gave a gritted-teeth snarl, *listen to him. He likes you. You like him back. I can smell things.* The canine's brown eyes fairly chortled at her, making a mockery of her morning. He wrinkled his snout at her, tipped his nose upward. *Impressive sniffer and all that.*

"No matter how wondrous your nose, fiendish dog, you cannot tell how much I like him!"

Can so.

"Susanna, sweet— Wait. Are you arguing with my dog?"

"Leicester! Derby! One ticket remaining."

Giving in to temptation one last time, she threw an arm about his neck—the man, not his contrary canine—and kissed his stubbly jaw. Tucked her face against his chest and inhaled down to her toes. Then she pushed off and wrenched the door open, running for the stage and that last ticket as if Homer's Scylla had escaped the sea and chased after her.

But she still could not outrun her guilt.

18

TO JAUNT WILLY-NILLY

No one took note of the big man, other than his sizable girth, as the carriage swayed when he coerced his bulk through the narrow door. But one person did take note of Susanna as she climbed in after him.

It didn't take Leo long to deduce what set the lass off like a firebrand to tinder.

They'd been intimate—remarkably so (if not completely) and she'd jolted far beyond his expectations upon realizing he knew her "secret shame" (her words, not his).

And the blame stage had chosen the worst possible moment to barrel through, thanks to some title holder who allowed it use of his land, his private bridge, avoiding the broken one (Mikey had imparted that).

The coach, both dislodging and picking up passengers, and heading straight toward Susanna's destination.

After at least two other stops.

Stops Leo was thankful for, as he saddled Nelson Rambler with more haste than care. He pulled the cinch. Yanked it again. Waited. "Come on now, girl." There! She puffed out the breath she'd inhaled to make his job harder. Now he could finish.

Over the horse's back, Mikey arrested his attention, coming forward with an aromatic package. A single nod toward Reaver, waiting a few paces away loosed words. "I know. He cannot come," Leo said, gleaning the question in that single glance, "not as far as I will be going. Nor as fast."

He had no expectation he'd be able to overtake the stage until after its first stop and change of horses, ten miles hence, mayhap farther.

Mikey nodded, called to the dog who loped over for a neck scratch, his pink tongue lolling out, giving his fierce canine a rare, relaxed and muzzy mein.

"My thanks." Leo tucked the wrapped food in his saddlebag, the rest of his belongings already tied up in his haversack and stuffed beneath. Then he turned to face his superior. "The twelfth?" He mentioned the date he was due in London. "Can I retrieve him them?"

A nod. "...you want..." His boss stopped. Gave a shake of his head, before starting again, talking slow, lips moving clearly. "Come sooner if you want. Fifth." He held up five fingers. "That's when... London."

Leo nodded. Then felt his forehead crease. "I am leaving you in the lurch," he acknowledged quietly. "Abandoning our efforts."

Mikey smiled, showing those horridly black teeth. "...saving your own...abandoning naught." A lift of his chin, indicating the inn, unseen from their current position. "Way I see it, your...turn...time. Did your service... Take care of yourself and Oliver's..." *Sister.* Some things did not need to be seen to be heard. Mikey knelt, still facing Leo, and pointed to the horse's leg where it met the ground. "I checked her." He accompanied this with a stroke down the length of Rambler's front legs. "Hooves. Watch out for ice... Christmas."

And since they weren't supposed to know each other, no hugs, no further smiles, but Leo handed over some coins, paying for the food and he did greet the ground with his knees to hug his dog, trying not to think of the cold slush soaking through his pants. "I'll miss you, Reaves. Be a good boy."

"Woof!"

Woof. Not heard, felt. Felt in the sloppy slake of tongue to cheek. To jaw. Leo didn't have the heart to push the canine away. Suffered another two—long—licks before he shoved back up.

When he rose to standing, Mikey met him with an abrupt motion, indicating a private conveyance that had just pulled into the yard. "Now get. Time... work."

So Leo got. Raced out of the inn's muddy yard after the coach. Took off like he and his horse had something riding on it.

A wager. A big one.

Because the way Leo saw it, they did.

His future. And his heart.

'TWAS ONLY A FEW JOSTLING, shuddering miles before Susanna concluded that today, *escape* equaled *mistake*.

A colossian, hugeous one. Running off as she had, in response to her own embarrassment, abandoning Leo and what he attempted to communicate? Why, she was no better than a town rudesby, rushing past and totally disregarding someone walking with a cane.

Not all afflictions could be seen. *Or heard.*

She should have behaved better. Not let emotions rule her actions and fuel her rash escape. But mayhap, after burying her feelings for so long, making decisions with her head, cramming her feelings deep so she wouldn't hurt, the freedom of the last hours spent in his company had opened her in ways she'd kept stifled for years?

Aside from the death of sweet Philip, she certainly hadn't felt this much angst toward how she'd treated another...ever.

Given the curious looks she had garnered thus far from the other passengers, she couldn't imagine what a riot she must present. Gloves missing. No cloak. Bonnet and dress? Pure catastrophes. Aye, yesterday's carriage mishap would explain all of that, but she could not imagine greeting her brother and new sister-in-law, much less her young nieces, attired thus. Why, the number and manner of questions would completely thwart the beginnings of what was supposed to be a joyful occasion.

Joyful? Her heart gave a painful squeeze. Nothing seemed joyful, not after her flurried exodus this morning…

Regardless, she would put herself to rights in Derby, before venturing on to Duffield. Decision made, heart still aching abominably, to distract herself from the turmoil of her thoughts, she made note of the others cramped alongside her within the humid environs of the coach.

Squeezed in directly next to her a young couple (who seemed to be having a bit of a wrangle, the female in something of a miff), traveled with a (thankfully) sleeping baby. Something about the tall fellow seemed vaguely familiar. But try as she might, she could not place his voice, and upon a second and third glance past his wife who huffed betwixt them, Susanna did not recognize the clean-shaven man, so it was easy to purge him from her mind.

Two men of heft and note resided on the squab opposite.

One of the gentlemen, the one nearest the door,

diagonal from her, his heft concentrated around his middle and beneath his chin, wheezed to such a degree that Susanna feared he might not last to their first horse change. He was quite loquacious, attempting to engage her in conversation (which she demurred) and then, with only a slight scowl—quickly erased—he turned his jovial efforts to the couple stashed in beside her.

Successful to the point that she now knew what prompted their excursions (his and theirs: "Business, what, eh?" and "Returning home after interviewing with my brother-in-law."), where they originated and where they would descend ("Not till Manchester, I'm afraid, what eh?" and "Our second stop, Loughborough. Hopefully baby will sleep through till then.").

The other gentleman, the one considerately angling his knees to give hers a spot of room, didn't *quite* remind her of Leo, but she could not help but think the comparison, given the second man's age and size. His heft of the muscular variety, despite the plain clothing that did very little to hide his fit condition.

Posh! Would she now be forever doomed to compare every mature, attractive gentleman to Captain Tucker? Their flirt might have been brief, but oh how her heart still yearned. Body still thirsted. Last eve's encounter nowhere near satisfying her hunger for intimacy with the man. Drat him.

Drat her.

Drat those pesky letters she hadn't yet brought herself to release into the rubbish bin.

After Mr. Harold Loquacious Harrell exhausted the young parents, unearthing the reason their babe slept so well now, after the child had remained awake crying all night, was a substantial dose of laudanum (something Susanna's mama would *never* have condoned in such excess), he focused, again, on Susanna. "So, tell me, miss. What is your name? Who are your people?"

And who did this big buffoon think he was, addressing her with such familiarity?

When she continued to decline the irritatingly persistent efforts to discover her destination, her origination and her reason for traveling ("I haven't quite decided yet." "Did I not board the stage right after you?" and a succinct, "Family," the only responses she deigned to make), he gave a sniff.

With a festivous smile and comment about snarlish females (one she took perverse delight in), the beefy man applied himself to quizzing the man beside him, the one sharing the space with her knees thus Susanna acquired knowledge about Mr. Trumbull, a vicar traveling back home for the holidays after partaking of a brief holiday himself.

The window flap between her and Trumbull was open, despite the brisk temperature, welcoming in the sunlight and slight breeze that helped mitigate the stuffy interior.

He didn't resemble any man of the cloth she had ever met, being significantly younger...and not necessarily polished in appearance. His edges seemed a bit rougher than one might expect from a minister; the thick mop of sable hair could use a good combing. But she instantly liked him, especially after Mr. Loquacious fixed his attention away from her and on the minister—who had given Susanna a pointed, private look of commiseration. Once the understanding was shared betwixt them, she knew that, much like herself, he was *not* interested in substantial conversing. But he continued to do so, to keep the other man from hounding her further, gaining her appreciation.

Because his unselfish sacrifice gave her solitude. Additional time to think over the last days of travel. The last hours of joy. The last minutes of regret...

Gave her time to consider her next best action.

"Approaching Leicester!" Their coachman's voice cried. "Loughborough after!"

As the carriage slowed, easing into their first stop for new horses, she could not help but look out the raised window, behind her, the way they'd just flown. More than tempted to abandon her reckless flight and return. To listen to whatever Captain Tucker might choose to say—if anything, now that she'd shown herself inconsiderate in the extreme.

At the thought, her pattering heart grew giddy, no longer filled with dread and regret, but now with anticipation. That is exactly what she would do! Exit the carriage, bespeak a parlor or private room at the posting inn, if there were any to be had, which she thought likely, given how the glorious, warmer weather of today had already melted much of the snow. No doubt many travelers had gone about their business as soon as it was light enough. She would await the next coach going the opposite direction, while setting herself a bit more to rights.

Now, with it approaching noon, the sun over-head? The roads might still be soggy, but they were passable, least the one they'd taken the last hour or more, after detouring through some lord's private land to cross the river. Surely that meant another stagecoach would be by soon?

The door opened, the coachman let down the steps with a barked, "Six minutes and we're off—whether you be back on or nay!"

Mere feet beyond the carriage steps, she heard the passengers up top exchanging quips, in the lower-cost section, and glanced upward. Only to hie straight back inside, staggering over big Mr. Harrell on her way to her corner. Instantly, she feigned a doze while her heart behammered with such fierce agony she feared surely everyone must hear. Suspicion it threatened to pound its way right through her chest.

Pound-pound-pound. Pound! POUND! P-O-U-N-D! Thumpthumpthump!

A man from *last night* was on her stage!

One of them that had circled tight about her. Taunted and endangered.

Had he seen her? She dare not risk leaving now, revealing herself to his gaze. From beneath slitted lids, she peered out the window, waiting for him to jump down and leave, but, contrary man, he did not. What did she do? What did she do?

'Twas daylight. Surely no harm would come to her now? *And last night, you were surrounded by people, hordes of them, yet only one could be troubled to come to your aid.*

Oh, Leo... Dear Captain Tucker.

She was still pondering her options, worrying over every mile, every *minute* since she'd left The Filthy Pig (which she'd learned from him), when their horses were refreshed—replaced—and they were off with a yell and snap of the whip. Drat. Now, any ease she might have claimed earlier vanished knowing who hovered in wait, only scant inches above her head...

19

A WHIT OF DIVINE INTERVENTION

PLEASE, God, let this overly inquisitive pryer stop talking.

Matthias Trumbull could not help but question the last few days. The ones that had landed him here, riding a delayed stage beside the most verbose man he had ever had the misfortune to meet. Chatty and so very corpulent, Thias's hinterlands commanded less than thirty percent of the squab where he'd paid for half. Mayhap the man grilling each of the passengers was really the regent in disguise?

The absurdity of that had him gritting his teeth and plastering a pleasant expression, however false, upon his countenance. *Why* had he listened to his aunt and uncle? Trusted them after their humbug of this past spring, when they gifted him a vacation, of all things, in Brighton?

Who went to Brighton in December?

What? Had they expected him to *fall in love* with the first woman he glimpsed away from his parish?

Nay, not love perhaps, but definitely *lust. Did Aunt Margaret not also gift you with new tooth powder before the trip?*

Thias barely suppressed a moan, recalling the sole female recently met—the one close to him in age, not nearly the young innocent he knew *they* thought he needed for a bride—he wouldn't have minded exchanging tooth powder with. But that was neither here nor there; "there" being not exactly Brighton, but instead the posting inn they'd spent the last evening stranded in, sharing a private parlor and more intriguing (lust-inspiring, to his dismay) conversations than he could remember having with anyone since he'd made his commitment to the church.

The subdued moan? One of unfamiliar longing. Of fleshly desire. Something he'd buried—with commendable success—these last years.

He hadn't dressed like a vicar for the trip, and that had nothing to do with Aunt Margaret handing him his bag at the same moment his meddling uncle gave him his ticket last week. Without the white bands about his neck, the white surplice or black cassock worn when sermonizing or officiating, his somber black attire beneath was nondescript. Away from the vicarage and his parish, he could blend in with other gentry fair enough.

When he was home, he gave his attention and time, the vast majority of his thoughts, to his flock and little else. It was only the rare occasions when he ventured beyond the vicarage and traveled, that his thoughts proved difficult to control. Almost as though discarding the trappings of his calling released his inner demons to jaunt forth.

Oh, come now. Desire isn't any sort of demon.

Mayhap not. But it sure can feel like one without a proper form of release. And ever since his little "outing" with Uncle Bamber this past spring… Desires of a different sort had begun hounding him. He'd learned, after the fact, he had unknowingly assisted England's now infamous Lady Scandal, and the little-known Lady Imposter, find their loves, officiating over vows he'd later insisted the two couples recite again, after they each purchased a common license, allowing him to do things in the proper order.

Havey-cavey was all well and good—lest it could get one in hot water. Any good parson knew to avoid putting themselves in peril with the Church of England.

Yet, ever since all that occurred months ago (no doubt aided by the *noises* he'd endured as the happy couples indulged in intimate acts he truly—sincerely—would have preferred his wattles *not* been privy to), Thias found odd thoughts of finding his own lady closer to the surface. And this surprise trip had not helped.

Especially after meeting the female he now secretly thought of as Lady Valiant.

His Lady Valiant. The timing was all wrong, she

being widowed not that horribly long ago. But that didn't stop him from dreaming, or seeing her everywhere.

The hair was completely the wrong color, as was the age, but the young gentlewoman that had joined them at the last moment, before the stage rolled out of East Crossings put him in mind of *another* female, the one he'd spent the last few hours developing an asinine, go-nowhere, *tendre* for. For this composed female, too, knew how to keep her pockets closed and private, didn't conduct herself as a flibberti-gibbet (much like the man seated next to him, signif-icantly older than every other passenger unfortunate enough to be snugged inside tighter than was comfortable along with his flapping jowls).

I cannot believe you thought that.

Aye, rather freeing, is it not?

For once, not having to mind his thoughts, his words, his every action... This whole week had proved a revelation.

And not of the biblical sort.

For was he not known as always available, whether his flock needed prayer over their souls, over their regrets (even over sins they *didn't* quite regret), or for their crops or any other trifle they came to him with? He was the *reliable* clergyman in the area (unlike the aged one a parish over who had become more enamored with tippling swill than saving souls).

A dependability he was now beginning to ques-tion, especially with each year added to his tally.

From the comments the older, grandmotherly sort of parishioners had filled his ears with since he turned forty—three years past, and still without a wife—a good third of them thought he harbored a secret fancy for one of the flock (inaccurate). Another third suspected he didn't favor women (wholly inaccurate). The remaining third? Those were the ones who wore on him. Who found trite reasons to visit the vicarage all week long, any excuse they could find to either try and entice him—should they be without a spouse—or to entice him *toward* their daughters, granddaughters or nieces...

No, thank you. It wasn't that there was anything particularly *wrong* with any of the women of his acquaintance, but none of them stirred him. Certainly not as much as he had been, hours past, sharing the private parlor with his Lady Valiant.

'Twas a true pity the recent widow who stirred him beyond what he would like to admit was in no position for a suitor. Even worse, that she lived, most incommodiously, on the opposite side of England.

Arranging his knees toward the coach wall beneath the open window, nothing dripping in the further north they galloped, the roads and air drying out, he looked again at the young black-haired miss that had joined them. The female, in complete disarray when she first climbed inside, had tamed her hair beneath a rather drab and drooping bonnet, pulled a snagged shawl around her shoulders—attempting to disguise where her dress had not been fastened (he knew because he was observant). Not only had she quickly righted her appearance, despite the stockings that were missing—giving him a glimpse of trim, forbidden ankles, but she kept her own counsel, seeming lost in her thoughts and content, if somewhat sad, to be dwelling there.

Her grateful, relieved look hardened his resolve as he continued to engage with Harrell, annoying jabber mouth that he was. At least his living had given Thias the talent of making small talk with only a part of his garret, leaving the rest to wander, to wonder...

As King Solomon wrote in the third chapter of Ecclesiastes, *There was a time to speak, a time to keep silent, and an eventual time to find one's mate.*

And I think all the blather has turned your brain barmy, if you are now misquoting the good book thus.

"Loughborough! Five minutes for new horses! On to Derby next."

When the stage rolled to a lumbering halt, the man next to him made his excuses about staying inside, "What, eh, knee doesn't like the stairs."

Thias rather thought his knee didn't like the amount of bulk Mr. Harrell carried, but was happy enough to stretch his legs. He waited until the young couple with the babe exited, then looked back at the other remaining occupant, the single female. She had not exited the stage at the prior stop. Might could do with a visit to the privy. "Miss? Would you like an escort to the office?"

She already knew he was a vicar; he'd not prevaricated about it when being peltered with questions by Mr. Heft and Jowl. "Require any sustenance I could pick up for you?"

Though her clothes were fine enough, and she too mature to be one of his many nieces and too young to be one of his aunts, he still felt a peculiar sort of protectiveness toward her. *Aye, in direct proportion to how many bladed questions the older man had pricked her with.*

She met his gaze with a tight smile. "Thank you, but nay. I will wait until the next stop."

"Mr. Harrell? Anything for you, sir?"

"Eh? Aye!" The man plucked a crown free from a bulging purse and held it out. "Get us both something, my good man."

Thias's eyes widened at the unexpected generosity. "Certainly, sir." He allowed his gaze to connect with hers, trying to offer whatever comfort he could at abandoning her now to the other man's exuberant personality. "I shall be back in a trice. Don't let them continue without me."

Which was actually a jest, for the stage waited for no man—nor man of God.

But three and a half minutes later, as he headed back, the bundled food just purchased warming his hand, a clasp upon his shoulder, quickly released when Thias spun and stopped, arrested his rush to return.

'Twas the hatted married gent that had ridden with them thus far. How peculiar. The man stood taller now, seemed much more imposing than he had within the crowded confines of the coach, and his missus and their babe were nowhere in sight.

"Aye?" Thias prompted. "This was your stop, correct?"

He had learned that much during Mr. Harrell's inquest of the couple.

"It is." The other man's eyes darted to and fro, and he lowered his voice to speak swiftly. "But the woman still in the carriage? The one seated across from you? *Watch her. Do not let her off the stage alone.*"

"What?" The unexpected warning startled Thias. "What do you know—"

But the other man was gone, striding off and disappearing around the side of the nearest building, and the coachman's cry gave Thias no time to query or investigate further.

What the devil was that about?

Brisk steps brought him back to the stage, eager to clap his peepers on the female, mayhap sit next to her for this next posting, inquire about her safety, about—

But when he climbed inside the stagecoach, wrapped bread and ham in hand for himself and Harrell, 'twas to find a burly brute crowding the female in question, his arm tight across her shoulders, whispering in her ear.

And the gentlewoman herself? Far from prompting recollections of his pleasantly strong and forthright Lady Valiant of the few hours prior to the stage, the black-haired miss now had a soured look of distaste puckering her lips and creasing her brow. A stubborn, rebellious gleam lighting her eyes.

"Hail there," Thias greeted the fresh comer with false gaiety, as the horses jolted forward, more than half surprised Harrell wasn't already conducting his own Inquisition.

His attention remaining on the female across from him, and the scowling man whispering into her ear, Thias handed over Harrell's portion of food without looking to the side. "Here you are."

If the brutish man's cloying regard was unwarranted—and with everything in him, he knew that it was—then Thias could be just as obstinate as another. "And you? Well met, good sir. You seem quite familiar with our other passenger here." Seeing her flinch when the rogue's grip tightened, Thias hardened both voice and posture. "Just who in blazes are you?"

<hr />

"WELL, well, little dove. Looks like I was right and you an' the cuff lied last night." The hugesome male wedged himself beside her, bringing with him a rife amount of malodorous scents. From his unwashed body that made her nose cringe to the sharp tang of onions blasting from his mouth that watered her eyes, her every breath was a struggle through fear realized.

She'd been found.

Shortly after Mr. Trumbull, and the parents with

their sleeping babe, descended, the threat above had barreled in and clamped unwelcome hands on her person, keeping her in place. After a single blink of surprise, Mr. Harrell had looked away.

"You wasn't claimed, not one bit." Hot breath assaulted her face. Fingers pinched painfully tight over her shoulder as he drew her so close not a flea could have squeezed between them. "But I'll see to that, I will. Just as soon as we get to Congleton fer the night."

Mr. Harrell coughed. Susanna wanted to plant her boot in the nosy's gullet—he *knew* she was traveling alone, yet did nothing to grate this newcomer nor question his unwanted presence. Instead, fixed his gaze everywhere but at them.

Everywhere...

Everywhere this unwanted scab pawed along her side crawled with disgust. What a difference the person made. At such variance from the closeness shared with another last night. For this nasty's touch brought nausea storming through her middle and bile up her throat.

More sneered threats followed. More ugsome promises. More vile words breathing filth into her ear over and above the noises of the inn yard as horses were led off and replaced. The new team full of energy, stomping the thick earth and jostling her prison.

Regret stormed her mouth like rancid meat. She clutched the handles of her valise, debating whether to slam it into his nose or thrash it against his groin.

Which might do the most damage? Thank heavens she had the gifts weighing her bag—

"Hail there." Mr. Trumbull climbed the steps, to the irritated shouts to "Make haste," coming from their coachman. The whip cracked overhead and they were off, practically before the vicar could gain his seat, the motion throwing her forward.

Mr. Trumbull's eyes met hers as he took in the restraintive hold—and no doubt her resistance to it. She gave a slight, very slight shake of her head. *Nay, I do not want him here. I do not want him touching me.*

A single slow and focused blink and she knew he understood. She did not release her grip on her bag, but the nausea eased enough she could at least swallow.

"Do not cry out against me," the varmint at her side said, squeezing her shoulder enough to leave bruises, "lest you want this one here to meet my chive."

Chiv. She knew he meant his knife, for she felt the edge of it pressed against her side, out of sight of the others. He moved and the point of it pricked through her dress. She couldn't stop her flinch.

Mr. Trumbull gave a growl-snort, something she couldn't imagine had ever graced his pulpit come Sunday, as his features firmed and he leaned forward, fixing the rook next to her with a glare. "Just who in blazes are you? Unhand the lady!"

20

RAMBLER FOR THE VICTORY

"Come on, girl," Leo encouraged, "just a bit more speed..."

They made better time now than they had after just starting out. The farther northwest they'd come, the dryer the roads, the storm saturated roadways south and east of here not stretching this far.

His horse had already done a good day's work, but the dig of Leo's heels in her flanks prodded for even more. Two changes, and still he had not caught up with the stage, and now they had fresh horses—*again*, Loughborough being several miles behind him.

He could have switched Nelson Rambler out as well, but couldn't imagine trying to learn another steed, not when he and this one were so attuned. Not when more than half his attention raced far ahead, along with the coach.

What do you think you are doing? What do you expect to say to her? Are you even assured she did not leave the stage at that last inn, the one you charged from after your single query was met with a negative shake from a young groom: "Did a young woman exit the stage that just came through? A black-haired lass?"

What *was* he doing?

Doubts grew the further through the Midlands they charged—without success. He really had naught to offer... Busted wattles, a somewhat broken naval career (albeit, with some decent prize monies earned), attitude and air of command that obviously hadn't done near what it needed to this morning, with her.

Quit whinging! You abandoned Reaver to come after this woman; you would not have done that did you not anticipate some sort of future beyond today.

True. What that future might look like, he wasn't yet quite sure, but he couldn't imagine dropping the astonishing hours they had shared together into the abyss of nothing.

There! Dust on the horizon. Not a significant amount, but as he'd gained miles and the ground had firmed, even Nelson's hooves kicked up a bit. What's more, a single rider couldn't account for what he saw.

"Up ahead, girl. Come on, Nelson Rambler." She knew; when he used her full name, she knew. As though wings lifted her belly, propelled her long, strong legs, his trusty prancer bolted forward.

———⋑○⋐———

THE THUNDER of hooves shouldn't have breached Thias's awareness, focused on the ragabash as he was, but they did, followed by one impressive bellow...

"Susanna!"

"What ho?" The big man chortled. "Highwayman?" It jarred him when Harold Harrell spoke. For the man had been unusually quiet since they'd left Loughborough. "Should we expect a 'Stand and deliver!' next?"

"Susanna!"

"*Yours?*" he mouthed at the female.

Eyes wide, frightened before the bellow, now closed in relief. A tiny nod.

"You're mine *tonight*, bitch, before I hand ya over. I'll be hanged before I let you 'scape again..."

Whatever else the cull might have threatened was drowned beneath the coachman's snap of the whip and cries of, "Move, ye bastard! Got time to keep."

"As if your schedule hasn't already gone to h—" *Hell and torments!* "Ah, *smithereens* this week," Thias murmured, barely catching himself in time. *My, this holiday must have agreed with you, likely too much, if you're ready to begin swearing this close to home.*

What he was ready for, given the look of terror that had so briefly filled the female's gaze once the royster started pawing her, was to rip the man off her and pound some sense into the brute.

"Halt! Susanna!"

Yea, in heart you work wickedness; you weigh the violence of your hands in the earth.

Nay. David had it wrong in that Psalm, at least where Thias was concerned today. Not wickedness, *righteousness.* Against evil. And the violence of his hands? The crick-crack of his knuckles proved audible.

"Halt, I say!" Thias shouted above the melee of horses, adding his voice to the other. Yelling until he felt the horses' gait hitch. "Halt the coach!"

Oh? And what happens when you arrive Sunday with torn, bruised knuckles?

He gave a grunt of satisfaction. For would that not take care of at least one third of his female congregation? The ones determined to marry him off to females in their family?

If they concluded their humble vicar had rough secrets of his own?

"Susanna!"

The roar was closer now, and before the stage had juddered to a complete stop, the narrow door burst outward.

Therefore now let your hands be strengthened, and be ye valiant... The words of Samuel came to his rescue as the lady, Susanna he now knew, was rescued by her man.

⸺◦⸺

"Susanna!"

Leo urged Rambler forward. Alongside the clipping coach.

Wind whipped against his face, flapped his coat out behind him.

"Halt!"

The coachman saw him. Scowled. Yelled something. But only pushed his team faster.

Nay. Not having it.

Leo's thighs tightened, heels knocked Rambler's sides, and with a burst of speed he'd owe his equine lady for the rest of her life, they overtook the team that had begun to falter.

Galloping across the road, in front of the coach, flustered the reined horses further.

"Halt!" He gave the order from the scary position of facing down a galloping team, but determination was on his side.

And a bit of foolhardiness, too?

Though Rambler strained against him at the coming onslaught, he made a nuisance of himself, confusing the horses and irking the driver until, finally, the coachman pulled on the ribbons, his lips moving and jaws flapping in unheard shouts.

Leo leapt from his horse while her hooves were still flying. Stumbled at the jarring *thump* that bounded up his legs. Flinging his gloves to the ground—because he needed to touch her skin-to-skin—he raced for the side of the coach and tore the door open. "Susanna!"

It had to be the right coach. It had to! He hadn't passed another this way.

Had to be—

The dark interior swam before his sun-drenched gaze. His body vibrated from the mad dash, the miles covered with little rest for either Nelson Rambler or himself.

The stage had come to a lurching stop beneath the canopy of a large tree, casting everything in shadows. After the glare of the last miles, his vision swam with spots. But he narrowed on his goal: liberating his woman from the stage.

"Susanna." 'Twas a low rumble, a growl this time, as he blinked into the darkness and thrust his upper body inside, past the squawking (red-faced, lips-a-blur) whinger taking up more than half the coach, to converge every ounce of his attention on the opposite corner where his black-haired, dirty-bonneted sweetheart was doing two very different things...

One that filled him with pure contentment: beaming him a smile of welcome that reached her eyes. And another that brought forth more rage than he'd felt since seeing one of his men needlessly dirked through the heart by footpads while on shore leave: fighting the white-knuckled hold of the pitted-faced nasty clutching her to him. Preventing her from moving.

One of Bowyer's worms, part of the filth fouling the inn last eve.

Leo didn't see red. Nor black. Nor any other color. Fury didn't screech through his head, blaring in his mind. His garret didn't instantly debate options and outcomes.

Nay, he simply reached forth and plucked her to him. Straightened, cradled her against his chest, and hauled them both free of the contraption.

His booted feet walked backward, the rest of him benumbed, stupefied by how she petted him, ran ungloved fingers over his head, hair, face, chest...

He inhaled her sweet, sweet scent and strove to calm the panicked cacophony that had made a bunk in his chest the last hours since she'd left.

He knew she spoke, the murmurings warm against his sternum. Knew she welcomed his presence, and that told him all he needed at the moment.

Relief. She would listen. He could apologize. He could tell her the thoughts he'd had for them, for a future together.

"Forgive me," Leo said the moment they were alone, after tugging her toward his horse. Hands to her shoulders, he set her away from him, so he could see her lips. "*Portsmouth.* We thought they would all be heading south. Never occurred to me one of them might be on your stage, else I would not have let you leave—"

"You cannot, can-not blame yourself. I did not really...a..." As though catching herself rattling faster, she took a hearty breath and spoke again, slower. "Gave you no choice, fleeing as I did."

"Susanna. I apologize. I never should have read—"

She interrupted, said something, but he knew not what, as she had plastered herself against him again, arms about his waist, fingers gripping the fabric of his shirt beneath his coat, as her warm breath "spoke" against his front.

She still had no cloak. No gloves.

And the sun might be shining now, but it was closer to the end of December than the middle. Seeing her bare hands when he pulled her arms from their clutch at his back, so he could read her face, her words...seeing the fragile, pale fingers cradled within the darker-hued nicked-up callus of his did something to his middle. He wanted those delicate fingers on his stomach, gliding up his chest, curving over his shoulders as he—

Leo cleared his throat, thick with all he wanted to say, needed to express, and met her gaze.

"I am pleased you are here," she said upon the instant. "Pleased you came for me." The flush on her cheeks said so much more.

The thickness hadn't receded, so he cleared his throat again. "Now isn't the time to say everything that is required. Will you come with me and Rambler? Allow me to escort you from here?"

A single nod.

"And I have something for you. Your little box? The wooden one you stored your letters and pencils in? It's in my saddlebags. I found that and one—one only *one*, mind—of my socks in the carriage after you left." She smiled at him, some of that alluring mischievous he'd noticed coming to the fore, but he knew better than to let her distract him. This was too important. "Your letters," he said with every bit of solemnness he could voice, "the ones I will never dare read again."

But she was shaking her head. "Nay...the quickest...you to know me. To *hear* me." She bit her lip, looked down, then braved catching his gaze again. "Other than running out without listening to you, I wouldn't change a moment since we met." And to make sure he "heard", she repeated it twice, pronouncing her words with care.

He grunted. "I would change things. For one, I would have put you on a stage with naught but angels for company."

She laughed at that. "I don't know... ...bit of devil, devil-ish-ness in this man just met...find quite intriguing. In-trig-gee-ing." Her sweet mouth contorted on the last bit, ensuring he saw every minuscule pronunciation. "You, should there ex-sist, exist any doubt."

"Come now, before delivering you safely to your brother's, I would see you fed, gloves and cloak purchased, your dress washed, if not replaced—a new bonnet if we are fortunate enough to make the next village before the mercantile closes, then see you fed again."

"And I would see you—all of you"—the way she swept her gaze over him left little doubt of her words —"by candlelight"—here, she mimicked the lighting of one—"if you will let me."

Even Leo could hear the growl that emerged from his throat at that brazen promise.

But before he could savor the peaceful, exhilarated feelings stealing over him, chaos erupted.

A howl behind her was the only warning Susanna had before Leo pushed her from his embrace and thrust her behind him. He crouched slightly, steady on his feet, as they watched the two grappling combatants roll in the dirt just beyond the coach.

The vicar had both hands clamped around the loutish oaf's knife-wielding arm, keeping the blade aloft—and not embedded in his chest.

But it was a struggle. Both men straining against the other.

"Mr. Trumbull!" Her cry was instinctive.

Before she knew what he was about, Leo launched himself into the fray. It didn't take her frantic screams to tell him friend from foe. He already knew, taking hold of the back of the scourge-mutton and flinging him a body's length hence. Mr. Trumbull popped to his feet, his brief "Thanks" to Leo going unheeded, unheard.

The other man rolled, came upright brandishing his knife, an evil grin splitting his ugly features. "Ye both want a taste? Come on, now..."

He motioned first toward Leo, and then the vicar. Inviting them forth, waving that chive between them. Boasting of his prowess, he tossed it from one palm to the other. Catching it every time. But the action was reckless.

Because Leo had been watching. 'Twas but an instant before he palmed his penknife, the one that had so carefully sharpened her pencil last eve. He had it opened and tossed before she could blink.

It landed in the fleshy part of the joint betwixt the villain's arm and shoulder, of his primary hand. Another howl, this one of surprise and pain, as his weapon—instead of being caught at the end of the arc, skidded to the ground.

"That's enough of that! All of ye!" The coachman, boasting his whip, snapped it down mere inches from the cull who would have retrieved his chive. Behind him, the horses stamped, snorted. "All of ye have made my day of shite e'en worse!"

He aimed the handle of his whip toward the vicar, and his words lost some of their angered informality. "You! Get back inside if you want to finish your journey. You!" The biting, tail portion of the whip came down against the coated arm of the fiend as soon as he bent toward the fallen blade. "Leave that. Be gone with you now!"

"And you!" This to her. "No refunding on unused tickets!"

"No need," she trilled, more than happy to be quit of the stage. She hustled to Leo, put her arms around his back, and held his heaving form against her front as she scuttled them both backward. His breath was loud. All of theirs were, her ears more aware since she knew she was hearing things he could not, and never would.

While the coachman stood guard, snapping the whip a second time—near the oaf's head—when the other man didn't move fast enough, Mr. Trumbull came to stand in front of Leo. "You have her now, good. Miss?" He leaned to the side to capture her gaze. "This is what you want? To leave with him?"

"Absolutely. Thank you for your assistance."

"And you shall be safe?"

"I will. With him, aye." She couldn't stop her lips from kissing the broad back in front of her.

With a single nod, the vicar held his hand out to Leo. "Thank you. I should not admit that I enjoyed that, but I did." A quick angle of his head indicated the fight they'd all witnessed. "Although, before you joined in, it did get more perilous than one might have wished."

She could only imagine how frustrating this must be for Leo, not having much of an inkling what the vicar said. He didn't know to speak slowly, carefully. But Susanna had a good ear and an even better memory. With one hand at Leo's waist, the other at his opposite shoulder, she gave him a quick, two-handed hug, hoping it conveyed her meaning. *All is fine. All is well. I will* sh*are what he said later. Shake his—*

As though he heard her, Leo did; clasped the other man's hand in his and gave a hearty shake, the two of them grinning at each other in accord, comrades after vanquishing a common adversary.

21

PIERCING TO THE HEART OF THINGS

ASTONISHING, really, how a good bout of fives could invigorate a man. Despite the exaltation bursting through Leo at having reached her at last, not to mention the primal urge to draw her to him and never let go, he possessed the wherewithal to release Susanna when the other man he'd fought *with* approached. He clapped his palm against the one outstretched before him.

"Thank you," Leo told to the other man. "Your intermeddling was most welcome." No matter that his very being buzzed with the need to toss her over his shoulder, mount Rambler and disappear into the horizon, he maintained enough presence to mind his volume, the words private betwixt the three of them. "In my haste to retrieve her, I failed to consider he might be armed."

A frown beneath the fight-deranged, dark shock

of hair and the other man, tall enough to meet Leo's eyes without tilting his head, responded with a flurry of words that whipped silently by."...gone awry... ...relieved when I heard..." His expression cleared and he glanced past Leo's shoulder, now including Susanna. "...my surprise when ... ...told me to watch...warned..."—had he just said *beware*? —"...dismayed..."

Whatever the other fellow said now—a Victor Tomball or something similar; he'd caught that much—caused Susanna's fingers to tighten at Leo's waist where she'd taken a position slightly behind him. *Worry not*, he fair sensed her conveying through her touch upon his side and shoulder. *I shall impart all he says later should you not wish to request he slow down.*

A heavy sigh gusted from Leo's lungs. Why not tell him? Why maintain secrecy about his hearing— lack of—here? Now?

Because you will never see him again. Why disconvenience the good fellow? 'Twill be a waste of time and breath...

Another gust, this one a bit easier, as he continued to watch the man's mouth—and eyes, not wanting to appear *overly* focused on another male's lips without reason—and Leo allowed his mind to fill with plans for the next few hours as Susanna and Victor Tomball spoke a handful of sentences more. Her gestures grew more animated and she had moved from her position behind him to stand more in front as they conversed, though keeping hold of his arm. Almost as though she sought to shield him. The notion tickled. Comforted.

How fantastical, that he had caught up with them.

Do you not mean that you just met *her?*

Pfft. What was time when one found the mate to their heart's longings?

At the first lull between them, knowing she was safe, he pulled gently from her grasp and stepped to the side, telling them both, "I will be but a moment."

He indicated the area surrounding the coach, where the other inside passenger—the swapping, bacon-fed gent—had come to ground, gesticulating wildly, likely berating the driver for the wrangle that caused further delayment.

Also compassing about, the half dozen or so jaunters from up top had jumped down, offering either encouragement or hindrance, he knew not which and cared even less when he spied Nelson Rambler grazing on downtrodden dry grasses near the ditch edging the road. 'Twas past time he found her some water and rest. "I would see to my horse, ensure she came to no harm. Thank you again, good sir."

At Susanna's understanding nod, Leo took his leave of Tomball and headed toward the stage, roaming his gaze over the road and clearing beyond the big tree where they'd all come to such a bounding stop. Forty feet distant, he spied his gloves where he'd discarded them. But the wretch was no longer in sight.

Where had Haggard and Bowyer's man gone? Had he been the only one? Or had others accompanied the weasel? Pity Leo hadn't realized she'd be in peril, else he'd have retrieved his case-knife from his haversack and been prepared to fell the fellow with one throw, not simply slow him down.

And where the devil was his penknife? He'd seen the other man yank the blade from his shoulder with a howl of rage and drop it on the ground just prior to the coachman's whip entering the fray.

Aiming for the pair—coachman and plump, irate passenger—Leo took a crankling, circulary path while, for the first time since racing off in frantic pursuit hours earlier, he allowed his mind to unclench, to drift, following the direction of his gaze...

The soothing rustle of enduring leaves dancing overhead, casting peekaboo glimpses of sunlit slivers to kiss the ground.

The snort and stomp of frustrated, impatient horses, ready to be quit of the lingering that marred their day.

The excited, relieved chatter of Susanna as she engaged with the other passenger, the helpful Tomball Leo would forever feel indebted to, and gladly.

He glanced up and around as he paused—and bit back a flicker of amusement, seeing how many now converged on the driver...

The shouts of crabbed passengers protesting the

loss of time—or mayhap the presence of the evil rip he and Tomball had rattled off.

After "hearing" it all, being soothed anew at Susanna's proximity, he focused on the ground, a few more steps and—

There! A sudden spark seen and gone in the whirr of leaves, and after a few paces, Leo bent to retrieve his penknife—

A boulder hurtled into him. Knocked him off his feet.

The hard ground collided against his knees and confronted his chin as fire erupted along his shoulder.

His upper arm screamed.

A roar of outrage—his own—and he flung his wounded arm back in an arc. His strong legs and feet gaining momentum as he twisted, slammed to his back, thumping the bastard into the dirt unseen.

But *seen* was the wicked blade heading downward. Aiming for another slice of his flesh.

Years of fighting, of sparring, of wielding his own knives, not to mention years of command and thinking through pain, had sharpened his ability to react.

His hands seized the wrist before the edge could carve into him again.

He rolled, taking the arm and the swine it was attached to beneath him. Thrusting up with a bellow, Leo smashed the hand against the ground until the chive slid free. One of his hands jailed the whoreson's wrist to the earth; the other slid to the miscreant's throat.

The pitted, red face struggling beneath his confining grip tried to gather saliva and spit at him. Leo firmed the shackle to his throat, subduing the heaving, bucking body beneath his bigger one with more ease than care.

"Bastard." He had no idea whether he yelled or murmured. "You don't go treating women that way." Both hands tightened around their fleshly prisoners. "And you made me lose my penknife again, by damn."

✦

FRAUGHT MINUTES LATER, Leo had a protesting Susanna atop Rambler, both her legs to the left, where he could not stop touching her limbs, heedless of how inappropriate.

As soon as he'd guided them a sufficient distance to put them out of sight of the others, he slowed his furious stride to glance upward and study her mouth. "You are injured...to ride."

"Stop your gruntling, sweetheart, lest you splinter a tooth. I am a hearty sailor, used to hours upon my feet. A walk of a few miles is not worth a single fret."

They traveled back the way they'd both come but without haste this time, the leisurely pace allowing not only Rambler to rest, but also granting for stolen touches and cherished words to be exchanged during the next few miles.

His little rescued, reckless female was determined to walk beside him; he was determined she not. One less thing for him to worry over, if he knew exactly where she was, given how a good portion of his attention was now to the sides and behind them, not only in front after that humiliating attack that had caught him unawares.

His preference something Leo had accomplished using his greater strength, simply picking her up and placing her where he wanted her, secure upon Rambler's back. "Nay, lass, I have other plans for you tonight," he told her the next time she protested, squiggling against his light hold as though about to slide down. He allowed the desire to heat both his voice and eyes. "Conserve your strength, hmm?"

That garnered her cooperation—for the most part.

"Let us put some distance between ourselves and that lot behind us. Arrive well ahead of darkness and hire a room before they are all let."

A slight nod from her and he exhaled in sheer relief. In amazement. At everything, as the events of the last twenty or so hours settled around him, stinging and soothing at turns.

He couldn't help but smile at himself as well. His own misunderstanding, one she had quickly put to rights after "Tomball" and the coachman had bound Leo's prisoner, and even now took pains to see the ruffian delivered to the nearest watch-house until the justice of the peace could be summoned. It felt good to have his hands washed of the miscreant.

Not *Victor Tomball*, he'd learned from her, with a bit of abashment, but Mr. Trumbull, a vicar—what a surprise, that: that a man of God proved so able with his fives, definitely a praise-worthy ally to have on one's side for a bruising.

"Nay, stay put." He patted the top of her thigh, spoke when he felt it tense again—in preparation of jumping down, he feared. "Any groan or laugh you might have heard was not due to pain nor amusement over your restrictive plight upon Rambler, I assure you." More amazement, as the chuckles continued to burst from his chest. Mirth that had been missing in his life ever since the accident. "'Tis rather, only a release of my own tensity. I grant, I am feeling more well-starred than I can remember."

Was another *ever* as fortunate as he?

A slight jostle of her ankle drew his gaze upward.

"...your arm..." Another frown aimed at his shoulder.

"Please, lass. I know you would see again to my wound, but what you did will work till we get to the inn. I shall let you have another tending-to there."

The layers of his coat and shirt had done little to dim the penetration of the honed edge. But even so, he'd seen enough cuts in his time to know this one wasn't anywhere near as deep as it could have been, the worst of it slicing into the muscle of his upper arm. Hurt like the blazes, but 'twas manageable. A good cleaning as soon as they hired a room, needle and thread—or mayhap only a snug enough wrap—and he'd be well enough.

The blood now? Not horridly copious, but enough to soak his shirtsleeve. To see his reckless lady turn as responsible as any cherisher...

He chuckled. For even now, he wore his sock, turned outside-in, the one she'd absconded with, snubbed against the wound and held in place by her shift, ripped and tied about his arm, his shoulder, *and* his torso to the point he felt like a trussed hog bound for the spit.

"It hasn't bled through your more-than-adequate efforts thus far." He attempted to soothe her jagged edges. "I daresay we can make the inn without me bleeding to my grave."

One of her booted feet kicked out, toes prodding his hand—as her eyes flashed at him. He grinned anew. "I know. No jesting about my grave. You're determined to keep me hale and hearty into my dotage. And for that, I thank you."

THEY COVERED another mile in pleasant accord, the only others seen upon the road a hugesome family in a pair-drawn conveyance, noiselessly singing-arguing-chattering without restraint as they clattered past unheard.

Minutes passed and all remained as it should; no surprise attacks nor unexpected, threatening travelers—from any direction.

Yet for him, the unspoken words battering about

his brain kept the everlasting silence from being anywhere near soothing.

The shift and creak of her slight weight atop Rambler's saddle (easily imagined).

The steady *tit-tat, clomp-clump* of the horse's hooves striking the earth (comforting sounds associated with the light puffs of dirt, even the light squishes of mud the further south they traveled).

The un-comforting *gulp* he made swallowing trepidation as he readied himself to speak from the heart (this one felt, not imagined).

"While I have you at a bit of a disadvantage," he began, his feet—and his horse's legs following—taking markedly longer, swifter strides, as though he sought to move beyond the nerves wanting to catch up with him now. "Alongside and at my whim, as it were, I need to take *advantage*. Listen and listen well, if you please.

"And when I am finished, 'twill be my turn to *listen*, aye?"

An upward glimpse revealed her slow, thoughtful nod; eyes beneath the bonnet's brim were curious, lips closed.

"Susanna, in the time since you boarded the stage—"

Do not be an idiot. Nor a coward. Halt the horse and face her.

His mouth practically still open, mid-thought, he did, indicated with a click of his tongue and a swing of one arm that Rambler should ease off the road, the very deserted road he could not help but be grateful for. He followed, stopped, and looked at her directly.

"Since you rushed off from the Pig, I have had plenty of time to think. To regret. I apologize for reading your letters without your express permission. But I cannot say I am sorry I did so. For upon evaluating your response, I have come to conclude that mayhap you misinterpreted my own.

"*If* you thought I harbored any ill regard toward you, you were misgrounded.

"If you thought, perhaps, that I wanted to do harm, Susanna, that I wanted to eliminate certain individuals off the face of the earth, you would have been accurate. Do you know what a horrible wretch I felt, seething with those emotions while holding you against me? While you slept so peacefully within my arms? 'Twas all I could do to control the urge to lock you in the carriage and rail off, to rip asunder every man who *ever* touched you without your invitation. Starting with the dead slag you wed."

Breath came hard at the end of that, face reddened, he knew, likely appearing to her exactly as he had that morning. This time, not hiding from her, facing her fully, honest in his ire.

LEO STUNNED Susanna's rampageous thoughts to a halt with that lengthy revelation. For whose mind would not be awhirl at all that had occurred?

From his fierce and instant rescue upon reaching

the stage, to the two separate bustles with the rat-faced, chive-armored threat, to the instant rapport full of ease and humor, and sensual awareness thrumming between the two of them... Despite her continued protests.

Leo was the one injured; did he not need to ride? A query he'd met with adamant refusal and a bark of disbelief that would have done Reaver proud. "After that impact of hard earth to my knees? Nay, lass, I shall walk out the aches and give my well-deserving mare a rest. Your weight? Pah. Will be as though she transports a feather."

Pah indeed.

So now both her legs were on the near side, as she perched upon a saddle intended for riding astride and marveled how Rambler did not require any sort of lead or direction at all to stay abreast of her master. The horse slowed when he did, sped when he moved faster.

Susanna? Struggled to take in so much at once...

His fierce mien of that morning, his anger, had *not* been directed at her?

Granted, she had begun to consider it might be so, but to have it confirmed? And with such deci-siveness?

'Twas like springtime hailed forth, blew aside winter's pall and burst upon her soul with all the light and echoes of love she'd lived without these past years.

"And my baby?" she asked, motioning to the air around her belly, shaping where he'd grown within her. "My precious Philip." It wasn't difficult to speak slowly; it was, though, a chore to keep the tears from her eyes, the wrench of guilt from trembling her lips. "Born from violence, conceived under the shroud of uncertainty?"

Something in her expression or the air—or mayhap her soul—reached him and Leo took the stride that separated them, placed both hands on her, his uninjured one at her ankle, his wounded arm—with only the slightest of twinges tightening his countenance—to her hip. His arms braced around her and exerted pressure in a hug, he laid his head along her thigh, the heat and heft of it doing strange, if welcome, things to her middle. Had they been on a picnic, his head would have been in her lap...

"Please, love, banish whatever shadows might still war within your heart, whatever their cause or source." He lifted his head and found her gaze beneath the bedraggled bonnet that shaded her eyes. The tone and volume of his voice lowered. "You think I do not have regrets for some of my actions these last years? Decisions made in the blare of battle? Decisions made to aid one, that might have destroyed another?"

As though both reliving the past and choosing to release it, he stood tall, his voice gaining strength. "We all do what our heart or head tells us is best—at that particular instant—and then must adapt. Whether with celebration or consolation, for life does not always adhere to our plans. As to plans..."

His stern manner relaxed, his beautiful lips quirking in a semblance of a smile, as he took in her mud-stained dress beneath the coat he had once again insisted she wear. "Really, I need to see you outfitted properly, *before* escorting you to Oliver's—lest I want to end up in yet another unplanned bout of fisticuffs."

The thought of that—Leo wrangling with her brother (and over her!)—brought a true laugh to her lips.

Bracing one hand upon his chest, she stretched to stroke her fingers beneath his chin. "He will know something is amiss, regardless. For you are bruised here." Then she touched his jaw and cheek. "Swelling here as well. Let me see your hands? I'm sure your knuckles have fared no better."

He ignored her request, instead grinned at her, flashed his strong teeth. "At least none of these beautiful grinders cracked."

"Well, if you can jest about it, then you're more intact than you look. Although, anyone we meet is sure to inquire about the hedgehog perched upon your shoulder." Where she'd bandaged the bleeding cut, to her partial satisfaction, but now the wadded fabric surrounding the bunched sock gave him quite the noticeable lump.

"No matter." He frowned at the protrusion drawing his shirt tight against the underside of his arm. The dried blood stiffening the fabric only increased the discomfort. "Hedgehog, eh? I shall retrieve my coat when we near our destination."

. . .

No sense alarming those we chance across.

Leo clicked to Rambler and got them both back on the road. "The inn, which we will not make by nightfall if we stay here *conversing*," he stressed, hoping his voice conveyed his desire to do so, "with me staring at your mouth. So, reluctantly, my attention is back to that covering distance.

"Fortunate for me, though, you can still listen." As he had noticed he did with Reaver, without intent he touched her. His hand settling itself upon the back of Susanna's boot-clad ankle, so he felt the tiny angle in it as she indicated assent.

Taking his eyes off the road ahead, he swept them to either side and behind, confirming—they continued to be the only ones in sight.

"Unless you have reason to protest, this is how I foresee things happening, and aye, I might be acting the controlling cull here, so I trust you will inform me should you disagree with anything I spout." An upward glance, toward her chin, echoed the tiny "nod" he felt from her foot.

"*After* we see our mired selves cleaned and secure a blessed night's rest, I will escort you to your brother's property, keeping myself out of sight while waiting for you to gain entrance. Not until I know you have met up with safety will I move off.

"I shall wait a day or two and then arrive with sufficient pomp at the Oliver household, as I *was* invited." He saw her gasp at that, felt the stiffness of surprise in her limb and didn't try to stifle his smile.

"Aye, that is correct. Your brother sent me an entreaty to spend the holidays with his family this year. I will join you there through Twelfth Night, and it will be everything I can do to woo you under his nose without alerting him to how very much I crave every part of you. *That* is how we shall salvage any potential taint to your reputation." Leo felt rather satisfied with himself for devising that plan, though the day or two away from her already loomed like a kick to his gut. "Speaking of, my dear Lady Reckless, were you *seeking* ruination gadding about England without a lady's maid?" Against his light, resting grip, her foot about spun off.

"Nay? Hmmm. All right."

'Twas all he could do to maintain his head and not guffaw till his cheeks hurt at the stinging look she glared his direction.

During their lengthy flirt of the night prior, he'd inquired the same, only to learn she had no personal servants nor the inclination (nor patience) to wait for her sister-in-law's escort, something he'd laughingly chided her over and then, with his lips upon her skin, had expressed his gratitude for, owing that—had she traveled with another—none of their interactions would have occurred.

The sharp kick of her foot—toward air, not him, but very distinct nevertheless—made it even more difficult to subdue his mirth. "Regardless"—he tried to firm both his lips and the dance of his heart—

"back to wooing you surreptitiously... When you are ready"—as soon as he could convince her, in fact—"I would love to claim you as my own, and take you to my home, where you shall meet my mother, my sisters, and their spouses and children. Where I hope you will live with me and be mine, and me yours—ah, I yours? I am not certain which is the proper grammar, but—"

And evidently she cared naught if his phrasing was of the highest order, because rather than kick out or angle her foot, she slid straight past his light hold, boots whispering to the ground as she embraced him on the way down. Her arms clung to his waist and she pressed an array of (he surmised) *delighted* kisses against his chest and neck and jaw— and his lips as soon as he lowered them.

Some minutes later, she managed to pull herself free. "But, Leo...tell them? They are going to wonder..." She ran her thumb over the growing bruises upon his face.

He just grinned. Grinned big.

Rather out of character, man.

Aye, and it feels grand.

"That, my love, should not pose a problem. Your brother knows me well. I shall simply tell him the truth: A bit of reckless living, and trouble found me yet again."

FROM FILTHY PIG TO
GOLDEN SWAN

THE POSTING station in Loughborough proved a jewel. The Golden Swan 'twas busy but clean and well-run by all appearances.

Aye, they had rooms to let. Would they (*Mr.* Tucker and his "Mrs.") prefer one facing the courtyard or the road?

Aye, a hip bath—and heated water, what a boon! —could be arranged for extra coinage.

Dinner? Ale? "Aye, sir, ma'am. My Janie can see to that."

"A lantern? But there is already a candle—"

"Nay? A lantern?" Followed by a bit of grumbling —even more than what the man had first released upon seeing the bruises blooming on Leo's face and his reddened, scraped knuckles.

But Susanna kept her serene smile in place, eyes wide and inquisitive, mouth silent as she had been since they arrived, allowing the big man at her side to manage things as he saw fit.

"*Full* of fuel, you say?" Another spate of grumbling; this softened when additional coins slid across the counter. "All right. Oh! Aye, this will *more* than suffice for payment. Yes, I will see that brought up as well."

Susanna loved watching Leo "negotiate" for what he sought. Since they arrived, he had politely, if decisively, stated each of his requests. And continued to *plunk* down coins until gaining the affirmative responses he'd desired.

"What of a physician? An apothecary?" Susanna interjected, staying Leo's retreat with a hand upon his arm when he would have bent down for their bags. "We had a, er, a *carriage mishap* and I would have my husband"—hmm, interesting she did not stumble over *that*, the husband part, despite the unusual grate of her voice—"tended. Not that I cannot see to his wound, but 'twould set my mind at ease if one were available to summon?"

"A wound, you say? Not sickness?" The innkeeper, who had been moderately pleasant thus far (made more so with each coin that disappeared into his keeping), a Mr. Wells, studied Leo anew, paying particular attention to the fighting bruises and then turning his skeptical expression to Susanna—after a pointed frown at the mounded "hedgehog" puffing one side of Leo's coat, the one he'd drawn on as they approached the village.

She nudged Leo's uninjured shoulder. "Look at

him, sir. Hale and hearty." With a bit of difficulty, she swallowed. "He is only not protesting my ask because I promised him a boon."

"Ah." The indulgence that gleamed from the innkeeper showed he suspected exactly what *sort* of boon. But the moment of levity did not keep his lips from turning downward. "Miss, you sound...awfy. *You* are not sickening?"

"Nothing of the sort," she said truthfully. Then lied. "Old throat injury."

"Well, your eyes look clear." After sparing them both with additional, evaluative glances, the man gave a *huff,* deciding to believe her, and then smiled.

"As to your request, you are in fortune, for we have a retired army surgeon staying with us. I will inquire."

"Thank you, sir."

❦

LITTLE MORE THAN a quarter hour later, hip bath delivered to their room, and heated water now filling it, Susanna waited (somewhat impatiently, for the rising steam beckoned) while Leo insisted on hanging a sheet. "For your privacy, lass."

Bah. She wanted to scrub, and she wanted him. And for once, she wasn't overly particular about in which order.

But it appeared as though he had his own plan. Stripping the topmost sheet from the bed, he knotted one corner around a peg in the wall and "stabbed" the adjacent corner in place with his recently cleaned penknife.

The knife found and retrieved after that last attack, along with his gloves, tucked away in his saddlebag. The attack that had seen her shouting such that she'd thought she'd go hoarse. It was the only time since they'd met she was relieved he couldn't hear, given how her ears still rang from the terror she'd screamed, watching the vile wretch stab Leo from behind and the blood drip from his arm.

How her throat ached still, raw at every swallow. The soreness growing worse with every mile she remained—for the most part—silent, once she stopped protesting his walking while she rode.

When Leo finally pronounced his barrier "fit enough" and gestured her toward the bath, her dirty dress, never completely fastened, quickly flew over her head, boots discarded with a bit more care until Susanna was sinking into the warm water with a heated moan of her own.

Beyond the "curtain" he created, Leo stated his intention of procuring food and supplies for them, then left her to her bath.

Had fresh water and a small cake of soap ever before been so very valued? Mayhap not, but she didn't dally, wanting the water to retain some semblance of warmth when he returned for his splash about.

Only when he came back, it was much quicker than she'd expected, returning not with food, but with a surprising stack of potential clothing for them both.

"Mrs. Wells, the innkeeper's wife," he explained, satisfaction on his face (keeping his averted as she rose and knotted the sheet from the peg, trundling it about her dripping form). "She allowed me to purchase several unclaimed things. Seems her daughter-in-law takes in laundry, and I retain hope that we shall benefit by finding something that fits."

Susanna made her way to him and quickly riffled through the pile. She might not have a new dress, but she did now possess a wearable shift— which was famous! "And stockings!"

Still wearing the sheet, she plopped on the bed and began to unfold the long woolen stockings. They didn't match, having come from two different pair, but it mattered not.

"I saw your feet this morning," he rumbled, his eyes roving over her damp shoulders and hair. "Think you I did not notice your wince when donning footwear? Blistered and sore from your trials."

She gave him a beaming smile, toes flexing as she drew on the pale stockings before donning the men's thick socks he gave over next. "For added warmth."

"Thank you." They might have been naught but simple socks, intended for her feet, but warmth from his cherishment spread through her like rare hot chocolate on a frosty morn. "Thank you."

"Tomorrow is Christmas Eve." He scowled, more

self-directed than not. "Given how late it already is, I doubt there will be a chance to obtain more, not if I am to get you to your brother without further delay. But Mrs. Wells did promise to see our things laundered tonight if we—"

In seconds, Susanna was shoving him back out the door, her dirty, wrinkled dress and ragamuff shawl and whatever else she could bring to hand, thrust into his waiting grasp.

BY THE TIME HE RETURNED, she wore her "new" shift, had the damp sheet folded and shawled about her shoulders, giving modesty to her breasts, because, "You, Leo"—she accompanied this with pointing and motions (and even a foot tap or two, making her insistence clear)—"are to bathe now. Wash. Posthaste. The water is already tepid, tep-id, weak, and I would have you clean and clothed before the healer knocks."

Because in between his errands, she had received word from the innkeeper's daughter that the surgeon, a Mr. Brooks, would be by once he finished his downstairs meal.

LITTLE MORE THAN an hour later saw both of them bathed *and* fed, the lantern's oil level tested and filled for the night, the sun thinking 'twas time to turn in, and Leo's injury washed and sewn, thanks to the gruff Mr. Brooks.

Before the surgeon's arrival, servants and Leo's good arm had seen the hip bath emptied and dragged off, so there was a modicum more space in the room by the time the former army surgeon tapped on the door and announced himself.

After completing his inspection of the wound, he first complimented their efforts at keeping the injury free from debris and the bleeding to a minimum, and then pronounced a good eight stitches should keep the edges together, and was it not fortunate that though he had no desire to ever return to the army nor see a battlefield again, he continued to keep a small plaster kit on his person, with needles sharpened and armed, and appropriate "thread" at hand.

The surgeon, a stern-jawed man with hair an indeterminate blond or grey, she knew not which, was younger than she'd expected. But confidently efficient. Talking while he worked, explaining what he was doing and why, even debating the benefits of waxed silk versus catgut when it came to seaming flesh.

His descriptionate words nearly enough to make her cascade.

Nay, be honest, Susanna. 'Tis not what the good surgeon says, 'tis the tools he wields driving into Leo's flesh that causes your stomach to roil.

She knew he was not trying to put Leo at ease with his detailed patter, for they had told him her captain no longer possessed hearing, so his words were all for Susanna. Mayhap his attempt to abate her disquiet. Despite that, each time the "square point stitching needle" pierced Leo's skin from either direction (something her man weathered with his countenance impassive, and through stoic silence) she knew the treatment, if not the injury itself, must ache like the dickens.

Given how 'twas her gut that bubbled mulligrubs, she could not have been more relieved when the deed was done, the last suture tied off and clipped. Finally, a full breath could fill her lungs.

Once Mr. Brooks was paid and the door closed after his exit, she turned, more than ready for her turn to touch the man seated at the table, where the lantern light had shone over the skin of his bare back and shoulder. His arms.

Glory be, his arms. If they were not the biggest ones she had seen, then they had to be close. The smooth muscle wrapped within his warm flesh drew her, made her fingers tingle for a touch unlike anything she could remember.

"Leo." He heard her not, in the act of reaching for his shirt, to draw it on—one of the shirts purchased from the laundress earlier, as their clothing would not be returned until the morrow.

The unclad skin of his back beckoned.

His muscled back and shoulders—and those magnificent arms—*everything* she could see beneath the careless fall of his wavy hair beckoned. Blazes, even his hair called to her, made her stomach dip, her fingers flurry, at the thought of delving through the strands.

"Leo." Swallowing past the excitement, the rawness still cloaking her throat, she moved from the door to seat herself on the mattress, across from him. She placed one hand on his unwounded arm and took hold of his shirt with the other.

His head swiveled, eyes swept up to hers. *What?*

She saw the curiosity he didn't put into sound. *What now, indeed?*

With a slight shake of her head, she tugged his shirt, pulling it toward her.

He refused to release it. More blue tonight than grey, his storm-swept eyes darkened. "I saw Brooks ask you something and point to his throat. What have you not told me?"

And in the quiet night, The Golden Swan's tavern suitably distant, nothing intruded, save her own agitation and unrestful body. She flushed at his question. Impressed anew at his perception.

"I yelled." Reluctantly, she moved her hand from his arm to mimic cupping her fingers around her mouth and shouting. "Screamed when you were attacked." Her eyes flicked to the plaster, the one Mr. Brooks adhered after adding some agglutinant powder, "to help everything hold and heal". Then she brushed her fingers over her throat. "Hoarse and sore now, 'tis nothing." She tugged again on his shirt. "Now give this over."

He did, finally releasing his hold.

"Thank you." Without looking, she tossed it toward the other chair, the one Mr. Brooks had used when he hadn't been standing.

"Now, strong and handsome Captain Tucker..." She took his hands and guided him to the bed. With a smile she could not help be aware of, she pushed his chest till he fell to his back and wasted no time climbing over his legs, intent on unbuttoning his falls, the draped-sheet shawl slipping from her shoulders unheeded. "I know you stare at my lips."

She flashed him a quick look, only to confirm his full attention upon her face, his eyes narrowed and glimmering, jaw and mouth tight.

"I shall endeavor..." Mmm, mayhap longer words were best used when she was writing? "*Attempt* to speak slowly and plainly but—drat it." She frowned at his falls, one of the buttons coming off, leaving threads behind in something of a knot, thanks to her fumbling, somewhat frantic fingers.

The length of his ready erection was hot beneath her efforts. What had caused her to fumble, surely...

Are you certain he is to blame and not your own impatience?

"Arrrrgh!" Frustrated—and aye, impatient—she sat back with a huff. Flashed her eyes up to his. "Your falls are knotted. Button..."

She held up the one that had come off in her hand.

"Boots, please." His rumbled reply.

"You make no sense but very well." Sliding to her feet she worked each of his boots free. Placed them out of the way along the wall and spun to see his grin as he—only then, knowing she watched, released his tangled clutch of the coverlet and brought his hands to his falls.

A sharp tug and a *snap* met her ears as he did away with any pesky threads that might have stood between them.

"Your shift, Susanna? I will dispense with these, if you..." A blink or two and his pants were off, sailing toward the chair, missing to land upon the floor, both his socks following a single breath later.

While she stood transfixed, in awe at the virile, masculine beauty. Roughened skin in places, enough scars to make a mama weep, but his muscling was sheer heaven. Glorious.

"I have to touch you." Forgetting all about disposing her attire, giddy delight storming her cells and stomach, Susanna leaned over to glide her palms against his chest, his stomach.

Crisp hairs met her palm, not too thick but tantalizing. Inviting her to stroke him, fingers splayed, all over. Heated, smooth shoulders, avoiding the plaster on one side, the swell of firm pectoral muscles, the solid slab of his strong torso and lightly furred stomach.

The paler, smoother skin below his navel... Angled muscles of his groin and—

"Oh heavens, Leo..."

Her exploring touch stuttered to a halt when she came upon his shaft.

Upthrust and reddened, proud and thick. Her fingers curved around what they could, to the song of his groan, and her body's hunger for his exploded.

"Lie back," she said, reduced to single syllables as she climbed over his legs. When he reached for her, she released him to capture his wrists and leaned over his torso, pressing his arms up by his head, flat to the mattress. "I'll not have you injuring yourself after just getting sutures."

Then she slid back down, her gaze going to his stand again, and the generous set of ballocks below.

Her hand shook as she reached—

"I think..." He snapped fingers on each hand until she looked up—tearing her gaze off his body to meet his. His tongue swept out to wet his lips. "I think that *you think* a rousing bout, or several, of sex will harm the stitches? Love..." He laughed—but she turned it into a moan when she centered herself over his groin and pressed against his hard, heated flesh, ready for exploring with more than her fingers...

"Do you forget I have seen battle?" His words were not quite steady. "However zealous we are tonight, lest you take a fork to my arm, I should be fine *sphdm-mmhpdm.*"

Her arms curved around the tops of his shoulders, along the muscles of his neck as far away from the plaster as she could, and she hauled herself completely over his chest and up—to his lips. He swore, garbled out more rimble-ramble, then warmed the air around them even more when, in between kisses, he confessed raggedly, "You shall be the death of me, lass."

She nudged to get him in place, and started

rocking her hips, her slick flesh parting to slide along his shaft. While she glided against him and gave a very unladylike whimper, reduced to flim-flam herself, he'd regained the ability to speak. "Before you dethrone me to batter, let me show you."

He whipped her shift over her head and flipped her over, bare back to the mattress, his body coming over hers as he leaned upon his arms, caging her within his embrace. He lowered to feather his lips along her throat, as though to erase any hurt. After mitigating any lingering ache along her neck, he supped at her lips, then spoke against them. "I want to taste you again, to lick and savor, yet 'tis a provocatory craving you have roused. One I am impatient to satisfy, for us both."

A deep-tongued kiss. A shift of his body, bringing one of his palms to the naked skin of her breast, where he cupped and molded and brushed his thumb over the tip till she writhed beneath him. He finished with, "I ache too much to dally about."

Reveling in his strength, his power, she panted heavy breaths in silence as he wedged his hips between hers, spreading her for his possession.

She opened herself, propped one foot on the bed and allowed her other leg to angle wide as he released her breast to sweep fingers along her slit, groaning deep when he felt how wet she was.

The slide of his hand against her folds was torture. Pure and exquisite.

A deeper slick of his dampened fingers

spreading her wet flesh and she started squirming against him in earnest. Her breaths coming faster as she arched into his hand.

And then it wasn't his hand. But less nimble, thicker flesh. A groan of welcome rattled her chest when he parted her and nestled forward.

Her body resisted... Hungered... A warm wash of desire dripped from her yet still he remained outside.

"Sweet Susanna. Give me your lips."

Her chin tilted up and his mouth claimed hers, tongue thrusting inside, hot and deep. Stroking alongside—

And *mmmmmm*.

With a keening noise that never left her throat, she rocked her hips toward him and her passage yielded in invitation.

He lunged inside, just a bit.

But enough that she pulled back and tilted to greet his lance anew.

The wet welcome of her loins eased his way and he filled her. Stretched her. Pushed inside and warmed every bit of cold she might ever have felt or feel again.

She clasped; she clutched. Embraced his shaft and warmed all over at the thickness sliding into her over and over again.

"The bed? How loud is it?" His question, by her ear, when he pulled away from her mouth, was full of heat and breath. "Are we like to be ejected over disturbing others nearby?"

He leveraged on one arm, raised his chest and caught her gaze so she could answer. The motion only pushed him deeper.

"The ropes," she gasped out, referring to the ones that supported the mattress, "they're tight enough, I wager."

Tight. She groaned as her feminine muscles tightened around his masculine one, then released, allowing him to sink down farther inside her. When he landed, she grasped his flesh, holding him close, **reveling** in how he filled her. Then she loosed her hold so he could lift free. Her hands clutching his buttocks encouraged more. *Again.*

He lunged inside.

Tighten, as he glided upward and nearly out. *Groan*, as he released his control and sank into her again. Over and over till it was a chore to recall what else she meant to say.

She lost herself, lost thought in the numbing pleasure flooding through her limbs. Met his tongue with hers when he returned to her mouth. Such desperate, debauched and dreadfully satisfying kisses.

She might have pitied other females, ones who didn't have a Captain Tucker in their beds, but nay—

Nay. Why spare a single thought beyond the grand and generous lover with her now?

She wrapped her arms and legs about his strong and heavy body, thrilling beneath his weight and hugging him tight as a squeal emerged and she ducked to lick his throat.

"Aye. The ropes are taut enough not to cause undue noise," she finally answered against his skin, gasping twice during her response, though he was no longer waiting for it, his lips busy against her neck.

But the bed, now?

The corner, where the wooden frame was slightly askew, thumping into the wall with every desperate, invigoured thrust? Aye, their neighbors could likely hear that—

And she didn't give a farthing.

Because with every second spent in his presence, in his arms, with every ravenous, ravishing kiss, he vanquished nights of fear and days of guilt, as he sank further and further into her body.

Into her heart.

LATER, when he thought back on it, Leo was never quite sure how he managed what he did. One moment, he was drowning in the bliss of Susanna's body, her slick heat surrounding him, providing just the right amount of friction as he powered into her, after that slow and tender beginning.

Nothing felt tender about him now, save for the ferocity of feelings peltering his heart. His body, though? An inferno. Had he ever wanted this much? Needed this badly? Nay, he had not. Every clasp of her core around him only hardened him further.

He yearned to shout to the heavens, to the ceiling of a certainty, his elation—had any man, anywhere, at any time ever found a woman so perfect?

He wouldn't have admitted it, not to anyone, but the line of fire on his upper arm prodded him to return to his back and draw her over him. Supporting his weight, so soon after, likely not his smartest action of late.

But once he was on his back, and she above him?

Glory be. His love rode his loins as though she had been born for it, her strong thighs gripping his hips as she glided over him, stampeding every thought straight out of his brain.

He'd thought her sweet before? A young-looking innocent who delighted his mind and sight?

Nay, with eager kisses such as these, with the heat of her bare thighs gripping his hips? With the way she damn near rode him, rocked the mattress beneath them both?

With the experiences of her past she'd shared? *Sweet* was not nearly all she was. His sweet Susanna had a core of steel and spirit of spice. Fortune had surely smiled on him.

Though the sight of her above him was so wondrous that nothing could compare, oddly, he found himself closing his eyes, simply savoring the sensations that rushed through him. He held her rocking hips with his hands, one of them at least. The other had lifted to support the slight weight of one breast, her nipple beaded and thrusting boldly into his palm.

His heart flapped like bird wings in a storm, fast and fierce, with all of the emotions bursting to the surface...

'Twas as though his body had known no others before her. No one had ever, ever enchanted him as she did, from her alluring scent, her saucy spirit, her sheer enthusiasm that humbled him.

And with his wattles out and his eyes closed, his other senses magnified. Amplified everything. When he caught the acrid hint of smoke from the lantern, he frowned. It should be nowhere near running low, not yet. Not after they'd filled—

But then the scent strengthened sufficiently to flare his eyes wide—and behind the majesty of the stript-bare, black-haired lass claiming him every bit as much as he'd dared to claim her, the muted orange glow told him something was amiss.

With a roar, he bolted upright, wrapped one arm around her waist and locked her to him. A lunge brought him off the bed. Two labored steps to the table, where he saw—

His shirt had caught flame. Alongside the lantern, the flare of fire licked several inches high and without thought—because some things were instinct—he swept down, captured one of his boots and "stomped" the flames.

Stomped and smothered till they were down to naught but singe and smoke, his nose now wrinkling at the unmistakable smell of potential devastation.

His heart no longer flying in bliss but tight in panic of what could have been, he thrust the smoldering fabric into the pewter chamber pot and watched it weaken, no longer near the heat.

The female against him had scrambled first to hold on, now in confusion as he reluctantly lifted her wet heat off of him—knowing he likely groaned loud enough to alert everyone in the tavern to his personal agony.

Once upon her feet, she spun to see what he'd been about. Taking it in at a glance and turning stark eyes up to his, a silent "*oh no*" met his knowing glance. And then guilt began brewing.

"No, you don't." He swept her back to him, confirmed the flame was out and the lantern now burning with ease, and fell back upon the mattress, his feet still touching the floor. He balanced Susanna against his chest when she would have scrabbled off. "No, you don't, Lady Reckless—Reckless Clod-brain just this once—appears you and I may need to review what sort of hazards lurk around lanterns, but that is for tomorrow. For tonight? Tonight, come here..."

And wonder of wonders, instead of the last few wrack-wrought moments destroying what they had been about, a few seconds of stroking his tongue against hers, of pulling hers into his mouth and drawing upon it like a man starved, of reaching his arms down, past the delicate beauty of her spine to the fleshy globes of her bottom, and pulling her tight against him... Sliding his fingers into the crease between and nudging lower...? A few seconds of that and she was panting against his neck, her feminine treasure rooting around for his bauble, ready to ride him once more.

And ride him she did. Until her eyes glazed over, a soft smile upon her lips... While she contracted, clasped even tighter around him as she approached her peak.

Reached it... And flooded his soul and body both with her release.

He didn't need to hear her gasp of delight, her moan of repletion to know the tightness that had coiled around him heralded her continuing and ultimate pleasure, for she melted over him, her frame going limp as she cuddled against him, now relaxed into the greatest ease he had sensed from her thus far.

Smarting shoulder or not, he arched forward, cradling her replete body, to stand on the floor. He turned, lowered her shoulders and head to the mattress while he leaned forward, over her softly smiling self and supported her thighs and hips as he plunged inside with his own reckless abandon until giving up his seed—and his heart, into her wondersome care forevermore.

BECAUSE YOU CAN NEVER RECEIVE TOO MANY LETTERS

BUT THE NEXT MORNING, when she awoke, 'twas *alone*.

Leo nowhere about.

And to a scratch upon their door. The door of their room at The Golden Swan, she recalled, glancing around with hazy, tired eyes.

Where had he gone? After sharing the hours and their bodies for most of the night, when they finally allowed each other to drift off, a hard and heavy sleep had claimed her.

The sound came again.

"A—a moment, if you please," she called, her tongue sluggish, as she dredged her mind up from the depths of sleep, the sheets a tangle about her bare limbs, her heart a twitter within her breast.

Could it be Leo at the door? Nay, for he would not scratch nor knock. Would know he could not hear any response she might make. He would come right in.

Pushing back the thick tumble of hair falling about her face—thanks, in part, by how reverently, how often, he had stroked his fingers through it during the night—she drew the sheet about her. Muddled both in mind and body, graceful coordination seemed beyond her as she stumbled from the bed, wrapping the sheet about her as she lurched toward the door. "Aye? Who is there?"

"Mrs. Tucker? 'Tis Mrs. Wells, ma'am. With your laundered things and a message from your mister."

The door whipped open, words and clothing exchanged, and scant moments later, Susanna was alone again.

Sitting on the edge of the bed.

Staring at the wall peg where her "still damp, ma'am, hang it so will dry" dress dangled, Leo's message, delivered verbally, ringing like a death knell in her ears.

"Says he has important business to tend and will be back tomorrow, weather permitting, and the next day if it proves unfavorable. Your room, and meals too, are paid through Wednesday, and I shall see you taken care of, I will." And before the woman had bustled off, "Did Mr. Brooks set things aright for you both last eve?"

Wednesday.

Paid through then, which was *four* days hence, certainly not tomorrow or the next should the weather "not prove favorable".

What if he did not intend to return?

Susanna, do not be daft. No escaping or fleeing this time, aye? Of course he means to return.

Of note, to her entangled thinking at least, was how, the further distant from her home in both space and time she had traveled, the less she heard Sarah's counsel and instead was beleaguered with her own.

Show some trust. Has he not earned it?

He had. And so she would.

But waiting proved difficult.

Challenging, indeed.

When the first full day eclipsed with nothing to mark its passing save the carriages that swept into the inn yard, holiday carols that she could have done without overhearing, and the two meals Mrs. Wells' daughter brought up. After her last unfortunate encounter storming into a tavern unescorted, Susanna had subdued that reckless impulse, at least.

The entirety of first December 24...

She exhibited patience and decorum, if only to herself.

And then...

Difficult more, the second day, Christmas, December 25. With louder carols, boisterous happy family rejoicings reaching her through the window she'd opened, still determined to remain in place, secured and safe—no matter how much the inactivity chafed.

The second entire day she spent alone. Alone and besieged by doubts and worries and crazed thoughts she could have done without. So very many... *It's too soon*, and *You have not known him long enough to depend upon everything he might have promised.*

But just as sternly, *Oh yes you have. You sensed his heart is true. Trust in that.*

But without anything else to dwell upon, to busy her time or her fingers, her own past occupied her mind far too much, allowed doubts to creep in more with every hour...

Such that, late the following night, just as she was debating blowing out the candle and seeking the oblivion of sleep, when the door knob rattled?

Rattled once and then again? Susanna eagerly bolted upright.

"Susanna," heard clearly through the door, that and Reaver's unexpected but very, very welcome muffled yelp of greeting.

Relief and joy—and a bit of shame for those doubts—rolled over her like a wave when the door opened and Leo's broad form presented itself over the threshold, his eyes eagerly seeking hers.

Though exhaustion lined his features, *his* relief echoed on them too, and in the second he secured the door, she leapt over the jumping dog and plastered herself against her man, her cumbersome-of-late, now-giddy heart finally at ease once he bound her up in his arms.

"Forgive me, lass." In deference to the hour, out of respect of the others near them, not to mention his entrenched habit of keeping his tone moderate at all times—so that in his ignorance, he did not allow his volume to grow beyond that which would be appropriate—Leo tendered his explanation as quickly as he could, and though his words might have sounded tranquil, he was anything but. "Deep toward morning, my mind cobbled together certain thoughts that I needed to make known to my superior posthaste."

The moment awareness had startled him awake, he'd recalled with complete clarity a supposedly *cursed* brooch by the name of Lady's Diamond, unearthed by an archaeologian some years ago. Was supposed to have been turned over to the British Museum, but it disappeared under mysterious circumstances.

Information Leo had raced back to East Crossings to share, among other things.

"How in blazes...know all of that?" Farnsworth had demanded, no longer dressed as, nor portraying, a stable master, but now in his finery and in command of his coach, the duke—and Leo's dog— had been about to return to London. Leo had just barely caught up with him beforehand.

"Sisters," Leo said succinctly, his breath and pounding heart finally settling, now that his messages had been delivered. "Three of them, if you will recall. 'Twas before they were married, so some time back, but I remember they were all agog over the whole thing, hoping to visit the museum while in town. What any of this has to do with our missing men or women, I know not, but it seemed precise enough of a potential match that I needed to let you know. Besides..." He finished this reaching down to pet his absurdly clean (for once) dog. "Figured I could retrieve this cur early and ask a boon?"

"Oh?"

"Aye." And while Tucker explained, Farnsworth's expression went from irritation to incredulity to assurety. "I suspected...was in the offing... Come." His boss gave a nod and spun away from the carriage.

Knocking Reaver's dusty paws off his chest, Leo followed, speaking to his dog. "Did I not tell you, no more of that? You cannot be behaving thus around ladies. It isn't done. And if I have my way..."

But I missssssssssssssssed you!!! his dog's frantic side hops seemed to insist, prompting both a laugh and a shake of his head.

"Manners, Reave. You need to gain some."

Because if Leo had his way, both he and his four-footed companion would be around a certain lady forevermore.

Back at The Golden Swan now, looking at Susanna, the energetical pup's paws once again propped against his torso, Leo gave the base of the dog's thickly furred ears a hearty scratch.

"I also decided to claim this bucket of dirty fur," he told Susanna, only a fraction of his attention focused on the lively canine. "I wasn't certain Mr. Wells was going to let him inside." Directing Reaver's front legs off his chest, with a stern reminder (*"Floor*, Reaver."), Leo reached in and wiggled a hand in his pocket, hoping he made a couple of coins clink. "Fortunately, I was able to clear the coast with our accommodating innkeeper. Despite the bath he received since we both saw him last, Reave decided to frolic in a ditch this morning while I was taking care of some other important business. And wait a moment—"

The sun had long since set, night embracing the land. The single candle she had burning next to the bed did not allow him to see any part of her to his satisfaction.

"I do not know what has gotten into him," Leo told her as he made his way to the small table, where the lantern he had requested upon their arrival still resided. "He's normally very well behaved, but the amount of travel we have done could explain his ill manners." 'Twas but a moment before he had it lit and the room brightened. "There, now." He turned to her. "Now I can see you enough — Wait. You're wearing my shirt."

A slight nod. "The one laundered and sewn." She pointed to the thin line of even stitches, a lot more than eight, along the shoulder and upper arm, then caught his gaze again. Her top teeth scraped against her bottom lip before she added, "Because it smelled like you."

Primitive urges roared to the surface. She was *his*.

By happen-so, he had claimed her when she fell under threat; by her own choice, she belonged to him now.

"My extreme apologies, Susanna. I thought to be returned by last night, but the more I rode with my clamorous thoughts, the more I wanted to see things put to rights between us. Without any uncertainty. After delivering my message to East Crossings, I found myself stabling Rambler for a well-deserved rest and renting steed upon steed, putting swift miles on the poor beasts so I could..."

His words faltered, so intently did she stare at him, her expression rapt.

Was this how she felt, when he stared at her mouth, studied her lips? Alive, exhilarated... Filled with disarrangement?

His heart followed his mouth, stuttering in place, and he firmed his resolve—and his voice. "Now that you, that *we*, are safe and time allows, 'tis appropriate to address some things between us."

Her face showed alarm, so he delayed not. "Some of my other important business, conducted since I saw you last..."

As he spoke, he bent to the haversack he'd tossed upon the bed, dislodging recently gathered paper and pencils, digging through until finding what he sought. "No, Reaver, I do not need your help." His big dog had jumped alongside, rooted his long snout inside the bag's opening and licked Leo's hand when he could have done without.

Standing, he inclined his head in a bow (on the sly, wiped the back of his hand against his pants, drying the unasked-for slobber). Lifting his head, he captured her still startled gaze.

"I believe, Lady Reckless, that you placed an advertisement for a kind, dependable man desirous of both matrimony and *your*self. One possessing both teeth and manners? I would apply for the position posthaste, if it is still available."

He waited, breath held—teeth clenched and manner straining—for her response.

She hesitated, perplexed.

Mayhap befuddled by the formal way in which he had begun? He suspected 'twas so, because what he thought she spoke next was nowhere the direction he had intended to point her. "Even... Knowing all that you do about me?" She frowned at the bed before catching his gaze again. "The...others?"

"Waste not a single concern nor thought about anything unpalatable in your past ever again. I mean it, lass." His response required no thought at all. Instinct guided him now. "For none of it—not one thing—could make my desire for you any less."

When she didn't speak soon enough to quell the riot climbing his throat, he revealed what he'd pulled from his bag. "Here. My own letters of reference."

That made her react.

Gasp, in fact, as she took the three letters from him. They were brief, the idea rather tickle-headed, yet so damn important...

So important.

Her reaction to them, surely.

WARY NOW, for had not *her* penchant for lettering nonsensical led them both into trouble more than once? Hoping a lightning bolt didn't await at the unfolding of it, Susanna dallied...

But then strong penmanship met her gaze.

Dear Lady Reckless,

She wasn't certain if this was in his hand or not, for all their scribbled conversations he had spoken while she wrote in double tides, with ferocity and vigor. Yet two sentences in she suspected; three sentences in and she *knew*—this was not Leo.

By the end of the short note, she possessed no lingering doubt as to whose carriage they had spent the night in.

I have known Captain Leopold Tucker for years. Considered him good enough to command the HMS Restless. Even good enough for my own daughter.

That should serve.

> *Yours, Farnsworth*
> *(Aye, the Duke of, if you questioned)*

The second note was in a feminine hand.

As she unfolded it with slightly less apprehension slowing her actions, Leo cleared his throat and leaned in to whisper, "I stopped by the house. Needed to talk with my sister and her husband. See how they felt about moving back to his abode. When Mama got wind of the whole to-do, she insisted I give you this."

When Susanna looked up at him, the letters tight in her clutch, his cheeks were ruddy. "I do not know what either of them said. Did not read them. I will not ever read anything of yours unless you see fit to shove it under my nose."

With that pronouncement prompting a smile, she turned to the letter, her nervosity a little less palatable.

Oh my lands a mercy, child, whoever you are, secure my Leo posthaste. Shall I bribe you? The garden house his father left us is nigh on begging for him to return home with a bride. His sister Liz and her spouse, John, would love nothing more than to move back to John's home, not stay here watching over me. Oh, what am I saying?

I need no watching over! Just give me some seeds, garden shears and a sunny day and I shall keep myself occupied handily.

Leo! You need to know of <u>him</u>, not all my blathering.

Sweet lass, whoever you are (he would not tell me your name—the wretch; said he'd not have you embarrassed if you didn't accept him), you will accept him, correct?

My Leopold Michael is steadfast, true, not given over to vast quantities of wine nor unduly chasing after women, nor even profanity. Getting him to church on Sundays might take a prod, but my Leo is truly a good man. I despaired of him ever finding a woman he wanted to wife, not after we lost sweet Ann-Marie (I'm sure he told you of her).

But now he's growling impatience at the doorway, telling me he must be off, and I am nowhere near finished.

Agree to wed him, Miss Reckless (he <u>did</u> tell me that much), and we can talk about him at our leisure.

I do so hope to meet you!

All my love, Abigail Tucker (Leo's mama)

Oh, her lands a mercy!
Susanna's.

For his mama, Abigail, sounded wondrous. So enthused and joyful, and after the years without her own mother, Susanna wanted nothing more than to wrap the other woman in a hug and be hugged in return. Well, nothing more than how very much she yearned for the man chafing beside her now, shifting his weight between feet, all that growling impatience his mother referenced only subdued at the moment.

"Now the last one." Stated in his deep tones.

Her lungs heaved as she opened the final letter, excited breaths panting from her lips.

Dear (<u>My Very Own</u>, I hope and pray) <u>Lady Reckless</u>,

Ours has not been a traditional meeting nor courtship, but rather than bemoan or regret, I choose to embrace it. To revel in your delightful, spirited ways, to celebrate the instinct that had me clambering to claim you upon an instant. (Mayhap the instinct to even tame a wee bit of that recklessness, hmm?)

Before that fateful act, I thought to spend the rest of my life alone, in silence. Your smile? It <u>speaks</u> to me. I cannot explain it. Because so does the sadness that at times has befallen your features.

Susanna, if you will let me, I will cherish your words, your sighs <u>and</u> your secrets. I would *banish your past hurts and give us both a future, together, at my modest home in Kniveton, the property that has been waiting for me to claim it —a simple cottage with ample room for any children we might be blessed with.*

My sister and brother-in-law will be relieved to leave—

And I digress.

Having (without express permission, I acknowledge) read what you desire in a spouse, I can confidently put myself forth as the Absolutely, Unequivocal Most Splendiferous candidate you might ever hope to chance across.

Yours, in heart and deed,
Leo

Too restless to wait a moment more, when the shift of her gaze indicated completion of his letter, Leo's words burst forth. "I know it's soon. Preposterously so, having only just met, but your light is too promising to ever again suffer the darkness of your past.

"*I* want to be the one to give you invited kisses. Hugs deep into the night so that you never have another second's worry again." He took the notes from her unresisting grasp, and tossed them on the table—the dog still in command of the bed—before crooking his knees until they were the same height and he could speak directly to the woman before him. "Selfishly, Susanna, I have a distinct feeling that if I did not do all I can to lay myself bare and keep you at my side, I would regret that to my dying day and miss you forever."

Spying the extra pages (blank) and three pencils (all sharpened) he had liberated from his haversack when he'd rummaged through it, she pushed an exhausted, slumbering Reaver aside and scrambled to scribble...

Kniveton? That is where you hail from?

Feeling the pinch between his brows, he held one hand up between them, fingers splayed, pointing to the scars on the back. "As lads, we were not inclined to play Knife Nick for naught. Gambling aside, calling Kniveton home meant being skilled with blades as much as our fives. And after *everything* you just read and what I just said— *that* is what you ask about?"

But then the page fluttered to the floor and she turned glistening, joyful eyes up to him. "Do you not...very close that...Nate's home now? His and Olivia's? My nieces..."

"I do realize that, lass. Not much more than an hour or so, and if it takes that knowledge to tempt you—"

"It does not." Her heart shone in her gaze as she stared up at him. "...tempted the moment you claimed me as *yours*. Yours. I am just—just"—she stopped speaking, simply stared—"without words. Speechless, utterly so, at the thought of—" Her fingertips slapped against her lips, halting the ramble for a few seconds, until they slid away, to his chest and her lips moved again. "Your mother—you —sisters!"

"Me...what?" He took a leap, recalling from her letters how much she missed her maternal parent. "Aye, to accept me for life means you may call my sisters, *my mother* your own."

And whatever bliss she might have voiced next got lost in her exuberance as she launched herself into his arms.

Fortunately, Leo had learned quickly how to "hear" the puffs of her breath against his skin. Words she delighted in chattering over his body for the next several hours.

Her welcome "chatter". Every syllable she either spoke or that puffed across his flesh, something he would cherish with his every breath.

With everything in him. As he would her.

EPILOGUE

∽∘∾

THE FOLLOWING SUMMER

KNIVETON, DERBYSHIRE

REAVER REMAINED IN ALT, his long tongue lolling past his lips as he savored the taste of the oncoming night. Kept his eyes on a family of chirping birds flying about with more haste than care as he debated rousing himself to snag one versus remaining right where he was, leaning against the old wooden chair, outside with his man.

What a blessed, exciting day!

Not only had the cart his man's lady sketched and requested Captain Tucker build worked beauteously (allowing either Tucker or his big mare to haul Reaver's magnificent self across more miles than his paws might want to travel)...

Not only had he enjoyed the attention of numerous younglings excited to see his freshly bathed self (and equally excited to sneak him ham from nuncheon)...

But the alluring bitch he'd sniffed out as they returned home and he'd abandoned his cart and run off to investigate had been *more* than amenable to an encounter with his impressively long—

Well, that was neither here nor there.

For satisfaction still thrummed through him.

Oh happy, happy day.

Happy dog, too. Pleased by how close his newly met, alluring canine lady was—less than a quarter mile!—but also thoroughly invigoured by the venturous hours since dawn.

Not that each of his days weren't enjoyable, for they were. Today had just been...special. More eventful than most.

But as for the others?

Now that he and his captain were no longer investigating rats—i.e., rat-faced humans? *Now* there was time to explore the nearby countryside together, time to lull about in the barn, where *Leo* (so sayeth the captain's lady) had created something of a workshop, a place for them both, he and his man, to tinker about...

Leo repairing furniture he brought out, building new things for inside, making garden benches (and drag-abouts for Reaver's quality self, heh heh)... whatever he thought might please his lady.

As for Reaver? An amorous meddle on the way

home late this afternoon? A bit of raw steak for dinner? And now his man's reassuring touch upon his flank...

Eh. The birds would live another day. For he would remain, right where he was.

———◦———

Puff, puff, puff. The sound of Reaver's swift pants.

The whistle of the wind, rustling through the trees, gliding through first his mama's perennial flowers, and then the ones Susanna had planted just this spring.

Thump-thump, bump. He thought that one with an audible laugh that cocked one of Reaver's ears. The sound (felt) of the broom handle hitting the ceiling just beneath their bed that morn when Susanna thought it was time he roused so they could be on their way.

Could he help it if holding her in his arms, if loving her during the night, if no longer being a captain on board an ocean-going ship had given him a tendency to sleep in *past* dawn, on occasion?

The broom handle had been her idea. But only *after* he had suggested she throw a log up the stairs, to land in the doorway, both of them testing the floor to see what he could feel, and potentially "hear". Even though it was the vibration of the old house, not the sound, they had turned the exercise into a bit of a game.

Something his nieces and nephews had joined

in during the earlier visit today, having him face the opposite wall while they took turns dropping things on the floor—to their mothers' (and even his)—dismay, given some of the, he gathered, exorbitant sounds they had made. Not to mention a couple of things shattered. (Which yes, dealing with his siblings, the trio had insisted *he* tidy.)

The memory, of a few hours past, spirited both his cheeks and chest upward.

Back home now, Leo sat outside on his father's old and favorite chair, repaired, sanded and varnished anew more than once over the years, appreciating another glorious day.

His hand stretched past the arm of the lounge-about chair, fingers resting against Reaver's side, feeling the steady pants that caused the canine's lungs to lift and fall in time with the gentle flap of his long tongue. Both of them relaxed, content.

The cottage at their backs, the overly gardened plot of land bursting with colors to his front. From trees to flowers to leaves—mayhap even a daring weed or two—Susanna had taken to gardening (to Leo's mama's sheer delight) as though she'd been born with a trowel in one hand and seeds in another.

Upon their marriage, his mama had moved in with Liz and John, saying she would help with her grandlings and give the "newly wedded couple a wee bit of time to themselves".

Thankful, were they all, that Mama Tucker was a smiling, blessed spirit to be around and not a harpy or a morose one, as he knew some siblings endured. His father? Susanna had asked of him when he'd joined her at her brother's.

Leo's father had been a stern, somewhat abrupt, but fair man. He had also been satisfied to leave the rearing of his children to his wife while he occupied himself with "manly" pursuits. Leo couldn't fault him for that, thankful to his sire for teaching him how to fight, either in the ring, or against bullies and evil. But neither had he grieved overly much when the man died shortly after Leo reached his twenties; nowhere near the grief he would feel when his mama's time came.

Fortunately, the spry female, who Susanna had pointed out Leo took after in temperament, showed no signs of slowing down.

Leo chuckled, relishing the wind against his face and arms where he'd rolled up his shirtsleeves as he watched the sun casting long shadows as evening approached its end. Nighttime ready to march forth.

And that knowledge brought no small amount of pleasure, now that he had no reason to dread the darkness.

For his love had explained their "private, intimate" language to him during his brief but earnest courtship, the one that saw them wed with Oliver's blessing (and continued surprise).

A language she continued to add to.

A tilt of her head toward her right shoulder? *Wait a moment, dear, and I will explain it all.* Often "said" when they were around others who didn't know Leo was deaf.

Two blinks and a quick wrinkling of her nose? *You completely mistook whatever was just said.* Whether it had come from her lips or another's.

He'd learned to glance at her after responding to someone whose expression indicated betwattlement, often needing to ask them to repeat themselves or to slow down. Other times, his wife could quickly speak for them in a way he understood.

His favorites, though? Were when they "spoke" betwixt each other.

Her nails along the back of his scalp, just above his nape, accompanied by a nuzzle to his jaw? *I am feeling amorous.*

Her palm, circling his heart and then tapping twice? *I love you so much, my big and strong and handsome husband.*

He'd twitted her over that one, but she insisted that is what it meant, and he could not love her more.

Tonight, when she joined him to watch the sun's final descent, making sure to walk in a wide arc so he saw her (not needed, as he had sensed her approach before he saw it), he gave Reaver a final scratch before tugging her down into his lap.

He imagined her squeal of surprise—for he'd given her no warning.

"All right, wife," he spoke as he pulled her against his chest, placed his hand, fingers wide over her belly. "*When* were you going to tell me?"

Now he imagined her startled gasp. Thrilled to the unladylike clamber that saw her pushing off from his shoulders and gaining her feet.

"You *know?* How? I only...last week...to visit Mama to confirm..." Why they'd gone earlier today after Susanna's impatient, broom-handled awakening: the convivial gathering of his family—*their* family—and great romp outside after nuncheon with his many nieces and nephews, along with his three brothers-in-law, while his sisters, Mama and wife stayed inside to jaw. "...to surprise you..."

The breeze riffled through the drying strands of her midnight hair, down just the way he liked it, after her bath.

"Mrs. Tucker." He gave her his best rumble, the one he knew fluttered her insides (because she had told him). "With a mother and multiple sisters, all *younger* sisters, mind, and every one of them adept at bringing life into this world, how would I not notice the changes in the woman I love most of all?"

Ah. And there it was.

She climbed back into his lap. Her palm met his nape, thumb stroked along his neck, up toward his ear where the sensation numbed. But unlike the scarred flesh that was deadened, Leo's soul alit.

For she'd just told him, in words he could hear, that he was her *everything.*

Howdy. Thanks for reading!

Sure hope you smiled along with Susanna and Leo (& Reaver!). What was supposed to be a quick holiday novella turned into the longest book yet in the Steamy Scandal series. Every time I thought I was nearly finished, both of them insisted I wasn't, that they needed more time together, *before* their happily ever after.

And yes, if you wondered whether that was Squirrel Beard accompanying his new, pretend "wife" on the stage with Susanna, it was! Stay tuned...

Meanwhile, ready for more steamy regency fun?

My hottest stories are the **Roaring Rogues Regency Shifters**. Check out Maggie Award of Excellence finalist ***Ensnared by Innocence***.

If you prefer something a bit tamer, **Regency Christmas Kisses** might be just the thing; start with National Excellence in Storytelling Award Winner ***A Snowlit Christmas Kiss***.

And if you want something in the middle, try **Mistress in the Making**, an extended-length novel full of humor, heat and heartwarming angst.

For more information on upcoming releases and all the cat and dog pics you might want, >^..^< sign up for my newsletter at larissalyons.com.

MISTRESS IN THE MAKING series (Complete)

Seductive Silence

Lusty Letters

Daring Declarations

Mistress in the Making - Bundle

Contemporaries by Larissa Lynx

SEXY CONTEMPORARY ROMANCE

Renegade Kisses

Starlight Seduction

SHORT 'N' SUPER STEAMY

A Heart for Adam...& Rick!

Braving Donovan's

No Guts, No 'Gasms

POWER PLAYERS HOCKEY series

*My Two-Stud Stand**

*Her Three Studs**

The Stud Takes a Stand (forthcoming)

**Her Hockey Studs - print version*

Lady Scandal

Sparks—and stockings—fly when an interview for a husband turns into a game of forfeits—played with articles of clothing—a scandalous lady and one handsome rogue learn how very right for each other they are.

Lady Scandal **awarded the Golden Nib!** "I can't praise this book enough. Regency fans, if you like gorgeous wit in with your devilishly superb, well written, sexy reading matter, Lady Scandal should be on your 'Must Read' list." *Natalie, Miz Love & Crew Love's Books*

Lady Imposter

He's not in the market for a wife. But she can pretend, can she not?

"Absolutely well written, full of love, drama, fun, laughs, society, family, steam, chemistry and so much more... So well worth the read and has some really great laughs to go it. **Fabulous story worth more than 5 stars.** Would strongly recommend to everyone." – 5-Star Reviewer

Lady Reckless

A mysterious sea captain aiming to stay out of trouble.
And a young widow who isn't your average damsel in distress...

CHRISTMAS KISSES

A Snowlit Christmas Kiss

WINNER! National Excellence in Storytelling Award, historical short novel category

A case of mistaken identity. One strong-willed, spunky female and one healing, heart-heavy lord. Two lonely souls stranded together during a wretched, snowy night...

A Frosty Christmas Kiss

She's blind but determined. He's grumpy but protective. Together? Pure holiday magic.

A Moonlit Christmas Kiss

He needs to walk again. But he may need her more...

FREE 40,000 word preview ebook available at all retailers.

MORE CHRISTMAS KISSES

Rescued by a Christmas Kiss

She's seeking shelter. He's hardened his heart. His cat just wants chin rubs.

ROARING ROGUES REGENCY SHIFTERS

Ensnared by Innocence
STEAMY REGENCY SHAPESHIFTER

Maggie Award of Excellence Finalist

Changing into a lion isn't all fur and games.

A Regency lord battles his inner beast while helping an innocent miss, never dreaming how he'll come to care for the chit—nor how being near his world will deliver danger right to her doorstep.

If Darcy had been a shape-shifting lion who thought about frisking—a lot...

STANDALONE ~ HEA ~ 81,000-WORD NOVEL ~ BOOK 1 - ROARING ROGUES REGENCY SHIFTERS

Deceived by Desire
STEAMY REGENCY SHAPESHIFTER

Meet a Shakespeare-quoting shapeshifter who wants nothing to do with love...

Cursed into the form of a lion without nightly sex, Lord Nash Hammond wants only two things—his liquor strong and smooth, and his wenches wild and willing. What he doesn't need is a virgin!

HEA ~ BOOK 2 – ROARING ROGUES REGENCY SHIFTERS ~ 97,000 WORDS

Changing into a lion is all fun and growls—until it isn't.

Mistress in the Making
A fun, emotionally satisfying, steamy tale told in three parts: Seductive Silence, Lusty Letters, and Daring Declarations.

Seductive Silence, Part 1
FREE at all retailers

Lord Tremayne has a problem. He stammers like a fool—at least that's what he learned from his father's constant criticism and punishing hand. Daniel now hides his troubles by barely saying anything. But then he goes looking for a new mistress and finds a delightful young woman who makes him, of all people, want to spout poetry. He thought he had a problem before? Avoiding meaningless dinner prattle is nothing compared to the challenge of winning the heart of his new lady lust.

Lusty Letters, Part 2

Thea's fascinating new protector has secrets—several. Hesitant to destroy her newfound circumstances, she stifles her longing to know everything about the powerfully built—and frustratingly quiet—Marquis. But then his naughty notes start to appear, full of humor and wit, and Thea realizes she's about to break the cardinal rule of mistressing—that of falling for her new protector. *Egad.*

Daring Declarations, Part 3

An evening at the opera could prove Lord Tremayne's undoing when he and his lovely new paramour cross paths with his sister and brother-in-law. Introducing one's socially unacceptable strumpet to his stunned family is *never* done. But Daniel does it anyway. And it might just be the best decision he's ever made, for Thea's quickly become much more than a mistress—and it's time he told her so.

ABOUT LARISSA

HUMOR. HEARTFELT EMOTION. & HUNKS.

A lifelong Texan, Larissa writes steamy regencies, blending heartfelt emotion with doses of laugh-out-loud humor. Her heroes are strong men with a weakness for the right woman.

Avoiding housework one word at a time (thanks in part to her super-helpful herd of cats >^..^<), Larissa adores brownies, James Bond, and her husband. She's been a clown, a tax analyst, and a pig castrator(!) but nothing satisfies quite like seeing the entertaining voices in her head come to life on the page.

Writing around some health challenges and computer limitations, it's a while between releases, but stick with her...she's working on the next one.

Learn more at LarissaLyons.com.